the rivals

by Daisy Whitney

LB

LITTLE, BROWN AND COMPANY
New York · Boston

Little, Brown and Company
Hachette Book Group
237 Park Avenue, New York, NY 10017
Visit our website at www.lb-teens.com

Little, Brown and Company is a division of Hachette Book Group, Inc.
The Little, Brown name and logo are trademarks of Hachette Book Group, Inc.
The publisher is not responsible for websites (or their content) that are not owned by the
publisher.

First Edition: February 2012

The characters and events portrayed in this book are fictitious. Any similarity to real
persons, living or dead, is coincidental and not intended by the author.

Library of Congress Cataloging-in-Publication Data
Whitney, Daisy.
  The rivals / by Daisy Whitney. — 1st ed.
    p. cm.
  Summary: Alex's role in the Mockingbirds, an underground student justice system at
her elite boarding school, is challenged when she tries to stop a group of students using
prescription drugs to help other students cheat, as school officials turn a blind eye to the
wrongdoing.
  ISBN 978-0-316-09057-5
  [1. Cheating—Fiction. 2. Boarding schools—Fiction. 3. Schools—Fiction. 4. Conduct of
life—Fiction. 5. Secret societies—Fiction.] I. Title.
  PZ7.W6142Ri 2012
  [Fic]—dc23   2011019227

10 9 8 7 6 5 4 3 2 1

RRD-C

Printed in the United States of America

For W and W.

You guys are the loves of my life.

Despite what I might tell the dog.

Chapter One

POSITIVE REINFORCEMENT

I will pretend I know nothing.

When she asks me about the Mockingbirds, I will deny everything.

I won't reveal who we are and what we do, even though she has summoned me here to her inner sanctum "to discuss matters pertaining to the Mockingbirds." That's what the note says, the one her secretary hand-delivered to me moments ago on crisp white stationery, sealed with the official emblem of the office of the dean of Themis Academy.

Ms. Ivy Merritt.

She is second in command here, and that puts her in charge of students, faculty, activities, and all disciplinary matters. Even though *discipline* is a loaded word at this school.

"Please come in," she says, and gestures to the brown

leather chair across from her desk. As I sit down, I quickly survey her office. Her desk is lined with photos of two dogs. Weimaraners. I've seen her walking her dogs around the campus. She lets them off leash, and they stay next to her the entire time, perfectly trained.

She notices me looking at the photos.

"Frederick and Fredericka," she says proudly. "Do you have dogs?"

"No," I say. When you go to boarding school, that whole "If we get a puppy, I promise I'll walk it" plea doesn't really work on parents.

"They're twins," she adds.

Twins? *They're called littermates, lady, as in brother and sister.*

"That's nice," I say, but I'm not really interested in her dogs' family tree. I'm just trying to ignore the nervous feeling growing inside me, the twitchiness of not knowing what the dean wants. I've talked to her before, heard her D-Day speeches, watched her happily overseeing student performances at the Faculty Club. Ms. Merritt is a Themis institution herself—she went to school here (the third generation in her family to attend) before returning as a teacher and then working her way up in the administration. She is the school's biggest cheerleader; she attends as many sporting events and student performances as she can, and she always cheers the loudest.

Of course, none of that gives me any insight into the *matters pertaining to the Mockingbirds*, and as far as I am concerned, any matter pertaining to the Mockingbirds must be kept secret from any teacher or administrator, no matter how much school spirit she possesses.

Maybe especially *because of* how much school spirit she possesses.

I look around some more, hunting out clues. The shelves behind her desk are lined with books, plaques, awards, but there's an empty space on the top shelf. It seems to have been cleared out, recently dusted and polished.

She's angling for something this year. Another award.

Ms. Merritt moves from her desk to the chair next to me, scooting it even closer. I watch her inch nearer still. I force myself to focus on something else—like the tight braid in her hair or the ugly glasses she wears. Ms. Merritt is pretty, but she's one of those women who try to hide their beauty by wearing glasses and pantsuits and never letting their hair down.

"First of all, thank you so much for coming. It's such an exciting time—the start of your senior year—so I thought we could begin our meeting by talking about your college plans," she says. I'm thrown off because I thought we'd be talking about the Mockingbirds, or at least the a cappella singing group we tell the administration we are. "Is Juilliard still at the top of your list?"

"Yes," I say, giving her only the briefest of answers so we can get to the real agenda: not dogs, not college, but the *matters pertaining to the Mockingbirds* she called me here to discuss.

"We haven't had a student admitted to Juilliard in four years," Ms. Merritt continues, then places her hand on mine. My first instinct is to yank my hand away. I don't like being touched by teachers, by adults. "But I have all the faith in the world that you're going to change that for us, aren't you?"

"Sure," I say, because what can I say? Of course I want to get into Juilliard. It's only been my lifelong dream.

"The school needs this, Alex," she says, and I detect a note of pleading in her voice. Then she presses her hand harder against mine. I look down at her hand, its veins all fat and blue, and then back up at her. I want to know why I'm here, because it can't just be about my college plans. But she's not letting on. Instead, she's just holding my hand tighter, and I don't like it. I start to wriggle my hand out from under hers.

She looks down, noticing my discomfort, and releases me. "I'm sorry. I should be more sensitive about your—" She stops, then says, delicately, in a whisper, "*Personal space.*"

It's as if she just dropped a tray in the cafeteria and now it's silent, dead silent, and we all wait for someone to break the seal with a sound.

I make the first move. "What do you mean by that?" I ask, because she knows something. I want to know how much she knows.

"What happened to you last year," she says, lowering her voice again, like this is a secret only the two of us know. "As if what you went through wasn't hard enough, I imagine there are students who don't really know what to think about it, seeing as the issue was never formally brought forth. And now you're having to live with people still having all those lingering questions of...*shared culpability*," she says, shaking her head, as if the thought disturbs her. "But I hope you know that had you decided to come to me about the situation with that boy, there never would have been a question about what really happened. And, of course, you can come to me about anything," she adds. "That's my job. That's why I'm here."

I am floored. I don't even know where to start, because I'm thinking ten things at once, but the first one is this: *Ms. Merritt knows I was date-raped by another student last year, even though I never told anyone in the administration.* I try to open my mouth to speak, but words refuse to take shape, and all I manage is "How?"

"There are many students here who share things with me," she says as she leans closer, patting my hand as if trying to set me at ease. But I'm not at ease. I'm not cool with students talking about me, and I'm definitely not comfortable with them telling her—especially since she doesn't seem very *sensitive* about my personal space after all. "And you should know that you can trust me too."

For a second I can feel the walls of her office looming closer, falling toward me as if they're going to enclose me too tightly. But the very thought of *anyone* insinuating I was somehow to blame for the assault strengthens me, and I push back. "How can you say there is any shared culpability?"

"Alex, you have to understand I'm not saying there was or

wasn't. But you and he never came to me, so I don't know the details. How am I to know whose fault it actually was?"

"Fault? It was *his* fault."

She waves this away, then nods to the desk photos of her dogs. "I find that positive reinforcement works best," she says, and I expect her to break out a basket of dog biscuits and maybe offer me one. "And that's why I say it's time to simply move on and focus on the good stuff. Like Juilliard." Now there's a beaming smile on her face. "The fact of the matter is, you are extraordinarily talented. You have an opportunity before you with Juilliard, and it's one we both want. Your admission there would mean so very much to me, and to you, of course. So let's not focus on the past, or any past troubles. Let's celebrate your talents instead, since not only are you our star piano player, but I see that you're also heading up the Mockingbirds singing group," she says, tapping a piece of paper on her desk. It's a list of the students who head up the various groups and clubs at Themis. I had to submit my name last week to qualify for a mailbox in the student-activities office and for the right to post flyers around campus. But does she know singing is just a cover for what the Mockingbirds really do?

"And that is why I have decided I want the Mockingbirds to perform in two weeks at our first Faculty Club event this year," she adds. "It's part of my purview to select the students who will perform, and it's imperative that the faculty have a good year. I want our headmistress to be happy, and I want all our teachers to be happy. We want them to love teaching here, and part of that comes from things like the Faculty Club performances. I do hope you will say yes." There's that hint of pleading again.

This is the reason she called me to her office? This is the matter pertaining to the Mockingbirds? It's not to tell me she knows I was assaulted, although she does. It's not to tell me the Mockingbirds need to cease and desist, as I'd thought. Instead, it's simply to invite us—*the a cappella singing group we're not*—to sing at the upcoming Faculty Club event in front of the teachers as they eat warm chocolate-chip cookies and drink hot cocoa and wax on about how wonderful it is to teach at Themis Academy? *Oh, the perks! Aren't they great!*

Call it positive reinforcement. Call it turning the other cheek. It amounts to the same thing: she knows what happened to me and she's dismissing it, wiping her hands clean. I'd like to say this makes me sad, or mad. But instead, I feel like it's business as usual at Themis Academy, where the record matters more than the reality and where the Mockingbirds are undoubtedly needed.

And if all she wants to see is one side of our story, if all she wants is the happy, chipper, cheery face of high school, then we'll give it to her.

"Ms. Merritt, it would be my pleasure to perform with my merry band of Mockingbirds before your Faculty Club," I say with a broad smile.

As she thanks me and says good-bye, I wonder whether she knows that we're not singers at all—that our true job is to police, protect, and prosecute other students. That we are the school's underground student-justice system.

I don't know which thought is more troubling: that the Mockingbirds are here in the first place to uphold the code of conduct because the school won't, or that she'd willingly let us exist to do just that.

Chapter Two

MOVIE IMAGES

"Can you sing?"

"Not to save my life," Martin says as he opens the door to his room and lets me in. "You?"

"Nope," I say.

He laughs.

"What's so funny about that?"

"Well, I have an excuse. I'm a science geek," he says. He's right. I even pilfered his favorite gray shirt with *Science Rules* in red letters to sleep in during the summer. It's well worn and reminds me of him. I wore it nearly every night, and still do. "But aren't *you* supposed to have every sort of musical talent known to humankind?"

I shake my head, because my musical talents stop cold when I step away from the bench. Despite being able to pick a note, any note, out of an aural lineup, my voice is an un-tamed instrument. "I am afraid my musical abilities are very specialized," I say, feeling momentary relief as I shift away from thoughts of Ms. Merritt.

"*Specialized.* That's such a PC way of putting it," he says, then turns the lock on the door. It clicks shut. He reaches for me, wrapping his arms around my waist.

"Decontaminate me, please. I was just in Ms. Merritt's of-fice," I say, and Martin obliges by pressing his lips softly against my neck and his hands firmly against my hips.

I relax into the feeling of him, something I didn't get nearly enough of when school was out for the summer. I saw him yesterday when I returned to school, and last night, and this morning, but we're still making up for lost time.

As his lips make their way up my neck, I let his hair fall through my fingers, remembering the first time we kissed, the first time I wanted to touch his soft brown hair, and how I still love the way his hair feels on my hands. As I watch the strands fall gently through my fingers, he pulls me to him, my chest against his, his mouth nearing mine, closing the space between us. Then his lips are on mine and all I can think is, how did I go a whole summer with hardly any of this? This kissing, this closeness, this boy.

And that's how the next hour goes by in about ten sec-onds, it seems. When we finally come up for breath, tucking in shirts and adjusting shorts that didn't quite come all the way off, because we haven't gone all the way yet, I tell him everything about my meeting with the dean. I don't leave out a single detail. Martin cringes, cursing her as I repeat the words *shared culpability*.

"But the thing is, I still have moments when I think I could have done something different. Like I could have shouted louder or pushed him off me," I say, and then tuck my face into his shoulder.

I feel Martin's hand on my hair, his whisper in my ear. "It wasn't your fault. It'll never be your fault. It was one hundred percent his, and I don't care what Ms. Merritt or anyone says to the contrary."

I breathe him in, the familiarity of him, this boy I know, comforting me. "And this is how people see me now. As the girl who was..." I stop because no matter how many months have passed, I feel like I've been marked with an *R*. "How do you see me? Is that all you see when you look at me?"

He laughs, but it's a reassuring one; he's not laughing at me. "It's the thing I never see. Because I see you, only you."

I can't help smiling, but inside I want to be where he is. I want to see me the way he does—without seeing *what happened* first. Sure, I can be all tough and *how dare you say it was my fault?* to Ms. Merritt, but she touched a nerve inside me that's still tender. Because as much as I don't have any lingering questions whatsoever, I know some students probably do, and the thought sickens me.

"And then I also see a totally hot piano player, because there is no way I can look at you and say *pianist*. Sorry, but too weird a word for a guy to say. And then I see this girl who still likes me and still listens to my science stories after six months. Which is pretty awesome. And I also see the head of the Mockingbirds, and then I remember, *Oh crap, Alex is in charge of me. I'd better be a good helper Mockingbird.*"

Then it's my turn to laugh, only I am definitely laughing at him and the way he's making fun of himself, since he's on the board of the Mockingbirds too—which means he helps decide which cases we take on. He's been a Mockingbird since he was a sophomore, working his way up to membership on the board. He's in the Mockingbirds because he believes in them, because he wants to help others.

But I'm brand-spanking-new to the group. And I'm the leader for one and only one reason—because I was raped. I didn't earn the post by putting in my time. I didn't work my way up or campaign. It was handed to me because the leader is always someone who brought a case and won it. And while *that night* when Carter Hutchinson took my virginity while I was passed out was many months ago, the memory of it can all come roaring back in an instant.

After Carter was found guilty by the Mockingbirds, I was sure I'd survived the hardest part. But then I went home for the summer and found that being away from school made me think about that night even more. I no longer had the buffer of classes, the daily regimen of a schedule. It was summer, lazy time, just the piano and me, and in that empty space the memories started surging again, like the sound of a fire engine that starts one town over, then grows steadily nearer, until it's blaring in your ear.

I thought I had moved on from victim to survivor, but

there I was feeling victimized all over again—this time by my mind, which betrayed me by replaying *that night* whenever it wanted, the memories turning on and off with a vengeance, like flashing neon lights. My sister, Casey, who's four years older, took me to a counselor, someone she found back home in New Haven. The counselor helped, told me it wasn't unusual for *survivors*—she always called me a survivor—to go through a period of time when the assault feels closer, fresher. It's like right before the wound can close, it has to be reopened one last time and flushed out.

With salt water, it seemed.

That's how it *still* feels at times, because randomly, out of nowhere, I'll see flashes of Carter's white-blond hair, his lips I didn't want on me, his naked chest I never wanted to be near. The worst part is when those awful images collide with Martin. Because here in Martin's room, where we've returned to kissing, I flinch as Carter's hands flicker in front of me, as I recall how they pressed down into the mattress on either side of my naked body.

I squeeze my eyes shut and try to push the unwelcome visitor away with more of Martin, like I can expel the memories through more contact with the boy I *want* to be with. But as my lips on his achieve a new urgency, he sees through me. He knows what I'm doing, so he extricates himself from my kiss to ask, "You okay?"

"Of course," I say quickly. Too quickly.

"Hey," he says softly. "We can slow down."

I shake my head and lean in to press my lips against his

again. He responds but then pulls back once more. "Alex," he whispers, "are you thinking of that night?"

"No," I say, closing my eyes and shaking my head, but soon, very soon, I'm nodding, managing a yes. Then more words. "I don't want to picture him when I'm with you. I hate it."

Martin props himself on one elbow. "I don't want you to either, but it takes time, right?" he says, reminding me of what the therapist said this summer. Time, time, time. Be patient with yourself. Be gentle with yourself.

Enough patience.

I want to be *healed*, not *healing*. Especially here with Martin. I hate that I cannot completely erase Carter from my mind. I want to own this space with Martin. I want it to be mine; I want it to be pure.

But I am not always in charge.

"But I want to . . . ," I start, then trail off. I try again, saying the words out loud this time. "I want to be with you. All the way."

His eyes sparkle. I look into them, deep brown, with these crazy green flecks twinkling, flashing. He pulls me closer, pressing his body against me to let me know he wants what I want. But he's more than just a *guy*. He's a *good* guy. "I'll wait for you. However long it takes. You're worth waiting for," he says, twirling a strand of my brown hair around his finger.

And with those words it's like one more of the dark shadows peels off the wall and leaves the room.

Another kiss, and there's only Martin and me here for this one. Then I whisper, "We'd better go."

Chapter Three

A LINK TO THE PAST

We leave together for D-Day, and the quad is bustling. We pass the bulletin board in front of McGregor Hall. It's stuffed with flyers for groups, clubs, and teams, including ones I posted this morning before the sun even rose. I posted them early because we're not supposed to be in-your-face, all swagger and bravado. The Mockingbirds are here to help, but the less we're seen doing our work, the better off we all are.

Obviously.

Running just as fast as you can, you'll find your way to the New Nine. Can you hit the right notes for the Mockingbirds? Let's hear your best song....

It's a recruitment poster; we're looking for new runners for the Mockingbirds. They're our on-the-ground members, and they're also the only ones who can move up to form our council, the New Nine. We pick the jury for student trials from the council, so we like to remind potential runners of the path up in the Mockingbirds.

Of course, the question really should be this: can *we* hit the right notes for Ms. Merritt in her Faculty Club show? And if we don't, will she see through us? And if she sees through us, then what? Will she just clap and cheer and keep looking the other way?

"Ironic, isn't it?" I say to Martin.

"Or a self-fulfilling prophecy," he quips.

Then I hear someone behind me.

"If it isn't Alexandra Nicole Patrick. The girl who just couldn't say no."

I grit my teeth, take a deep breath, and then turn around. It's Natalie Moretti. She testified against me last year in the Mockingbirds courtroom, painted me as some animal in heat. *She was kind of rubbing up against him*, she told the council. Her eyes are every bit as cold as they were that day. Her brown hair is pulled tight at her neck, and she's wearing a sleeveless shirt, showing every smooth, toned muscle in her arms. Natalie is the überathlete here. Lacrosse superstar in the fall, track goddess in the spring. I don't think her lean muscles would even permit an ounce of fat to reside on her body. They'd attack any fat molecule that dared appear, eating it up and spitting it out like a victorious cannibal.

"Hello, Natalie," I say coolly, determined to be the picture of poise, even though I'm burning up inside because her name, her face, her voice dredge up the worst memories of the trial. She is the face of judgment and, worse, the judgment of another girl. She is more living, breathing proof that there are people who think I asked for it. She is the reminder that I wasn't raped in an alley at gunpoint, that I was drunk, that I flirted with Carter, that I kissed him.

Before I said no. *Before* he went too far.

She is the face of all my shame.

I bet she's the one who tipped off Ms. Merritt.

"How was your summer? Plenty of time to think about all the stories you told, or were you too busy entertaining more young men?"

"You can shut the hell up, Natalie," Martin says, staring hard at her as he clenches his fists.

"Oh, so cute. Your boyfriend defends you," she says to me in a sickly sweet voice. Then she turns to Martin. "If I were you, I'd be careful, though. She might turn around and prosecute you next."

It's my turn to get a word in, so I say to her, "You don't have a clue about us or me or anything, Natalie. And you never will."

"Are you allowed to talk to me that way, Alex? Isn't that bullying? Should I file charges with the Mockingbirds?"

I want to slug her. I picture a fat red welt appearing across her cheek courtesy of my fist. I've never hit anyone, and have no clue how to land a punch, but it's a nice image. Somehow I rein in the overwhelming urge to practice a right hook for the first time. "Feel free," I mutter.

"Maybe I will, then," Natalie says, leaning closer to me, her breath now inches from my face. "Maybe I'll be your case this year, and I'll accuse you. How would that feel, Alexandra Nicole Patrick? How would it feel for you to be the accused?" Then she lowers her voice, her mouth coming closer to me, and more words slither out in a low hiss. "You're only leading the group because you couldn't keep your legs closed."

My entire body coils, every muscle and nerve ending tightening and then snapping as I start to raise my right hand to slap her, to whack her across the face for real this time.

But before I can even lift my hand, there's another voice.

"Who's excited for D-Day!"

I turn around and see McKenna Foster. I stuff my hand into my pocket. I brush my other hand against my shirt, like I'm wiping Natalie off, getting rid of the coat of filth she breathed onto me. Even though neither Martin nor McKenna could hear the last thing Natalie said, I can't help but wonder if other students will blame me for what happened last year. If they'll think I asked for it, if they'll think I don't deserve to lead the Mockingbirds.

If they all believe in *shared culpability*.

I wonder if McKenna knows why I'm a Mockingbird and if she has an opinion on it too. But for now I'm just glad she's here, defusing Natalie. McKenna and I have had a few classes together, including government in our sophomore year, which she killed in. She's a senior and on the student council, maybe VP or treasurer, I'm not sure. She has wild, curly black hair, and she's always pulling it back, putting it up, wearing sunglasses on her head to keep her hair off her face. Today she's twisted the crazy strands with a pencil, though a few errant ones have come loose. She's standing next to a younger version of herself.

"C'mon, guys! It's not as if *your* parents are going to embarrass you by making a dumb speech," she says, and rolls her eyes, cutting through the tension. Her parents are world-renowned research doctors—behavioral psychologists, I think—who get big bucks to travel and lecture around the world. McKenna's mom is a Themis alum, and our D-Day is on their lecture circuit, though I'm pretty sure it's the one pro bono stop.

The girl next to her clears her throat.

"Sorry," McKenna adds, with a nod to her companion. "Alex, this is my sister, Jamie, but you'll probably get to know her soon enough because she's in the orchestra too. She plays flute," McKenna says, and there's a touch of pride in her voice.

"I'm a freshman. I just started here," Jamie says, and she has an eerie confidence for a fourteen-year-old. She looks like McKenna except her hair is straight, the follicular opposite.

"And Alex here is the kick-ass leader of the Mockingbirds," McKenna adds, and somehow I manage a combination of "thanks" and "hi" before McKenna keeps going. "C'mon, enough gabbing. We've got to go see Mommy and Daddy. Oh, and don't forget to check out my awesome signs for student council," she adds, this time to me, as she points a thumb at a poster positioned right next to my Mockingbirds one—on hers is a drawing of a gavel with a smiling cartoonish face on it.

She heads off with her sister to the assembly hall. I notice that Natalie is right behind them. It crosses my mind that McKenna only introduced her sister to me, not to Natalie. Please don't tell me McKenna would be friends with that evil witch. McKenna's got to have better taste than that.

Martin turns to me and sees my jaw set tight, my lips pressed together hard. "What did Natalie say when she whispered to you?"

"I don't want to repeat it," I say quickly.

"But I already heard the first thing she said."

"And the second thing she said was far worse. Which is why I don't want to repeat it," I say, but I wonder again if people see me as someone who stood up for herself, or if they picture me in Carter's room, drunk, legs open, on his bed?

Either way, I have become fused to the crime against me. That's what happens when you take a stand, because then everyone knows what you were taking a stand for.

Martin and I walk into the auditorium together, and I see McKenna slide into a seat near the front and say something to Jamie. Jamie glances quickly back at me. I look down at the hallway into the auditorium, feeling a pang of longing for the way my life was before my past became public.

Chapter Four

THE THEMIS WAY

An hour later, D-Day is in full swing. Technically, the school calls it *Diversity Day*, but we've coined our own special nickname. It's like a pep rally, only the energy is radiating from the teachers, the administrators, the headmistress, and the dean herself. All the adults are hooting, hollering, whooping it up from their seats on the stage. Ms. Merritt is leading the show, and she has been trotting out each and every teacher to wax on and on about each of their subjects and how history, philosophy, French, calculus, and so on can all lead to the betterment not just of our nimble minds but, by golly, society as a whole!

My roommate Maia's sitting on one side of me, wisely using the time to read her favorite news blogs on her phone— gotta stay current on politics, government, and all that jazz for Debate Club. Her focus is the stuff of legend. She hasn't once looked away from the stories she's reading, or sighed, or whispered a comment to one of us. She is machinelike as she digests information, storing it up so she can call upon it at any moment.

Martin and Sandeep are on the other side of Maia, and from the looks of it they're using Sandeep's phone to make fantasy football trades. If Martin can segue from Natalie's insults to pretend sports team ownership, I should perk up too. Besides, if I don't want others to linger on my past, I shouldn't either. I should put on my best game face. So I tap T.S., my other roommate, on the shoulder and roll my eyes when she looks my way. She rolls her green eyes back at me, and we proceed to keep ourselves occupied with eye rolls and fake gags for the next few minutes as Mr. Bandoro, the school's Spanish teacher, effuses about the Spanish language, promising fluency for all students who apply themselves fully to his curriculum and declaring that said fluency will make us better global citizens.

I hold up my hand at T.S., lifting four fingers. "Fourth time I've heard this," I whisper. "And I'm still not a good global citizen."

"Oh no? I hereby sentence you to four readings of the school handbook and a recitation of it on the quad in front of the entire student body this evening. Backward. And while wearing sunglasses."

"Is there even a school handbook to read from?" I ask.

"Collecting dust somewhere," T.S. whispers, her bob-length blond hair swinging against her cheek as she leans in.

"Being sold at a garage sale," I say.

"Used as a coaster in the Faculty Club," she says.

"Being peddled as an artifact at a boarding-school exhibit in some museum."

"You totally win," she says, giving me a high five.

The voice of the headmistress, Ms. Vartan, echoes through the auditorium. She informs us that she will spend most of the semester visiting prep schools around the world as she gathers best practices to implement here at Themis. "But before I go, let us take the honor pledge, as we do at the start of every year. The honor pledge is the foundation of our academic excellence. We must always keep honor above all else, and your pledge on all tests, examinations, papers, academic activities, competitions, and assignments is that you have neither given nor received any assistance in completing the work. And now...," she says, holding up her right hand as if she's testifying in court.

We recite the pledge along with her. "I will not lie. I will not cheat. I will not tolerate any dishonorable behavior on behalf of myself or others."

Ms. Vartan nods and then gestures to Ms. Merritt. "Our beloved dean will be acting in my stead while I am on my journeys. And she has some very exciting news, so I will pass the baton to our very own Ms. Merritt."

Ms. Merritt thanks the headmistress and then says, "Some of you may know this is potentially a very special year for Themis, and I personally am so thrilled that the amply decorated debate team is in line to compete for a very prestigious honor with the Elite." That statement catches Maia's attention; she pops her head up from her phone and taps me on the shoulder.

"*The Elite*," she whispers to me, and then grins. The Elite is a very specialized tournament for debaters that occurs the last week in October, just in time to be reflected in early-admissions apps, which are due in early November. But here's the catch—invitations are harder to come by than Ivy League admission. You have to be handpicked by a supersecret selection committee composed of former Elite winners, Nationals winners, and other past debate stars. Maia's been praying for an invite since her freshman year. She *finally* landed one for this year's tournament after taking the Themis team to Nationals, where they placed third, in our junior year. That alone constituted an invite to the Elite.

"Well, you know, you have to live down the shame of that third-place victory at Nationals," I tease.

"I *so* know," she whispers. "I will do whatever it takes to win the Elite."

"You totally will win," I say.

Then I tune back in to Ms. Merritt, who's rattling off the rest of her hopes and dreams for this year. "I also have it on good authority that we are one of the contenders to receive the J. Sullivan James National Prep School of the Year Award."

There's an orchestrated hush throughout the auditorium, as if it were written into the stage directions. I scan the teachers' faces, wondering if they too are salivating for this award, and most of them are enrapt, their eyes glossy with desire. But there's one teacher up there who's not quite buying it, although it takes a practiced eye to tell. *I* can tell that Miss Damata, my music teacher, doesn't have J. Sullivan James's picture taped to her locker. She sits gracefully, with her hands in her lap, but she looks out at the students in the auditorium rather than at Ms. Merritt at the podium.

Ms. Merritt continues. "It's exciting, I know! It's been ten years since Themis received such an honor, and I don't think I need to remind anyone here that the J. Sullivan James Award is indeed the highest honor a prep school can achieve, because it's voted on solely by our peers in the world of preparatory-school education," she says, and I do a quick mental calculation. Ms. Merritt started as dean exactly nine years ago, so this would be the first time in her tenure that the school is in contention for whatever this silly award is. I wonder if a win would catapult her to the headmistress level here or elsewhere, and if she's gunning for it to get a promotion. Maybe she's even planning a coup while Ms. Vartan is touring the world of academia. "And I have no doubt that your tremendous academic achievements, extracurricular activities, and, of course, rigorous code of excellence in all matters related to character and community will help us bring it home."

Right home to her office, where she's prepped and polished the shelf space for this trophy.

"The award is also determined by excellence in the arts. So let us not forget that we must aim for the highest stars when we dance, when we sing, when we play piano. Which is, of course, what you wonderful students do already!"

She claps heartily, turning to the faculty to urge them to join her, and they do. Then she gestures to the students, and we clap as well. I make a mental note that the instrument she singled out was the piano. Somehow, this feels like another message: *Please get into Juilliard, Alex. You're my only hope.*

"On to other matters," Ms. Merritt says, this time with a sober look on her face. Which means it must be time for Bring-on-the-Experts. "There are, of course, aspects to Themis Academy beyond the intellectual rigors, challenges, and opportunities an education here affords, and they include character. Hand in hand with the honor pledge is character, one of the key pillars of a Themis education. We have an exceptional student body, and our students are exceptional not just in their intellect but in their character. Because they know how to behave..."

T.S. leans close to me, imitates Ms. Merritt's pregnant pause, and then says on cue with our dean, "...the Themis way."

Ms. Merritt goes into her introduction of Dr. and Dr. Foster, McKenna and Jamie's parents, who bound up to the stage from the first row. They're here to talk about hate speech, bullying, cheating, respect, individualism, and other assorted blah-blah-blah. Look, it's not that I don't believe it's important to talk about those things. I do. But Themis faculty are like the parents who say to their daughter, *Now, be careful not to get an eating disorder*, and then don't notice when she heads to the bathroom and yaks up every meal.

In my Mockingbirds notebook, I have documentation of every time the faculty looked the other way. Because there's a common thread with all our prior cases—nearly every time, a student had tried talking to a faculty member before coming to us.

"Peer pressure is intense," Dr. Foster says, and he sounds like Tony Robbins. "It is scary and dangerous, and we are here today to help you with strategies for dealing with it."

The other Dr. Foster chimes in. "We have to encourage an environment of trust and honesty and mutual respect, where students can say no to drugs, stand up to bullies, and speak their minds without putting others down."

Then Ms. Merritt weighs in. "You know I have an open-door policy, and you can always come to me to talk about anything."

Right. The only door that gets knocked on is the Mockingbirds'.

Then I sit up straight in my chair, realizing I forgot to add my name and contact info to the Mockingbirds mailbox so students would know how to reach me.

"I have to go," I whisper to T.S.

"Ooh, Mockingbirds business?"

"Kind of," I say back.

"I'm going to be a runner this year, right? We're still on for that, aren't we?" she whispers, referring to the feeder system for the Mockingbirds. Runners collect attendance slips from classes and can deduct points from accused students. Losing points sucks because points net you off-campus privileges. Above the runners, and chosen from among them, is the council. We pick our juries from the council. Running the show is the board of governors, who investigate charges and decide which cases to hear. The board is made up of two former council members and one person the Mockingbirds helped. Me. But it's what the runners do that gives us any power at all.

"Of course," I say, then gesture to Martin that I'll call him later. He gives me a curious look, but I keep going and slink up the side aisle and out the doors before anyone can notice I'm gone. I race to my dorm, grab some masking tape and a Sharpie, and then head back across the empty quad to the student-activities office in McGregor Hall.

The office is unlocked, naturally. Themis wants us to feel free to enter the student-activities office at all hours, to thumb through the course catalogs, check out the brochures for clubs, learn about drama group, debate practice, sporting events. We can even kick back and have a cup of coffee while perusing all that this fine institution offers to stimulate our extracurricular glands, because an actual espresso machine is perched on an end table. To set the mood, there's the alternative radio station from nearby Williamson College piping in through some unseen sound system.

I take the roll of masking tape from my back pocket, rip off a two-inch section, and place it on the bottom of the mailbox marked *Mockingbirds/a cappella singing group*. With the Sharpie I write my name, *Alex Patrick*, followed by my e-mail address. Want to register a complaint? I'm your gal.

I linger for a moment on what my first case could be. I don't *want* anyone to come to me, only because I don't *wish* the crap I've gone through to happen to anyone else. But I know how the world works. We do horrible things to one another. Will my first case be brought by someone like me, or like Amy, who led the group before me? Amy's case was so cut-and-dried—another girl held her down and carved the first two letters of the word *Queer* in her back before she could get away. Amy pressed charges in the Mockingbirds court, and the girl was found guilty. Then Amy tattooed the last three letters, finishing the job and creating her own badge of honor out of the mutilation, taking back her skin, her identity, her whole self.

She's probably going to lead some national movement or rally for sexual-identity equality someday. She'll be a spokesperson for equal rights or gay marriage or something. I wonder if Amy had the same fire, the same drive, before she was cut. Or if the Amy I know now was forged by the crime. If she's tougher than the Amy who existed before, and if somehow her complete determination to do the right thing was grafted onto her along with the letters on her back. I've never really talked to her about it, but I'll have to the next time I see her.

I put the cap back on the Sharpie and drop it in my pocket. That's when I hear a noise, a door opening, then quick, determined heels clicking down the hallway toward me. A girl appears in the doorway. Her hair is pulled back in a thick black headband that sits right above her hairline. Her face is framed by square silver glasses with sparkly little rhinestones on the earpieces. She wears baby-pink plastic boots with massively high and thick heels, a white jean skirt with safety pins down one side, and a gray T-shirt that says *Property of Detroit*.

"Alex," she says. Her voice is raspy, but it's a natural rasp—not the kind from crying, or from a cold, but from just having one of those husky, smoky voices. The effect of that voice—from only one word, *my name*—is like the scuffing of boots, the planting of feet, fists raised and ready to fight.

I have a feeling I'm about to get my first case, only I have no idea what to say, what to ask, what to do.

"Are you from Detroit?" I ask just to say something. Then I want to kick myself. Because why am I asking her where she's from?

"Yeah," she says, tilting her chin up at me, as though I just insulted her on her turf or something. Like the next thing she'll say is *What of it?* as she whips out a knife. "You don't like Detroit or something?"

"No," I say quickly, realizing my skin is prickling and my heart's beating a bit faster, like the way I feel in those tense few minutes before I step onstage and play the piano. I tell myself to calm down. Except this isn't a piano recital where I know all the notes, all the music, when I sit down at the bench. Because there's no checklist of questions to ask when someone tracks you down in the student-activities office. "I mean, it's fine. I've never been there. I was just asking."

Then she's fiddling with her headband, pulling it back farther. I notice her hair is mostly purple.

"Cool hair," I say, hoping I can deflect attention to her colorful locks.

"I did it myself," she says.

"I thought about dyeing my hair blue a couple times. But it's a lot of upkeep, right?" I ask. Sure, I have thought about it once or twice, but I mostly just want to keep the conversation on the innocuous.

"It is, but it's worth it. You have to bleach it out pretty regularly, but people notice it."

"Maybe I don't want it blue, then," I say.

"You could just do a streak, then. Streaks are easy. I can help you. My mom does hair."

"Oh," I say, wondering if this is what it feels like to visit a foreign country where you don't even know how to say *hello* in the language. Because I have no freaking clue what to say to her or why we're talking or why we're discussing *hair*.

"Seriously. You'd look awesome with a blue streak."

"Maybe," I say, reaching a hand into my straight brown hair.

"Anyway, that's not why I'm here," she says, and finally she's speaking English. "I came here to find you," she adds, but the gravel in her voice is suddenly softer as she glances around, making sure we're alone. "To tell you something."

"How did you know I was here?" I ask cautiously,

wondering if this is how my role with the Mockingbirds starts. Students coming up to me, knocking on my door, tracking me down, catching me after class. I picture throngs of them, stumbling over one another, tripping on the next person, grabbing shirts and backpacks, pulling fellow seniors, juniors, sophomores, freshmen down into a giant mosh pit.

"I was sitting behind you at D-Day. I saw you leave."

"So you're following me?" I ask.

She nods. "Hell yeah."

I find myself wishing once again that I could just slide back to last year, to the way it was before I went to the Mockingbirds, before I became one, before everything about me was made public. "How did you know already that I'm head of the Mockingbirds?" I ask, because it's not as if the Mockingbirds publicized my appointment with skywriting when my junior year ended a few months ago. Sure, word about my case—and my victory—started spreading, but not everyone here heard or cared that I was next in line to run the group. I was never tracking the comings and goings of the Mockingbirds roster before I needed them.

"I knew you had your case last year, and I knew it was a big one. So I figured you were the one they asked to take over. I'm right, right?" she asks.

"Yeah, you're right. It's me."

"He deserved it," she says, narrowing her eyes, and I find myself softening, because she's not like Natalie; she's not like Ms. Merritt. She's on my side, and I'd like to think that means she's also on the good side, that she believes what I believe about the Mockingbirds—that we can help. "And now you get to be the enforcer. It's poetic justice. It's karma, you know."

I nod, liking the sound of *poetic justice*, but mostly liking the fact that though this girl knows my history, she sees me as a survivor, not a victim; a leader, not a slut. She may know my past, she may be privy to the report card on my sexual history, but she sees beyond it. I like her.

"So how can I help you?" I ask. "And while we're at it, how about a name? You know mine. What's yours?"

"Delaney Zirinski," she says, and the name clicks instantly.

"Delaney, you're the girl who—" I start, then catch myself before saying more.

"Yeah, I'm the girl *who*," she says, throwing it right back at me.

I'm embarrassed as I fumble around on the job. And I deserve to have my words tossed back at me. Because here I am identifying her by the legend that precedes her, when I, of all people, should know better.

"I'm sorry. I'm really sorry," I say, because I don't want to do to her what people are doing to me.

But, like me, she is twined to her past. Everyone knows her here. Or knows *of her*, at least.

"It's cool," she says, and then she stands taller, straighter, prouder as she continues. "I'm the girl who got kicked out of Matthew Winters. I'm the girl who got invited back. I'm the girl who said *you can take your lame-ass apology and shove it.*"

I want to be like her. I want to *own* my past like she does. I want to say *let them talk* and then walk away without caring what people might think about me.

Delaney Zirinski descended on Themis Academy last year in a cloud of controversy. She *had* gone to Matthew Winters in Exeter, New Hampshire, and had been accused of cheating by other students. The school investigated the claims—there was even a full disciplinary hearing with teachers and students jointly presiding over it—and found her guilty. She was promptly kicked out in what became a very public display of the school's vaunted *zero tolerance* policy. But then, lo and behold, it turned out Delaney had been framed. Set up by the other students. The school's headmaster made another very public display—this time of humility. He said all the right things: *it's our fault; we're so sorry; you are welcome back.* But Delaney and her mom would have none of it. Then Ms. Merritt swooped in, offering Delaney a slot at Themis Academy and embracing her with open arms.

Did I mention that Matthew Winters is one of our biggest rivals? Both our headmistress and the dean were thrilled to grant *asylum* to the student one of our biggest rivals shouldn't have disgraced. They made sure to point out that Themis would never cast aspersions on a student. What they didn't say was that Themis would never do anything about anything, period.

Delaney takes one more look down the hall, then says in a low voice, "So you can probably figure that cheating—in any way, shape, or form—is one of my least favorite things."

I nod.

"You can probably also figure I would want to stay as far away as I could from any accusations of cheating."

I wait for her to say more. I picture Amy talking to me for the first time last year and do everything I can to channel her calm and her warmth.

"That's why what I am going to tell you can never be associated with me in any way. I need to be far away from this."

"Okay," I say. "What do you want to tell me?"

"There is a group of students here plotting out how to methodically, systematically, and regularly use drugs to cheat this semester."

"Already?" I say, and it comes out as a snort and a scoff and a laugh all at once. It's doubly ironic, considering the pledge we all just took. "But classes don't even start till tomorrow."

"I know. But it's Themis, so they're prepared," she says, waving her hand in the air, separating herself from the rest of the school.

"You mean they prepped over the summer? Like summer reading?"

"Yep. They called it summer training. They want to be ready, in top shape for the second school starts."

"What are they doing exactly?" I ask.

"Prescription meds. You can guess what kind, right?"

I nod, because I can. "So is this like a cheating ring or something?" I ask carefully.

"Yeah. Several students already. And it's about to be a lot more."

"Why do you say that?"

"Because of the deliberateness of it. The planning. They're like an army, plotting how to use the meds to cheat in a very specific way," she says, and an image flashes by of Themis students huddled together in a sort of war room, a mastermind-y general type holding a pointer, tapping a blueprint of a bunker, barking commands at some elite group— Delta Force, SEALs, that sort of thing—so they all think they're untouchables. "And it's every day, several times a day. Taking more, using it in *different ways*," she says, sounding out those words slowly, and I nod again, because I have a feeling I know what she's talking about without her having to say the words *snorting it.*

"Are you talking about Anderin?" I ask.

Because it's got to be Anderin. It's the latest ADHD drug, the new Ritalin, the new Adderall, but better, stronger, faster. It's like steroids for the brain. I know that plenty of college students think nothing of popping an Annie before a big test, saying it makes you perform better. My sister, Casey, who's a senior at Williamson, has told me Annie is pretty much the rage over there. Still, there's a difference between taking a pill every now and then before a test and taking it every day. And there's an even bigger difference if the cheating is so premeditated. Because at the end of the day, it is what it is—an amphetamine.

Delaney nods.

"Who's doing it? Can you tell me?"

Her phone rings, the opening notes to an Arcade Fire song. She grabs it from her back pocket, looks at the screen, and says, "Crap."

She doesn't answer the call, though; the song keeps playing and the vocals start. But it's not the band's voices I hear. It's someone else—raspy and gravelly. It's Delaney doing a cover of "Wake Up."

"You can sing," I say, trying to mask a grin, thinking we should recruit her for our Faculty Club performance.

"Yeah," she says in an offhand way. "I'm in an all-girl band back home."

"An Arcade Fire cover band?"

"We have our own songs too. Listen, I totally have to go," she says, holding up the phone.

"Wait," I say quickly. "I need more. Can't you tell me more?"

"Not now. But you can start looking into it, right? Investigating it? Just don't say the tip came from me, all right?"

"So why are you telling me, then?"

She gives me a look like *duh*. "Because it needs to stop. Because I can't have this touch me again," she says, and I instantly understand where she's coming from. I understand deep in my gut how much you can want to get away from your past. And for the first time, this leading thing feels natural.

But only for a second. Because I still don't get why this cheating ring would affect her.

"But why would it touch you? Are you involved?"

"No," she says, and sneers at me. "And I'm telling you because I cannot afford to be even remotely associated with this."

"But why would you *be* associated with this?" I press.

"I'm not associated with it! Other people are, and you need to stop it," she says, and her raspy voice has that same toughness it did when she first said my name. I picture her as the type to twist your shirt collar, jam her forearm against your chest, and say, *Don't say a word.* "And you cannot, under any circumstances whatsoever, say this came from me."

Even though I feel a kinship with her, even though I plan to do whatever I can, I'm pretty sure I don't have to agree to every directive sent my way.

"If you want our help, I'm going to have to tell my board members," I inform her.

She's silent for a moment, then says, "Fine. I have to go," and just as quickly as she clomped down the hall, she's clomping the other way now, leaving me alone in the student-activities office with my first tip.

School hasn't even started, a bell hasn't even rung for a single class, and there's already stuff going down.

That's the Themis way.

Chapter Five

EXTRA CREDIT

I perform my next official act as leader of the Mockingbirds and call an impromptu board meeting, texting Martin as I leave McGregor Hall. That's what our rule book says to do. Tips should be shared with the board to be vetted and discussed. That's why we have a board, so it's not one person making all the decisions.

Got tip. Can you round up Parker for a mtg in 15 min?

His response comes seconds later.

Justice never sleeps. We will be there.

I head downstairs to the basement laundry room of Taft-Hay Hall, scratch out a note that says *The Knothole is in session*, and slap it on the door. I claim the dingy red chair in the back, flip open my Mockingbirds notebook, and say hello to Martin and Parker when they arrive moments later. They opt for the couch. Not only is Parker our third board member, he's also one of Martin's roommates this year, along with Martin's best friend, Sandeep.

"Our first official meeting," Parker says, rubbing his hands together and flashing a toothy grin. He could be the poster boy for Whitestrips. He's a senior, but he looks younger. He's tall and lanky, but not in a rock-star way. More in a Mormon-knocking-on-your-door way. His short blond hair is the color of sand. His face is smooth, stubble-free, and I don't think you'd find shaving cream or a razor in his medicine cabinet.

And he thinks he's fried gold because his daddy is a senator.

He was a council member for all of last year, so he was eligible to move up to the board. The night before final exams started in late May, we gathered in here and met with all the contenders. There were four of us who decided—Martin and me, and also Amy and Ilana, who served on the board until she graduated last year. Ilana's final official act before leaving Themis for Columbia was to vote on who'd replace her.

Parker said he'd served *loyally*—he emphasized that word several times, and it grated on me exponentially with each successive mention—since his sophomore year and had done so at great risk to himself and his family. His dad had survived a tax-evasion scandal, narrowly winning reelection the year Parker started here. His dad's a Themis alum too, and Parker promised Dad he'd do nothing to bring further shame on the well-heeled political family. But, really, his dad had done plenty of that himself. Something about Parker—his defensiveness—made me think the apple didn't fall far from the tree.

"If anyone besides students found out about the Mockingbirds, if this ever got out somehow, this could seriously hurt my dad," Parker said that night, adjusting his wire-rimmed glasses, a worried look on his face, as if we were discussing state secrets. "It would be one more thing for him to have to deal with. To him this would be totally subversive. He believes in working *inside* the system, not against it."

I wasn't all that impressed. Weren't we all doing this at personal risk? I risked everything by coming to the Mockingbirds in the first place.

Anjali Durand made a much simpler case for herself. She handed us a list of all the trials and investigations she'd played a role in and said she hoped we'd give her fair consideration. I knew Anjali through the Mockingbirds and because she lived two floors below me. She was always tossing off some pithy observation about classes and teachers, something that made me think or laugh or smirk. Plus she was involved in the Chess Club, which was so coolly ironic because she's this tall, willowy European beauty with freckles like an American. Not that tall, willowy European beauties with freckles like Americans can't play chess, but she defied the stereotype of nerdy chess boys, *and* she beat them most of the time in late-night competitions in the common room. After she handed us her list, she flexed her right biceps, winked, and said, "And I've been lifting weights, so I can totally replace Ilana as the muscle."

That won me over for two reasons. First, Anjali didn't have a muscle to speak of. Second, Ilana was something of a toughie. You didn't mess with Ilana. She was a powerful protector. I knew Anjali could fill that role on chutzpah alone. Ilana and I sided with Anjali. Amy and Martin went with Parker. Two against two. A classic stalemate.

Amy said, "You have the deciding vote, Alex. You're the leader. You can override all of us."

"They both have good records," Martin pointed out. "Really, either one would be fine. Either one would be great."

But overriding the other remaining board member—Martin—and the outgoing leader—Amy—wasn't a good way to start my new role. So I backed down. "Let's go with Parker," I said, conceding.

Now here he is, eager and ready to serve at *great personal risk*.

But if I'm going to lead, I have to put any reservations I once had behind me. So I say, "I'm glad you're our newest board member, Parker. Actually, we're both kind of the new board members."

He smiles and nods. "True! First term for both of us!" Then he pulls out a small reporter's notebook from the back pocket of his shorts. "Though I *did* serve on the council last year."

"True," I reply.

"And I was a runner the year before," he adds as he flips open the notebook and uncaps a pen.

"That you were."

"So it's not really my first term."

The message is clear. I'm the newbie; he's the veteran. And I feel knocked down, once again, like with Natalie. Neither one thinks I'm fit to lead. Neither one thinks I *deserve* to lead. Do I have to defend myself yet again and explain to everyone that *date rape, well, IT SUCKS, PEOPLE!*

Comparisons to Amy flood my mind again—her case was so black-and-white. No one would have questioned whether or not she deserved the post. But with date rape, everyone sees it in some shade of gray. Did the fact that I flirted with him early in the night mean I gave consent? Did being drunk make me responsible for what he did later, while I was passed out? I thought these shades of gray would *only* matter in our courtroom during the trial. But they reappear, in unexpected ways, every day, every hour.

Like now, as I trip through a fresh set of questions: what leadership reserves do I have beyond the big fat *R* that's been branded onto my chest? What have I done that would give me any skills in this job? I am the very definition of introvert. Seriously. Look it up and you'll see my picture. Before all this I was just a girl who loved her friends, who liked school, and who'd been having a mad, raging affair with the piano for her whole life. That's who I was—pianist, friend, and good student. Where's the leadership training in that? I'm not captain of any team or head of any club. My God, I barely even read the news. I only notice politics when there are scandals, like with Parker's dad. Someone like Martin would be a much better leader, and I'm not saying that because he's my boyfriend. I don't think he's better than me or smarter than me. With a judge for a father and a prosecutor for a mother, law and order runs in his blood. My body ticks in time to chords and octaves.

So Parker's not-so-subtle dig strikes a nerve. Especially because I don't have a response, a clever retort. I'm not even sure how I'm supposed to be sticking up for myself here, so I choose the path of least resistance—I ignore the thinly veiled barbs from the senator's son, pointing instead to his notebook. "Yep. You've even got a notebook."

He laughs lightly. "I'm pretty much a fervent note taker. My parents have given me notebooks and pens every Christmas as stocking stuffers. I know, I know. It's the height of the Christmas spirit."

"Mine give me Chap Stick," Martin offers.

"Socks," I add. "The Patricks are all about socks. Usually argyle socks."

"Ooh, I can't wait to see your argyle socks," Martin says to me. His teasing voice lightens my mood.

"Maybe I'll show them to you."

"Now, now, guys," Parker jumps in. "I know I'm going to get kicked out of my room plenty of times this year, but let's not get started in the Knothole too."

We all laugh—I'm relieved that at least Parker has a sense of humor—and then I decide it's time to get down to business. I tell them about Delaney and what she just told me.

"That's not much to go on," Martin says when I'm done.

"We don't even know *who* we're supposed to be investigating. It's pretty weak evidence."

I know he's not dissing me like Parker did, but his matter-of-fact appraisal of my first tip is yet another reminder that I don't have a clue how to lead.

But I *can* be quick on my feet. I'm a Themis student, after all. I'm a fast learner.

"Right, but that's because she walked away," I point out.

"Then why are we even meeting?" Martin asks.

"Because isn't that what we're supposed to do when someone brings us a tip? It says so in the notebook," I point out.

"Sure, but I'm not really clear on what the tip is, or what we're supposed to be discussing."

Oh, I'm sorry. Was I supposed to put together a whole game plan before coming to the board? A presentation with slides and an overhead projector?

"The tip is," I say in a louder, firmer voice, "there's some sort of cheating ring going on here, and they're using Anderin."

"But *who's* the victim?" Martin says crisply. "That's all I'm asking."

I open my mouth to speak, but I have nothing to say. The room fills with my own awkward silence as I fumble for an answer, because who *is* the victim here? Who's the Amy? Or even the Alex? I'm not so sure I'd say Delaney is the victim. The crime's not against her.

"Because that's our job. To defend people who need help,"

Martin adds, this time gently, this time his tone a reminder of why he joined the Mockingbirds in the first place when he was a sophomore—to help.

"But then is a crime only a crime if there is a victim?" Parker asks, and in this second I am grateful that our board is a threesome and not just Martin against me. I'm glad someone else is here to vet the tips. "There are obvious crimes, like bullying, where there's one person or a group of people hurting someone else. Or even hate speech. Same deal. Victims and attackers. Even theft has a perpetrator and a victim. Assault, rape, obviously do as well. And what they all have in common is—"

But Parker doesn't finish because Martin jumps in. "And *those* are the type of cases we've tried so far. The seniors who bullied the sophomores, Alex's case, Amy's case."

"But those aren't the only type of crimes," Parker continues, tapping his pen against his notebook. "Those are what we think of as *blue-collar crimes*. Crimes that involve violence. But there are other crimes too, crimes without violence, more *white-collar crimes*."

I quickly shift my eyes to Martin, wondering if he's thinking what I'm thinking—that Senator Hume's name is about to be invoked. Because isn't tax evasion the classic white-collar crime?

And just as the girl predicted, Parker says: "That's what my father was accused of. Cheating on his taxes. He didn't do it, of course. But the point is, those types of crimes— the kinds that involve deceit—they're crimes too. They might not be violent crimes. They're not one-against-one crimes. They're more about a moral code and how we treat one another."

Thank God for Senator Hume. Thank God for that tax scandal. Because for whatever reason, my weak tip is no longer the focal point of this Knothole session. I feel like I have front-row seats to a boxing match, but a gentleman's kind, as the boys keep up the jabs in their debate on morals, decency, and the good of society.

"Right, but a lot of times with so-called *white-collar crimes*, there are still victims," Martin says. "Think of all the people Bernie Madoff screwed over. Who lost their life savings. They were the victims."

I see a chance to jump in. "Shouldn't we then be thinking about who would be getting screwed over by cheating, then? By that same Bernie Madoff logic," I add.

"That's my point," Parker says, nodding in agreement. "Because cheating is a crime against a group of people. It has the potential to hurt students who don't cheat, who try to do the right thing. What if their grades are pulled down? What if they don't get into college because of those who cheated? *Everyone* here at this school has the potential to be affected by this. Not just Delaney. And that's where the whole idea of a greater moral code comes in. That's the whole point—these crimes can hurt everyone."

Martin furrows his brow. He's not convinced. "But is that what the Mockingbirds are supposed to uphold? A greater moral code?"

"Why not?" Parker tosses back. "Why are we just a police force for one particular type of crime? We all took the pledge tonight, but it ends there, as far as the administration is concerned. Because even with something like cheating, Merritt would still brush it aside because she wants a perfect record. She wants to say, *We have zero incidences of cheating here at Themis Academy.* And isn't that why we exist, then? Because the administration doesn't do a thing?"

Then Martin looks to me, their tête-à-tête over for now. "It's up to you. You're the leader. Do you think we should pursue this?"

I'm momentarily taken aback, because part of me thinks it's odd that he went from saying the tip was weak to asking me if we should move forward. But I also know he's not just changing his tune because of Parker's ability to argue a point. Martin respects the pecking order. At the end of the day, he knows the leader has the final word.

I pause for a moment before I answer, wanting to make sure my answer is the right one. But the truth is, I *know* the answer in my heart. Delaney may not be the victim. But she sought me out, she tracked me down, and she asked us to do something about the problem. That's why the Mockingbirds started. That's why the group was founded. It's not up to us to judge whether the crime is big or small. The simple act of someone needing us makes this cheating tip our jurisdiction.

It is one of our rules.

"Our first rule is we must give help to students who come

to us. She came to us. She asked for help. I think at the very least we should look into her tip," I say.

Martin nods. "Let's get into it, then."

"Good," Parker says, and if he had on a long-sleeve shirt he'd be rolling up his sleeves right now, digging in. "I think the next step should be to address what Delaney's motivation could be in tipping you off."

"Well, obviously it's because of what happened to her at Matthew Winters. She doesn't want to take the chance of being framed again."

"But why *would* she be framed?" Parker asks curiously. "Why did she feel the need to tip you off? If she's tipping you off, she probably thinks there's a reason she could be framed again. So, why would she think she'd be accused again?"

Did the board ask these questions about me last year? Did they ask what my motivation was in telling them what happened to me? Did they dissect not just my case but whether I might have any ulterior motives too? I feel a brief flicker of anger at the Mockingbirds, now that I am seeing things from the other side. But then, I had the same thoughts about Delaney. I guess this is what the good of the whole is all about. Looking into every angle.

"The thing we need most is info. So, what do we know about Delaney?" Martin asks.

"She has purple hair. She's from Detroit. She's a junior. She's in a band at home," I say, rattling off everything I learned earlier. But none of that points to why she'd be concerned about a repeat accusation. So I quickly add, before anyone else can suggest it, "Who's she dating? Who's she rooming with? Who's she friends with? Who would she want to protect? Who would she want to see punished?"

Martin grins at my litany of questions, rhetorical though they may be, and I know I'm hitting on something, heading in the right direction.

Parker chimes in. "She's been on and off with Theo McBride since she started here," he says, and I know that name better than I knew Delaney's. He's an incredible dancer, the only other student I know here who has Juilliard in his crosshairs. He's a senior, and he's been a regular fixture in dance competitions all over the country, handily winning most, and he's been scouted by the Alvin Ailey and Martha Graham dance companies. He's worthy—I've seen him perform here at Themis, and his moves take your breath away; he dances like air, like water, like fire.

I wonder if our dean gave him orders to get into Juilliard too.

"The dancer!" I say quickly, like I'm on a quiz show, banging the red light. *I know the answer! I know the answer!* "He's amazing," I add.

"Not anymore," Parker says. "Didn't you hear? He had an ACL tear over the summer. Landed wrong or something."

"He did?"

"Yeah, he came to Hopkins to have surgery. My mom's head of orthopedics," he adds.

"Did she do the surgery?"

"No, one of her colleagues. I hear he's not dancing anymore."

"That's so sad," I say, and I suddenly feel an intense pang for Theo. If I were sidelined from the piano, I'd be lost, like a wanderer roaming the desert for years, thirsting for water but never finding it. I might as well be dead if I couldn't play. Then my mind shifts back to Ms. Merritt and what she said to me earlier. I wonder if she knows about Theo's injury, if she's aware that the other Juilliard aspirant is out of commission, and if that's why she's putting her chips on me. If that's why she sounded just a little bit desperate.

"Regardless of how sad his injury is, I don't think we should be assuming he's in any way related to this cheating ring, guys," Martin says, the voice of reason, of measure, like he was before. "I mean, she might have just heard about it in general. And naturally, given her history, she wouldn't want to take a chance. We need to talk to her again. Find out more about what's going on."

Then Parker offers another idea. "Do you think it's possible Delaney's actually involved in the cheating? And by tipping us off she's hoping to not be implicated?"

"You mean maybe she wasn't so innocent after all at Matthew Winters?"

Parker shrugs. "I'm just saying…"

It's a nefarious suggestion, but I wonder if he's onto something. Yes, we have an unbreakable rule about helping those who need it, and we're clearly going to do our due diligence. But I'd be foolish if I didn't keep in mind that there's also a ruthlessness to this school—to any prep school—and it's not out of the question that even with her history Delaney could be playing us, maybe establishing her own early alibi by tipping us off to the cheating ring. This is Themis—we are all driven here, we are all relentlessly pursuing excellence, and we can all be calculating enough if we have to be.

And because I'm like that too—maybe not calculating, definitely not underhanded, but *driven*, driven to excellence—I do the natural thing a Themis student and the Mockingbirds' leader would do.

I volunteer for extra credit.

"I'll talk to her again tomorrow," I say.

◆ ◆ ◆

"I sort of feel like I'm dating the boss," Martin says after Parker leaves the laundry room. We're alone together on the beat-up couch.

"Is that bad?" I ask.

"Nah. I'm a postmodern man. I'm like the guy who doesn't mind that his girlfriend makes more money than him."

"I believe that's called a trophy husband. Or a kept man," I tease.

"I could be good in either role, don't you think?"

I laugh, then ask, "Do you think it's weird, though, that we're working together and not always agreeing?"

"Why would we always agree?"

I shrug by way of an answer, then shift to another question. "So, how do you think I did with my first meeting?" My voice rises. I realize I'm nervous. I want to do a good job for so many reasons, but I also want Martin to think I'm doing a good job. He's been doing this so much longer than I have. "I mean, it's my first official meeting."

"You were great."

I laugh, a disbelieving laugh. "Seriously."

"Yeah. Seriously," he says, his brown eyes fixed on mine.

"I don't know. This is hard," I admit, and when I do I feel lighter—just voicing some of my worries out loud makes them weigh on me less. So I unburden more. "It's very trial by fire. I feel like I'm just making it up as I go along. Besides, how can you say I did great when you were all, *Why are we having a meeting? Why are you bringing this tip to us?*" I ask, imitating him.

He laughs. "Is that what I sound like?"

"Yeah. Totally," I say, punching him on the arm.

"Ouch."

"So. Answer the question, Martin."

"Because one does not preclude the other. I thought you did great, and I also didn't agree with you. But then you convinced me."

"I think Parker was the one doing the convincing," I say.

Martin rolls his eyes. "Parker was fine. But you," he says, and places his index finger on my chest, where my heart is. He pushes lightly. "You have what it takes in here."

I feel warm all over, but it's not only physical. It's deeper, and it comes from knowing he's not just into me on the outside; he's into all of me, and he sees all of me. I grab his hand, and with my hand on top I press his closer, imagining that he can feel how his words have turned the temperature up through every square inch of my body.

"Maybe I should disagree with you more," he says, moving his body closer to mine.

"Let's fight and make up."

"Over and over. Terrible fights, horrible fights," he says, and buries his face in my hair. "The worst."

"Because it bothers you so very much to be beneath me in the chain of command."

"I'm so bothered by it, Alex. It makes me want to fight even more," he says, then runs his hands through my hair the way I like. Everything he does is the way I like.

"Mmmm..."

He shifts me so I'm sitting on his lap. "Now I'm literally beneath you. So fitting."

I pretend to swat him, but he pulls up for another kiss.

"I like you beneath me," I whisper to him.

"I like it too," he says, and right now, in this moment, it's just the two of us here. No one else is in my head.

Then as soon as I think that, an image flickers by. Quick, fast, like a burglar outside a window. But I've spotted the thief and, try as I might, he keeps looking through the glass. So I shut my eyes and rest my head against Martin's chest. He wraps his arms around me tight and holds me close. And now we are not Mockingbirds. We are just us. Just a boy and a girl trying to move beyond what happened.

Chapter Six

WORKING GIRLS

When I was younger, I was a baseball fan. My father was a fanatic, a diehard, so he felt it was necessary and vital to take my sister and me to ball games. He taught us how to keep score, and by age seven I was tracking the number of errors and base hits and the batting averages for every professional baseball team. I know—it was an unusual habit for a piano girl. But I liked the numbers, the history, the strategy.

Then I stopped.

I went cold turkey when I learned about the sport's modern history and how steroids had radiated across nearly all of professional baseball, touching virtually every player. The sport was tainted; they were tainted. Their records didn't matter; their scores didn't matter. I could sit there and tally up RBIs till the wee hours of the morning, but there would be asterisks next to their names.

Because they doped up to get ahead.

"You just don't do that," I told my dad. "So I'm not going to follow baseball anymore. And I don't think you should either."

It broke his heart, but he agreed and joined in my boycott.

I was just a fan, though. So while I understand the broader philosophical stance—success of any kind needs to come on its own terms, by its own merits—I also *want* to understand the personal one. I want to understand why Delaney's so worried about a possible déjà vu that she'd seek me out the second school started.

When classes end the next day, I head straight to her dorm.

I knock and knock and knock.

There's no answer.

The music is blasting from her room, so I bang louder. They're probably rocking out to her tunes in nearby Connecticut too.

"Delaney!" I shout as loud as I can possibly go.

The music stops, and she yanks the door open.

"What? Oh. It's you," she says.

"Yeah, it's me."

"What are you doing?"

"I'm here to see you," I say. "You came to find me yesterday. I came to find you today."

She narrows her eyes at me, looks me up and down, then scans the halls. She nods and lets me in, quickly shutting the door behind her.

Her bed is piled with clothes, T-shirts upon jeans upon jackets with ironed-on patches all over them. Her floor is littered with suitcases and duffel bags. The one thing that's neat is the row of nail polish bottles on her desk, easily twenty or thirty of them. I notice she's holding the brush of one of them—a sparkly sea green. I glance down at her nails. Every other one has been painted sea green; they alternate with cherry red.

"I like your nails," I say.

"Want me to do yours?"

"Sure," I say, and I sit down on her desk chair. She grabs another chair and pulls it up next to mine.

"What color do you want?" she asks.

"You pick," I say.

"Blue," she declares, and reaches for a color the shade of a cloudless summer sky. "You are definitely a blue."

"You must be the Color Oracle. Yesterday you said I should do a blue streak."

"Yes, but that was because you told me you'd thought about dyeing your hair blue," she says, correcting my memory.

"True," I say as she brushes on a daub of nail polish, spreading the color perfectly in one, two, three strokes. She continues across my right hand with the same precision and I say, "You're like a pro. Wow."

"I am a pro," she says. "I do this for a living back home. And on weekends at a salon down on Kentfield Street."

"You do?"

"Yeah. Why? Does that bother you?" The raspiness in her voice is its own question mark.

"No. Why would it bother me?" I ask, but I know why she's asking. Because she has some sort of chip on her shoulder, some sort of defensiveness, like she did when I asked her about her hometown. She thinks it should bother me because it must bother other people, other students.

"Because I have a job, unlike the rest of the students here," she adds.

"Then you should let me pay you," I say.

She shakes her head. "No. I offered to do your nails." She reaches for my left hand. "Blow on your right," she instructs, and I do as I'm told. With her practiced hand she applies the color to my left hand, and I realize Delaney and I are similar. We both work with our hands. We both have chips on our shoulders. She thinks people will judge her for her past. I think people will disrespect me for not having earned the Mockingbirds job. And maybe that's the reason the Mockingbirds pay it forward, because when you've been through something yourself, it's much easier to connect to someone else. Maybe that's why I don't need a leadership pedigree or a lengthy résumé of captainships. I'm here because I had my training by fire.

"Delaney, is Theo involved in the cheating ring?" I ask as she finishes my pinkie.

She keeps her head bent over my hand, not meeting my eyes. "Why are you asking about Theo?"

"You're dating him, right?"

She shrugs. She's uncharacteristically quiet.

"Should I take that as a yes?"

A nod.

"So, is he the reason you reached out to me?"

She looks up now, her blue-gray eyes behind her glasses meeting mine hard. "You think I'd rat him out, don't you?"

I stay calm. "I didn't say that. I just asked if he's involved."

"I'm not a rat," she says, her voice low but still full of smoke.

"Hey," I say softly, and I have this impulse to reach out and touch her knee to reassure her. But I don't do it. "I know you're not a rat. I would never think you're a rat. I think cheating sucks too, Delaney. And if someone I cared about was doing it, you damn well better believe I'd try to stop him."

She looks up quickly, her eyes blazing at me through her silver-framed glasses. She points at herself. "You think I didn't try to stop him? I tried, but he just totally denied it. Completely, one hundred percent denied it. And besides, I hardly know anything," she fires off.

"Can you tell me what you do know, though?" I ask gently, thinking of what Martin said last night, of how when I lead from the heart, I know what I'm doing. This is what I zone in on—just talking to her, just connecting.

She breathes out hard, pushes her hands through her purple hair.

"Yesterday I saw some of his e-mails. But I didn't read

them," she says defensively. She takes a beat, then continues, "Okay, I mean I looked at them. But not like looked *through* them. They were just up on his screen, and I saw bits and pieces about"—she stops to sketch air quotes—"*the plan.*"

"The plan to . . . ?"

"What I told you yesterday. I don't have any more details. He was e-mailing other students; they were setting things in motion about competing again. That's all I know. He said *competing again.*"

"Like dance competitions? I don't think Anderin helps you *dance* again," I add.

"No. It doesn't. That's why something else is going on and I don't know what, because once I saw those e-mails I asked what was going on."

"What did he say?"

She steels herself for the next thing. "To stop snooping."

"What'd you say?"

"I told him not to leave e-mails up on his screen," she says proudly.

"So is he the one supplying?"

"I don't know. As you can imagine, he was kind of pissed."

"So why'd you come to us?" I ask, wanting to finish the conversation that was truncated yesterday, wanting to hear from her what we only surmised in the Knothole.

"Because I told him to stop. I said whatever he's doing needs to stop, but he just said he wasn't going to talk about it. Wasn't going to discuss it with me. And I can't take a chance of this thing blowing up again. I'd never get into college then. Sure, it's all fine and good that Matthew Winters apologized, but could you imagine what would happen if I'm even remotely connected, even through my boyfriend, to another accusation of cheating? I'd never get into college. Never. That's why you can't say it came from me. You can't let on, okay?"

"I won't," I say, reassuring her. I will protect her like the Mockingbirds protected me.

"If people ask why I'm talking to you, I'll say I'm a runner or something. I'll say I'm in the Mockingbirds. But if you're going to press charges against him or anybody for this, it won't be from me."

"But you do want us to investigate him and see if we can figure out where it's coming from and who's behind it?" I ask, because I want to hear it from her. "Do you want us to help you?"

"Yes. I want you to help. And I want you to stop it, obviously."

"Then I will. Look into it," I say, and blow a long stream of air against the fingernails on my left hand. "Now, I have to ask you something."

"What?"

"Are you involved?"

Her eyes go wide. "No!"

I hold up my hands. "I have to ask."

"I would *never* do that. I thought that was clear."

I give her a hard look. "I need to trust you. I need to know you're not messing with us."

"Alex, I did your nails."

"And I love them. But I need to know you're not playing with us. You want us to protect you, and we will. But we're about to go out on a limb and investigate a far-reaching cheating ring because of what is effectively an anonymous tip. And I need to know we're not being played."

"I swear I'm not playing you."

"Good. I'm glad," I say. "You know, Delaney, I could give you a really good cover-up for being seen with me."

"Yeah?"

"Yeah."

"What is it?" she asks warily.

"Come sing with us at the Faculty Club in two weeks. I thought we could do something," I begin, then pause for effect, "*ironic*."

She smiles. "Hell yeah."

"Good. We're going to practice this weekend. I'm thinking subversive songs."

"How about protest songs?"

"How about songs that rage against the man?"

"How about 'Another Brick in the Wall'?"

I smile, nodding a few times, then I think of something better, something apropos for many reasons. I tell her my idea.

"Perfect," she says, and we shake hands.

Chapter Seven

THE SCENE OF THE CRIME

And so the investigation begins.

I spend the evening rereading notes on past investigations that the Mockingbirds have conducted. As I flip through pages in the notebook, it's clear there's not really a secret sauce to them, especially ones at such an early stage. The one rule—guideline, really—is to *be respectful.* Which means we aren't supposed to cross lines. We aren't supposed to trip people up or try to catch them on hidden cameras or go snooping through their things, their phones, their bags. If we did that stuff, then *we'd* be the bullies, *we'd* be the bad guys. So my job right now is just to find clues, and according to my sister's own handwriting here in the Mockingbirds notebook, we're supposed to do that simply by *keeping our eyes and ears open for clues.*

Not easy.

I shut the notebook and look at my watch. It's eight at night, which means it's way past midnight in Barcelona, where Casey is studying abroad for this semester. I want to call her and ask her what she meant by *keep our eyes and ears open for clues*. And could you be a *tad* more specific with this whole *be respectful* directive, big sis?

My sister founded the Mockingbirds when she was a student here four years ago. She was consumed with guilt over the suicide of a girl in her dorm who'd been bullied. That girl—Jen—had tried to talk to Ms. Merritt but was roundly blown off. Jen went to Casey too. She didn't tell my sister she was thinking of shuffling off her mortal coil, but even so Casey felt like she didn't do enough. She felt responsible. So she created the Mockingbirds to give students options.

Now it's my job to live up to her legacy.

And since it's too late to ask Casey what this all means, I give Amy a call. She's a junior here, and lives a floor below me. Her advice is simple, but it makes sense. "Just keep an eye on Theo and look for clues, signs, evidence. That's all you can do right now at this early stage. You can't cross any lines," she tells me.

"But what does that mean—cross a line?"

"It means you can't start following him around until you have something concrete on him," she says. "You don't want him to freak out and think he's being tracked or about to be tried or anything. Because he could very easily not be guilty, and we don't want students thinking we're out there following everyone without cause. You need to have a reason to follow someone. I mean, we're not the government, wiretapping and profiling and all. So, for now, you have to keep it casual, observe him in class or in the caf or when you see him in public places."

"So what you're saying is keep an eye on him without letting on we're keeping an eye on him, and hope I happen to find a clue?"

Amy laughs. "Yeah, something like that."

I shake my head. "This isn't easy."

"No, it's not."

I say good-bye and look up Theo McBride's name in the school directory to see where he lives.

Richardson Hall.

The name itself makes me shudder.

Richardson Hall is where Carter lives. Richardson Hall is where Carter date-raped me. I haven't been there since that night. I've barely even seen Carter since the trial. After he was found guilty, he practically went radio silent for the rest of last year. It was like he was the one walking the long way to class, he was the one staying as far away from me as he could, because I hardly saw him.

I like hardly seeing him. No. I *freaking* love it.

So there is no way I am going to that dorm to keep my eyes and ears open for clues. No way am I setting foot in that building ever again. If the memories come crashing down when my boyfriend touches me, I'm not going to walk into the combat zone and let the flashbacks unleash a full-scale assault.

Besides, I have boys for fellow board members. They can do it. They can stroll through Richardson Hall—dorms are open to all students—and keep their eyes and ears open. I'll tell them in the morning.

But when morning rolls around, I rethink the decision to send the boys. I feel weak. I feel afraid. I feel like I'm right back where I was last year. Afraid to go anywhere. Afraid to leave my room. Afraid to walk around my school.

And I didn't go to the Mockingbirds to be afraid.

Because this is *my* school. This is *my* senior year. This is *my* life, and I took it back last year and I plan to keep it.

So as I shower, I tell myself to snap out of it.

As I get dressed, I remind myself I can set foot at the scene of the crime without this feeling that everything's a drive-by shooting and I'm left with bullet wounds on the side of the road.

As I grab my backpack and literally march across the quad to Richardson Hall, I repeat that I am not doing this for the Mockingbirds, for Delaney, for the greater good or anything like that. I am going to walk into Richardson Hall *for me*.

I open the doors to Richardson Hall. Theo is in room 103, just a few doors down. I grit my teeth and push ahead, turning down the hall. There are boys everywhere; the place is teeming with them, and I feel exposed again, as if they all see the crime against me, as if they all look at me and think, *There's that girl who was date-raped.* Or maybe they think of me now as Martin's girl, his damaged goods, and feel sorry for both of us.

It's then that I see him.

Carter.

All the way at the other end. He doesn't see me—not yet, at least. He's walking with his head down, maybe toward the bathroom. I'm here and he's here and there's one long, looming hallway and many dorm rooms and many boys between us.

But I keep walking.

Then everything happens quickly. It's not like in the movies, where it's slow-motion. Here in real life, things happen in a snap. Carter looks up. He spots me. A door opens. It's the bathroom. Theo steps out. Carter opens his mouth. Theo glances down the hall. Carter shouts, "Get out of here, whore." Theo turns to Carter, then to me. He puts a hand on my back and nods to the open door to his room, guiding me inside.

"How about *you* get out of here, douche bag?" Theo shouts back down the hall to Carter.

Then to me, gently, "You okay?"

I nod because I can't speak. Because my skin doesn't feel like mine. My bones don't feel like mine.

"He's an ass," Theo adds.

I still don't say anything.

"Are you okay?" he asks again.

Then I realize Theo knows what Carter did. But he's on my side, and I have to stop acting like a mute.

"Yeah, I'm fine," I manage. "But thanks. Seriously."

"Anytime. Are you going to class now?" he asks as he

grabs his backpack from the floor and slings it over his shoulder. "Or did you need something here in Richardson? Are you meeting someone?"

"I have English," I say, answering his first question, but not the second or third.

"Me too," he says, and gestures to his door. But before we leave, he reaches to his desk and grabs something. I glance back, and when I do I see it's a pill bottle and it's full of little orange pills.

Now I feel dirty in a whole new way, because as we walk to class, I keep thinking I have a secret I don't want to have, a clue I wish I hadn't uncovered. Because now I'm spying on the guy who rescued me this morning.

And even though I didn't cross a line, it *feels* like I did.

I try to tell myself the pill bottle proves nothing. That this is not a clue whatsoever. That everything is totally circumstantial, coincidental, and happenstance.

But I can't shake the feeling, especially when he stops at the water fountain outside class, roots around for something in his pocket, then takes a drink.

◆ ◆ ◆

Mr. Baumann begins English class with a statement. "When you are sixteen, adults are slightly impressed and almost intimidated by you."

He's seated on the edge of the desk at the front of the classroom. Perched, really. He's one of the younger teachers here, though *young* is a relative word, because I'm pretty sure he's in his mid-thirties, which makes him twice as old as us. His hair is blondish, or it had been, at least, but last year it started to turn gray, and now you can see more streaks creeping in every day. I wonder if that means this job is wearing him down already or if he was always going to go gray now.

"Do you think adults are impressed or intimidated, or both, by you?" he asks, then gestures with an open palm to us.

I look around and notice Theo is eager to answer the question. His hand is straight up in the air. But Maia's hand juts up too. Mr. Baumann nods at her.

"But we're not sixteen. We're seniors, so we're seventeen, and some of us are even eighteen."

"But of course. Let us never forget the facts," he says with a grin, and then taps the cover of a paperback book on his desk. I can't see the title. "However, what I am more interested in are not just the facts but how we exist with them, especially when the facts are bent and shifted. In this case, the question is not so much about the age or the number but about the experience of being a teenager and how adults see you. To that end, perhaps I will rephrase the question. Are adults slightly impressed and almost intimidated by the likes of you?"

Theo's practically waving his hand back and forth like a flag. But another hand shoots up. I turn around and notice Anjali Durand, the New Nine member I passed over for appointment to the Mockingbirds board. She's no longer on the council—she served her one-year term, but she did choose to stay on as a tier-two runner this year. A wispy red scarf is wrapped stylishly around her neck, her dark blond hair clipped back, her straight bangs falling just above her eyes. The effect is striking—both youthful, with the bangs, and sophisticated, with the scarf.

"I think they are intimidated by what they have lost and what we still have," Anjali says. She has the slightest trace of a French accent, just enough to be interesting, not enough to be overly distracting.

"And by that, presumably, you mean youth?" Mr. Baumann asks.

Anjali nods. "Yes, but also an openness about the world, right? We're still malleable and receptive to new views and new opinions. We can change more easily than adults, without as much moaning and creaking of the joints."

A smile lights up his face. "Moaning and creaking of the joints. Very nice, Anjali." Then he adds, "Are we impressed too?"

Theo's still going at it, raising his arm higher and farther than anyone, almost like he could touch the ceiling—and even like that, with his arm lifted in class, he has a natural grace and fluidity to him. Now that I'm out of Richardson and removed from the shock of seeing Carter, I feel as if I can see things clearly again. Like Theo and how he moves—like water; his long, lean frame flows in and out of space like he's one with the air around him. Even his hair looks as though it's dancing—it's caramel brown and wavy, and I would swear a breeze is blowing through it just so, just around him.

"Theo. It seems you have something to say," Mr. Baumann says, inviting the eager boy to answer.

"Why would adults *not* be impressed with the accomplishments of the young? The way we balance a million different things, the way we must navigate between being no longer a child but not quite an adult. The way we often have to figure this all out on our own," Theo says, in an astonishing fit of eloquence. It's not surprising to hear eloquence from a student, nor from Theo. But he doesn't sound like the Theo of thirty minutes ago. He sounds like an adult. He sounds like he's giving a speech. It sounds like the orange pill he just took has kicked in.

But why would he be using Anderin for an advantage? The advantage he wants is the one he evidently can't have yet—to dance again. Anderin doesn't restore an ACL. Anderin doesn't help you compete in dance competitions or ace auditions for Alvin Ailey or Martha Graham.

"Well said, Theo. Well said." Mr. Baumann nods. Then he picks up the book on his desk, but he's holding it on his lap so I still can't see it. "As some of you know, I also advise the debate team, so you can expect that we'll be enjoying many hearty debates in this class this semester."

Maia straightens up a bit higher as he says that. Nothing could please her more than the chance to sharpen her skills, especially with the Elite on her radar screen.

Mr. Baumann chuckles slightly. "Well, I shouldn't

presume you'll enjoy them. You might be bored stiff, but I suspect not, because I have selected a series of books for the next few months that I believe should speak to all of you. Because you all will have something in common with these books. *Jane Eyre, Nicholas Nickelby, Tom Brown's School Days*," he rattles off. "We'll also read *The Chocolate War* by Robert Cormier and *A Separate Peace* by John Knowles. What you have in common with them is they, either in part or in whole, are set at private prep schools, usually boarding schools," he adds.

Oh. Well, that *is* a bit more interesting.

"And I want you to look for yourselves in these school stories. Boarding school in particular is an unusual experience. You live away from home in dorms with your friends. You're given all sorts of freedom but even more responsibility. What do you do with that freedom? What do you do with your responsibility? What did your fictional counterparts do, and what does that say about truth in fiction? That will be the overarching theme of this semester—truth in fiction. And perhaps then we will better understand what John Knowles meant in *A Separate Peace* when he wrote, 'When you are sixteen, adults are slightly impressed and almost intimidated by you.'"

He holds up the paperback, then adds, "In this context, it was about war. Which is why you should never take things at face value. Because Knowles wasn't just talking about the experience of being a teenager. He was talking about teenagers getting ready to fight a war. A war the adults would only watch. 'When you are sixteen, adults are slightly impressed and almost intimidated by you. This is a puzzle, finally solved by the realization that they foresee your military future, fighting for them. You do not foresee it,'" he reads. "As you can see, context is everything and nothing at the same time. Words both stand alone and with each other."

When class ends, I notice Theo leaves with Anjali. They fall quickly into what looks like a deep conversation. Maia and I leave together.

"That was a headfake if I ever saw one," Maia says, and it's clear she approves.

I look at her out of the corner of my eye. "A headfake? You mean because he set us up to think he was talking about teenagers, and then it turned out he was talking about war? And then it was as if he was talking about the first thing again?"

"It was bloody brilliant. I am totally going to use that strategy in my next debate. It's like your opponent thinks you're going one way with the football," she says, then demonstrates by turning her head to the right, "then, boom! You're off and running the other way." She finishes by turning her head to the left.

"Did you actually just refer to football, as in *American football*? I thought you had a long-standing practice of spitting on American football."

"I still spit on American football. The headfake is an English football strategy too, my oh-so-American roommate. And besides, it's properly known as *footy* in the homeland," she says as we walk across the quad to our next classes. "Speaking of the homeland, did I tell you Ms. Merritt wrote to me this summer about the Elite? Several times actually, asking if I was prepping for it yet, if I was going to be ready, if the other debaters would be ready," Maia says.

"Creepy. Did you delete her messages?"

"Yes," Maia says proudly. "Though I finally relented two weeks ago and answered *one* of them. But get this! I made it seem as if I hadn't received the ten other e-mails because I live in London, hence the *homeland* connection. Like the Internet doesn't work there or something. I told her I had *spotty* Internet access at our country home, and I was so dreadfully sorry I hadn't replied to her notes."

I laugh. "You don't even have a country home!"

"I know. That's the irony of it."

"But you know, she *loves* thinking you do."

"Oh, she ate it up. I'm pretty sure the next e-mail she sent was to my parents asking for a donation. She probably figures they're *lords*."

"Shall I call you Lady Maia, then, in front of her?"

"Oh, please do. In fact, I command you to as my royal subject."

"It's all because of that stupid J. Sullivan James Award. She made it pretty clear she's pretty much dying for me to get into Juilliard," I say.

"There are three criteria to judging the winner of the J. Sullivan James Award. Academic excellence, athletic excellence, and artistic excellence. So debate, theater, music, dance—they are all part of the artistic portion of judging for the award. I looked it up," Maia says.

"You research everything."

"You have to know the enemy," Maia says.

◆ ◆ ◆

When I arrive at orchestra later in the morning, my friend Jones is waiting outside for me, lounging against the railing, sunglasses on. But the strange part is he's actually holding his violin in public. Even stranger is when he lifts the instrument to his chin, then gently, like a painter, an artist, Monet himself laying a brush to canvas, massages the strings with the bow.

I recognize the first notes immediately, Tchaikovsky's 1812 Overture, and I'm about to shout it victoriously, but then he shifts into something else, something more Jones's speed, opting for a little Vampire Weekend.

"For a second I thought you might actually play Tchaikovsky. More than a few notes, that is," I say, and give Jones a reunion hug, then a quick once-over. With his brown hair now reaching his shoulders, he's totally got the whole rock-star look going on. He's the most amazing classical violinist, but he'd rather be jamming on his electric guitar. I have no doubt he'll make his way back to New York City for college when we graduate, and start some awesome band. I can picture him in cool little indie clubs, the kind where beer has sloshed onto the wood floor so many times, the place smells permanently of hops. The lights'll dim, he'll come onstage with his bandmates, and then he'll jam out an epic opening chord sequence on a sleek silver Fender Stratocaster.

The crowd will go wild. The girls will swoon.

"I heard Delaney Zirinski is in need of your services," Jones says, then gives me a wink.

I'm shocked, but then I'm not shocked. Nothing gets by Jones. He notices things, sees things, then sees what lies beneath. Like he found out some shady stuff his dad's company was up to this summer and now they're engaged in some kind of standoff. It's a shame Jones isn't a Mockingbird. He'd make a terrific investigator, an unbeatable secret weapon.

Still, it's my job to protect Delaney. God knows, I wouldn't have wanted Amy giving up my name, rank, and serial number before I was ready last year. So I will myself to keep all the muscles in my face still, to not grin, to not frown, to not give a thing away.

"Not sure what you mean," I say.

A full-blown grin fills his face, like a kid whose dad just handed him the keys to the car. "That is really adorable. How you do that whole stony-faced denial thing."

I press my lips together, fighting harder to remain a blank. "How was your summer?"

Now he laughs and points a finger at me. "This is good. It's like a show. I want to see more."

I look away but can feel a smirk starting to bloom on my face.

"Ah, there. I knew I could break you down."

"I'm saying nothing," I say, but I can hear the laughter breaking through my voice.

"It's okay, Alex. Don't feel bad," he says, and wiggles an eyebrow. "My ability to put two and two together knows no bounds."

"You are the worst," I say, teasing him.

"But don't you want to know how I knew she was in need of your services?"

I hold up my hands as if to say yes.

He taps his forehead. "You leave D-Day. Two seconds later, she leaves D-Day. Ergo." Then he adds, "Besides, I hear the same things she hears. It's so Themis, isn't it? Anderin is like the drug of choice for overachievers."

Which is pretty much an apt description for anyone who goes to this school. I can only imagine what'll happen at Themis if this gets out of hand. A whole student body amped up on speed. It's like giving a cheetah a triple espresso when it's chasing down a gazelle. The cheetah doesn't need another advantage, but the cheetah will take it.

Predators, all of us.

Jones returns to Vampire Weekend, tucking his violin back under his chin. He sings quietly, plays quietly in the final moments before the bell rings, but I still recognize the words and the music. I also recognize an opportunity when I hear one.

"Hey, Jones. Would you come to the Faculty Club with me? Ms. Merritt wants the Mockingbirds—the a cappella version of the Mockingbirds—to come sing."

He straightens his head but keeps the violin on his shoulder. "You're crazy. I only make Faculty Club appearances if I have to."

I give him a light punch. "Do it for me?"

He plays a few more notes. "We'll see," he says.

"You'd do it if I told you about the morning I had," I say, rolling my eyes to make light of things. But the fact is, that run-in with Carter still lingers, like the scent of sliced onions left in the garbage can for too long. So I tell Jones what happened, the way Carter spewed those words out—*whore*.

"God, I hate that guy," Jones says. "Why can't he leave you alone?"

I shrug, then sigh. "I don't know."

"If I ever see him or hear him say anything like that to you or anyone, well, it'll be the last time any words come out of his mouth for a long time."

I give Jones a faint smile. I love the protector in him, though I don't mention Theo played that role earlier today.

"But what were you doing in Richardson Hall?" Jones asks.

I look away. I don't want him to see me as I lie to him. "Nothing," I say.

"Nothing? Why do I have a hard time believing that?"

"Jones, it was nothing, okay?"

"I'm sure this *nothing* had everything to do with your case."

"Yes, it did, and that's all I can say because I shouldn't be talking about it," I say. Because I have to do my best to protect people's privacy. No one's been charged with anything.

"Playing by the rules," he remarks.

"It's the least I can do," I say.

"You won't even bend for your old friend Jones? Maybe I can convince you with a little of this," he says, then returns to the violin, to the 1812 Overture, a musical gesture just for me. Then he stops playing and lays a hand on my shoulder and it's as if Tchaikovsky radiates from it, like notes are seeping out of his fingertips, and my skin beneath the fabric of my T-shirt absorbs the music, shoots it through my body and turns me into a human tuning fork. This must be what they say about great guitarists, extraordinary violinists. They are "hands men," and there is something simply electric in the way his hand feels after he's just played.

"Did it work?" he asks, taking his hand off me. My shoulder goes silent, and I don't like it. I want it bursting with sound again.

"Nope. I'm a vault," I say, making a motion to zip my mouth closed.

"Damn. I'll have to try harder next time," he says, and holds the door open for me for our music class.

But before I go in, I say, "Of course, it should be noted that I would gladly tell you *almost* everything if you'd just join the Mockingbirds."

"Ha," he laughs. "Like that'll happen."

I give an exaggerated sigh. "I know, I know. You operate alone."

He shrugs. "I am a loner, as they say. But, you know, not in the creepy, dark-raincoat way."

"Right. More like the leather-jacket-and-motorcycle way," I say, picturing Jones rumbling down a long stretch of deserted highway, perfectly content with himself and the road in front of him.

"Something like that."

"Well, if you ever change your mind, you have an open invitation to join. I wouldn't even make you go through all the hoops."

"You'd bend the rules for me," he says, then winks.

"Only for you," I say.

As the door closes, I find myself touching my shoulder ever so briefly as if I can feel a lingering vibration. Then it occurs to me that when Jones touched me, I didn't think about Carter at all. When he touched me, it was as if his hand had silenced all those memories and the only thing I felt or saw or heard was music.

Chapter Eight

STATE'S EVIDENCE

I keep my eye on Theo. So do Martin and Parker.

We can report that he and Delaney are very hot and heavy. Everywhere I turn, I see the two of them. But not where you'd expect—never in the caf, or on the quad. Martin will run into them at the library, pressed up against each other, down in the stacks. Or I'll spot them way down by the side of one of the buildings in between classes, when they think no one is looking, and he'll be running a hand down her leg. One night after I leave the music hall, I see them slipping off campus, and she's touching his hair as they walk off into the night.

She's hooked on him, that much is clear. She may hate cheating, she may want to have nothing to do with even the mere suggestion of it, but she can't seem to resist the boy she's saying is doing it.

I can also tell you that Theo spends his afternoons in the dance studio. I know this because it's right next to the music hall, where I spend my afternoons. That first week of school I see him slip in with the rest of the dancers every day, wearing dance clothes like the rest of them.

But then one afternoon I hear the door slam and the sound of feet in the hallway. I take a chance it might be him, so I pop out of the music hall to get a drink from the water fountain. My hunch was right. Theo's practically marching toward the door now, fire in his eyes. I take a quick drink, then say hello.

"Hey, Theo," I say.

He looks taken aback. "Hey, Alex."

"Thanks again for that morning." I still feel kind of weird knowing he helped me out of a jam and yet now I'm *keeping an eye* on him.

"Has that douche bag left you alone since then?"

"No more run-ins."

Theo squints for a second, glances down at his knee quickly, then back up. My heart caves in a bit, aching for what he's lost, what he's losing. Now is not the time to question him about the pill bottles. Now is the time to just be there for him, like he was for me.

"I keep meaning to tell you that I heard about your injury. I'm really sorry."

"Yeah, me too."

"How bad is it?" I ask.

"Bad."

"Are you dancing, though?" I ask, and nod toward the studio.

"I'm not supposed to. But I do it anyway."

A pang of sympathy shoots through me, knowing that's what he's been doing for the last week, dancing through the pain. "What did it feel like?" I ask, and in this moment I'm not a Mockingbird at all. I'm just another student, another aspiring artist.

"When I got injured? Or just now?"

"Now. When you were trying to dance through the pain."

"Like shrapnel in my leg. Like a grenade exploding in my knee."

I wince, and he puts a hand on *my* shoulder as if *I'm* the one in pain. "Hey. I'll survive," he says, and gives me a half-hearted smile.

"Are you still going to apply to Juilliard?" I ask, and I can't hide the hopefulness in the question, like maybe there's a way around this, a way out for him.

"I don't know. I don't know anything," he says, then sighs. "Want to hear something funny?"

"Sure."

He brushes a hand through his caramel-colored hair, and I watch as the pieces fall through his fingers. "Ms. Merritt wrote to me over the summer when she heard about my knee," he tells me.

The name of our dean causes an instant reaction—I roll my eyes. "What did she say?"

"She was *saddened*—that was her word—to learn that

my dreams might not materialize. And she had some *suggestions* for what I might be able to do with my *creative energy*."

"What were those suggestions?" I ask cautiously, my antennae now up where Ms. Merritt is concerned.

He shrugs. "Not worth mentioning," he says. "Anyway, I guess it's up to you to carry the torch for her. You're her only hope," he says playfully, but we both know there's a sick truth to it.

"What about you? Are you done with dance forever?"

"I have no idea."

"So what are you going to do?"

"The way I see it there are two options: find something else or die."

I nod, knowing I would feel precisely the same way if I were him. And in knowing this, I don't know how I can think of him as a cheater right now. I don't know how I can *investigate* him. Because all I can think is we are one and the same. He is my mirror.

"See you later, Alex," he says. I watch him as he leaves, and even with his hobbled knee, barely noticeable when he walks, he still moves like a mountain stream. Beautifully.

All that talent, all that skill, wasted because of one bad landing.

It could happen to anyone.

I return to the music hall, thinking that there is probably a vital clue in our conversation and I should tell my fellow board members.

But something about sharing it feels like a violation. Because Theo doesn't feel like a defendant; he doesn't feel like the bad guy. He seems like a friend. So I tuck the exchange away, keeping it personal, keeping it private.

◆ ◆ ◆

Mr. Friedrich scribbles out a painful-looking equation on the whiteboard, then instructs us to graph it.

I do as I'm told, but it's hard for me to take my math teacher seriously.

Okay, Mr. Friedrich *does* know his way around differential equations and asymptotes, I'll grant him that. But I'm pretty sure numbers and limits of functions are all he cares about.

Last year there was this math genius whose roommates were forcing him to do all their homework. He came to the Mockingbirds, but only *after* talking to Mr. Friedrich first, saying he was feeling pressure from his roommates. Mr. Friedrich sat him down and explained—as the Fosters did at D-Day—that peer pressure is intense and it's best not to give in to it. *No, really?* Then the teacher sent him on his merry way. I can even picture the jovial smile on Mr. Friedrich's face, maybe even an encouraging pat on the student's head before he swiveled around in his well-worn leather chair and returned to the advanced integral derivative quadratic equation Fibonacci sequence or whatever he was working on before.

It's not that Themis attracts the callous kind when it

comes to instructors. It's that this school breeds institutional blindness. "Smile and look the other way" is the school's own creed, handed down by the dean herself. The teachers follow suit. The more they look the other way, the easier it is to keep looking the other way. Blissful ignorance fosters more blissful ignorance.

Ah, but at least we have the best math scores in the prep-school world!

Mr. Friedrich assigns us several more migraine-inducing equations to graph over the weekend. Then the bell rings and the classroom fills with the sounds of books snapping shut, backpacks zipping, and a sprig of excitement that the week-end is here.

T.S. and I leave together.

"I am in dire need of a lip-gloss reapplication," she declares, so we head to the nearest bathroom. "Can I borrow yours? I don't like my color anymore."

This is typical of T.S. She changes her mind constantly about makeup. I root around in my backpack and hand her a shimmery dark pink gloss. "No fair. This is for brunettes," she says, giving a playful toss of her sun-streaked blond hair, then puts it on.

"So color your hair brown, then," I say as I look in the mirror and adjust a few strands of hair. "I might do a blue streak."

"That would rock," she declares as she smacks her lips at me in the mirror. "I bet Martin would be into it." Then she winks at me.

I give her a playful shrug back.

"C'mon. He'd totally think it was hot."

"You think so?" I ask.

She nods.

"Why do you say that? Has he said something about liking girls with streaks in their hair?" I ask, and I feel my stomach fluttering, a bit of nerves taking flight because she knows something about Martin I don't know—something about girls.

"Because he's Martin. Because he's into you, dork."

"Oh."

"He'd be into you even if you suddenly decided to shave off all your hair."

"Well, he doesn't have to worry about that because I'm not going that far."

"Speaking of how far you're going," T.S. begins, then lets her voice trail off as she raises her eyebrows.

I hold out a hand for my lip gloss but don't answer right away. She knows what I see sometimes when I'm with him. She knows the memories still crash back into me. But still, she wants me to be able to move on. She wants me to be like her—carefree and happy-go-lucky, all the wounds erased, all the baggage packed up and shipped off. She's not naive, though; she knows she can't wave her magic wand and wash last year away.

She shakes off the levity when I don't answer. "Are you ready?" This is the T.S. who took me to the Mockingbirds last year, the T.S. who can be serious, certain, determined. I can feel a weight start to fill up the bathroom as her casual self vacates the room.

"I don't know," I say.

She places a hand on my arm. "Don't rush into it. Just let it happen when it happens, if it happens."

I nod.

"And if it doesn't happen, that's okay too. You don't have to do anything until you're ready, and when you're ready is totally up to you."

"I know. Martin knows that too."

"Of course he knows that. I want to make sure *you* know that," she says, and she's got that look in her eyes that says the lip-gloss conversation might as well have happened in another lifetime.

"I do. I do know that," I say, and then let out a long breath. I look away briefly, then back to T.S. "I really want to with him, T.S. I really do."

She lets out a small squeal and almost bounces on her toes.

"You are the dork now," I say, laughing.

She slings an arm around me and we leave. "Whether you do the deed or not, nothing could make me happier than just hearing you say the word *want*."

"You like it so much, you'll buy me a macchiato right now?"

"Make mine caramel and I'm there," she says, and starts to break toward Kentfield Street, where the nearest coffee shop is.

I point to McGregor Hall. "I have to stop by the student-activities office. To check the mailbox."

When we're inside the office, T.S. grabs some flyers from her soccer captain mailbox. In mine I find a few random notices from the school on how to book space for your meetings, as well as the school's official roster of members of every club, group, and team. Then there's a blue index card folded in half and taped shut with red masking tape. On the front is my name in slanted black writing.

"What's that?" T.S. asks.

"Nothing," I say quickly, and slide the card into the back pocket of my shorts.

She puts her hands on her hips. "Oh, Alex, I forgot to tell you: in the last twenty-four hours I turned stupid," she says. "I saw the note. What is it?"

I shake my head. "I don't know. It's taped shut."

"Well, open it."

"Not here," I say quietly, because other team captains and group leaders start squeezing into the student-activities office, including McKenna. This time her hair is pinned back by a pair of cranberry-colored sunglasses. When she sees me, she wags a finger at me. "Hey, Alex! I have been wanting to talk to you because I have the *best* idea," she says, stretching out *best*, making it like a declaration, an announcement unto itself.

"Okay," I say, waiting to hear about this best idea.

"Since my sister, Jamie, is in orchestra too, and she's in your music class, what if you were to be her mentor this year?" McKenna asks.

I had almost forgotten about our Senior Mentor Program, in which the school pairs seniors with freshmen who have the same interests. I was matched up with a saxophonist back when I was a freshman, fellow musicians and all. We should get our mentees any day now.

"I don't know how much say we have. Don't the teachers make those picks?"

"That's what they say," she says, then blows air out her lips to show what she thinks of that. "But I'm betting if *you* made the request, Miss Damata would totally go for it. My sister said Miss D. *loves* you. And I want my sister to be paired with the best," McKenna adds. She leans in closer to me, like we've got a secret or something. "It would mean so much to me. It'd be like a little gift I can give her. She is always talking about the music competitions you've won."

"Sure," I say, feeling at once flattered and a little freaked out to have a fan, especially one who knows my musical curriculum vitae. I've never been one to advertise it. "I'll make the request."

Thank you, she mouths, then turns to her mailbox.

I grip the note tightly in my pocket as T.S. and I walk down the hallway. As I step outside, I feel something hard and muscle-y slam against my shoulder. "Ow," I say loudly.

When I look up I see Natalie. Her fingers cover her mouth and she says, "Oops, so sorry," in a faux dainty voice. "I must not have seen you coming."

"Right, Natalie. I'm sure you had no idea it was me." I have a feeling there's going to be a fat bruise on my shoulder tonight. I think Natalie's muscles might be made of sheet metal.

Once we're out on Kentfield Street, T.S. asks again, "Are you going to open it?"

"I can't."

"What? You said you would. You said *not here.*"

"T.S., I can't show it to you," I say.

"But I'm in the Mockingbirds. Why can't I know?"

"Because I'm not supposed to."

"Where does it say that? I'm officially a runner. You and the rest of the board approved me as a runner, and aren't runners supposed to be helping the board? I mean, it's just a note anyway. Why can't I see it?" she pleads.

"What if this were last year and someone left something in the mailbox about me? Would you want Amy to share it with just anyone?"

"But I'm not just anyone. I'm your best friend. Don't you remember the BFC?"

The Best Friend Code is the keeper of all sorts of secrets, like how every now and then when T.S. kisses her boyfriend, Sandeep, she thinks of the hot TV star of the month, or how I'm really, truly petrified that I might not get into Juilliard and the possibility feels a bit like death, or like life as I know it would be over. Or how when she thought she might be pregnant last fall (she wasn't), what scared her the most was knowing she wouldn't abort. These are the things only I know, only she knows.

"Of course I remember the BFC. But this isn't about the

BFC," I say, and now I'm some sort of traitor to my best friend, a turncoat. "It just seems wrong."

"Fine," she says, and looks away.

"I'm sorry, T.S. I want to. I really do. But…" My voice trails off.

"It's nothing," she says, putting on her game face. "I get it. It's Mockingbirds business. It doesn't involve me."

"T.S.," I say.

"It's no biggie," she says brightly. Too brightly. Then she glances down at her watch. "Hey, I gotta go. I forgot I'm meeting Sandeep."

"But I thought we were getting macchiatos," I say. It comes out like a whine, and I hate the way I sound.

"Next time," she says, and then takes off.

I'm left in the middle of the quad, just me and my clue, and my best friend mad at me. I slide my index finger through the red tape, breaking it. I unfold the note and read it silently: *I have information to share about Annie. Meet me in the dressing room Saturday at noon. Stage left. Alex only.*

Looks like I have a meeting at the theater tomorrow.

Chapter Nine

DRAMATIC GESTURES

Like an operative, I embark on my mission. I should be wearing a catsuit and carrying high-tech gadgetry to communicate back with headquarters. *I've apprehended the thespian and am questioning him beneath the spotlight. Indeed, the glare of one thousand watts is wearing him down. I'll have a confession soon at center stage.*

But I stop short before I reach the theater, nearly tripping as I duck behind a nearby bush, because Carter's leaning against the theater doors looking the other way, his whitish-blond hair slicked back, his thumbs tucked in the front pockets of his khaki shorts.

My heart slams against my chest, pounding, pounding to get out.

It's all so clear now. It's all so stupidly clear. Carter set me up. Carter wrote the note. I close my eyes, running through my regrets. I should have gone with my gut instinct last year when Amy asked me to take over. I should have said thanks, but no thanks. But I said yes, said it in a moment of triumph, a moment that's now dissolved. I'm reminded again that I'd be better off being the quiet, private piano girl I once was, not this public figure I've become.

A public figure who hides in bushes.

I open my eyes and see Carter kissing a girl. And the girl kissing back. The girl *wanting* it. He has one hand on her cheek, one on her waist, and this redheaded girl is leaning into him. Her arms are around his neck. I feel like someone just took my insides and twisted them like a kitchen towel, harder, tighter. I grab hold of the bush, grasping leaves and thin branches to hold on to because I'm about to rock back, to fall off this planet, to plummet through the dark of space.

Doesn't she know he's a rapist? Hasn't she seen the book in the library? Hasn't she heard?

Or maybe she doesn't care.

Or maybe she blames me, like Ms. Merritt, like Natalie, like all the others who don't say it but do think it.

Carter and the girl stop kissing, then switch to holding hands, and walk away from the theater and toward his dorm.

As the door to his dorm shuts behind him, I exhale because he wasn't the one who wrote the note. But it's not really relief I feel.

Drained is more like it.

I enter the theater, then walk down the aisle and into the wings. I rap on the dressing-room door, stage left. I'm greeted by Beat Bosworth. He's a sophomore. Last year as a freshman, he and his good friend Simone were cast as the understudies in *Evita*. But they had stars in their eyes and felt they should have played the lead roles of Evita and Che, so they began drugging the leads. Trouble was, the other freshmen theater students caught on and told the drama teacher. The teacher's response? *There, there. It's best not to make false accusations against your fellow students. Perhaps next year you'll land bigger roles.*

Typical.

The informer came to the Mockingbirds. Once the investigation began, Beat and Simone quickly confessed, taking a lesser punishment of only one semester on the theater sidelines rather than a whole year.

"You're here," Beat says, as if I'm the nurse on the battlefield bringing him his pain meds. He peers out, glancing side to side, checking to make sure the enemy's not watching. No one is, so he closes the door gently behind him.

"Please take a chair," he says, and pulls up a director's chair for me. He takes the chair next to the dressing-room mirror and I watch as he arranges himself in it, crossing his legs, leaning forward just so, pushing his hair off his forehead. He looks like an old-fashioned movie star. With dark locks and the most smoldering eyes, I could see him in a tux. No, a *dinner jacket*. A white one. Like the kind you'd see Humphrey Bogart wear, with a bow tie and combed-back hair. He'd talk out of the side of his mouth, toss off some quip we'll all be quoting back to one another for the next hundred years about life or love or friendship. I could see Beat existing only in black-and-white, with the snappy sound of an old film reel as his background sound track. But he's firmly in the here and now—jeans, black lace-up boots, and a well-worn red T-shirt that falls against his chest and stomach just so.

Just enough to hug his belly in all its glorious flatness.

Holy crap—I am checking him out.

And I have a boyfriend, so I shouldn't be checking him out.

But then I forgive myself because Beat is a gorgeous specimen. So really, what choice do I have? I mean, it's not like I'm going to jump him. I make one final sweep of his arms, chest, and stomach before settling on those perfectly dark, deep brown eyes.

"I need your help, Alex," he says, and though he speaks in the crisp, perfectly enunciated voice of someone who's taken diction classes, there's an underlying desperation in his tone. I feel for him.

"What's going on?"

He breathes out heavily. "Obviously you know who I am. You know what happened last year to Simone and me. You know what I did."

"Right. You confessed last fall, so your punishment was reduced. I've read about your case."

He swallows, blushes for a second. "Look, I'm not proud of what I did," he says, his eyes hooking into mine. "And I'd like to think I've learned from my punishment. I had no choice but to learn from it, because it sucked not to be acting. I felt like a part of me was missing. God, it was awful. But cathartic in a way, because it was the reminder of what I'd done." He presses his teeth into his lips for just a second, then looks away, blinks. "Do you believe people can change?"

"That's kind of an open-ended question."

"Like do the things we go through truly change us?" he asks, his eyes locked on me still.

"Of course. Sometimes you have no choice but to change," I say, because what I went through last year is still coursing through me like a poison, and the doctors are waiting, watching to see if I can flush it out, if I can recover.

"I think so too. I really do. And I know this might sound cheesy, but I feel like I've changed for the better. And isn't that *also* what the system is supposed to be about?" Beat says, and it's as if he's turning a shirt inside out, showing me the reverse side, the side we rarely see. Because it's not just the victims who can change. The bad guys can too.

"Definitely," I say.

"That's why I told you in my note that I have info, because I know you guys are doing some investigations into the Anderin ring going on right now. And that's why I'm kind of freaking out that I could be accused again. But I didn't do it. I'm not involved. So I want to show you I'm innocent."

"Why would you be accused, though?"

Beat shifts around and reaches into a backpack on the

dressing-room counter. He takes something out of the front pocket, then turns back. He holds up a pill bottle. "Because of this," he says, dangling the bottle between his thumb and forefinger. He unscrews the cap, reaches inside, and pulls out an orange pill. It's long and oval, and its gel cover is half orange, half clear. Inside the casing are hundreds of tiny little orange balls. He offers me the bottle carefully, meticulously, like it's a dangerous and highly combustible wire he wants me to defuse. And it is practically a flammable substance here at Themis. "They're mine. I have a prescription. The same one I've had since I was twelve. The same one my parents fill for me every month. The same one only *I* use," he says. He hands me the bottle next. "See? Look at the label."

I read it carefully. *Beat Bosworth. Prescribed by Dr. Dunn in Ridgefield, Connecticut.* I hand the bottle back to him. He drops the pill he's holding back in, screws the cap on, and tucks the bottle into his backpack.

"I don't want people to think it's me just because I'm on the debate team now. I joined while I was serving my time," he says, explaining why he is suddenly mentioning Debate. "But just because I have a record doesn't mean it's me who's behind it. Someone else is selling and supplying to the debate team," he says.

Debate Club.

The words are fully registering now.

Debate Club. He's in the Debate Club.

"What did you say?" I ask, hoping I heard him wrong,

praying that the thing my roommate loves most is *not* the epicenter of this cheating ring.

"It's sick, Alex," he says, his lips curling in disdain. "They're trying to gain an edge in winning the Elite. The Debate Club has engineered and implemented a detailed and specific plan of regular use solely to win the most prestigious award in the sport."

The Elite. The thing my roommate wants more than anything. It's her Juilliard, her World Series, the thing she has spent years training for.

But something doesn't add up, and that's Theo. Because as far as I know, he's not on Debate.

Unless he's new to the team.

I reach around for my backpack, grabbing the activity roster from inside. I should have looked at it yesterday, should have scanned the list of every group and club for Theo's name. A thoughtful, diligent leader would have prepped for this meeting, would have memorized the rosters of every activity. But I didn't, so I go straight to the Debate Club listing now.

There's a star next to Theo's name, indicating he's new to Debate this year.

My heart sinks. This is what Theo meant when he said, *Find something else or die.* He found something else; he found his replacement, his new adrenaline rush. But is he really calculating enough or desperate enough to try out for Debate his senior year for the sole purpose of bringing home a victory in the Elite?

But now's not the time to ask. Now's the time to make up for not preparing last night. By asking more questions, better questions, than I did with Delaney. By not letting Beat get away too soon.

"How widespread is it?"

"It started late last year with one or two students, and then I think a bunch were in touch over the summer, but literally since a week or two before school started it's become about half the team."

"How often are they using?"

"Every day. Several times a day."

"Who's selling?"

Beat holds his hands out to show they're empty. "I wish I knew. I seriously wish I knew."

"Is Theo McBride selling?"

He shakes his head, but it's not a *no*. More like an *I don't know*. "I have tried to stay as far away as I possibly could. I don't want to be connected to this. I don't want to be assumed guilty because I have a record," he says, reminding me of Delaney.

For a second, it strikes me as odd that two students here are so worried they'd be implicated that they'd come to me for help. But then again, maybe that's the point—maybe they are the nameless *victims* we're supposed to protect. Maybe they're the ones who could get hurt by what's happening. But even so, I have to make sure I'm not being played.

"How do I know you're *not* the one selling, though? You could be behind it all. You could be telling me because you think that'll remove you from suspicion," I say, because now I am determined to make up for my lost ground, to ask the questions I should have methodically planned out and written down in my notebook in advance of this meeting.

"I was worried you'd say that because of my past," he says, and I guess whatever side of the Mockingbirds you've been on, you've got a past. "But I'm not doing it, and to prove it you can take my pill bottle and keep it under lock and key and dispense the pills to me every day twice a day."

I move into the next question. "How would I know you don't have more? You could be selling and refilling."

"Check the prescription. Call the pharmacy. Monitor my refills," he says, holding me steady with his eyes. In those dark eyes, I can tell he's laying himself bare.

"I totally appreciate that, Beat," I say. "Really I do. But I don't think I'm going to put your pills under house arrest. If you say you need them, I'm going to trust you. Am I right to trust you?"

"Absolutely." A warm smile fills his face, and he presses his hands together like he's praying. "Thank you. I can't thank you enough." He pauses, then says, "So what's next?"

"I'm going to keep investigating," I say, and at first the words feel foreign, like I'm playing the part of the chief of police when I'm just making this up as I go along. But then I repeat them in my head—*I'm going to keep investigating*—and they feel strangely comfortable, like this is how I do the job, this is how I'm supposed to lead, supposed to help.

Beat nods, then takes a deep breath, his chest rising up and down. He opens his mouth to speak, then shakes his head.

"Is there something else you want to tell me?"

He pushes a hand through his hair. "It's just...," he begins, then trails off.

"Just what?" I ask.

"It's just, I don't even know if you do this, but since I showed you my pills and all, and since I told you what I know, and since I *really* need your help, I was hoping I could have immunity. When it all goes down."

Immunity.

Is that even an option? Is that even something we do? I think back to the notebook, to all the entries, the words I've practically memorized. There's nothing in there on immunity. No one's ever asked for immunity before. But no one had ever brought a date-rape case to the Mockingbirds before I did, which means there's a first time for everything. Which also means rules sometimes must be crafted on the spot. And I believe him. Because I believe people can change. I'm living proof, and I'm changing every day, so why can't he? He *wants* to move beyond his past. I know that feeling. God, how I know it well.

I also know how people behave when they don't want to change, because that's when someone calls you a *whore* when you walk down the hall. There's a big difference between Beat and Carter, and I don't just mean their crimes. I mean their actions now. One is contrite; the other is not.

"You have immunity. For now."

Chapter Ten

IDENTITY SHIFT

This will be simple. Maia will know what's going on. She will want to help. Together we can get to the bottom of this and clean up the debate team. We will be partners, just like we were last year when she acted as my student lawyer in my trial. This case will be over in no time and Maia can lead her team to victory, unscathed, untouched by what could potentially be the next big boarding-school scandal. And I will have successfully led us through our first case, no fuss, no muss.

With laser focus, I walk back to my dorm and I ask Maia point-blank if she knows anything about Anderin abuse on the team.

"I don't know a thing about it. But I'd sure like to know who's spreading those sorts of rumors. *Who* exactly is telling you this?"

"Just people," I say, but my face turns a shade of pink

because I feel a bit foolish protecting Delaney and protecting Beat—people I barely know—while questioning my roommate.

Maia gives a dismissive laugh. "Just people? Well, that's typical, isn't it? *Unnamed sources.* People—including *just people*—should just have the guts to come forward, especially when they're casting aspersions on the whole team."

"I know. But that's what we're supposed to do."

"Protect people who can't come out and point fingers directly? I'm sorry, Alex, but I think that's kind of lame. Nothing against you. It just seems if people are going to make an accusation, they should have the guts to do it without the guise of some sort of anonymous protection."

Or immunity.

She doesn't say that, since she doesn't know about my immunity promise, but now I am doubting whether I'm making the right decision, trusting the right people, protecting those I should be protecting.

"Are these *unnamed sources* pointing fingers at me?" she asks, the tiniest bit of worry in her question.

"No! God, no. No one has mentioned your name."

"Good. And if I find out they're trying to win illegally, I will smash them," Maia says with a wink, slamming her hand down on the desk in a pretend show of her pugilistic punishment. "But seriously, Alex. Keep an eye on this one. It all sounds a bit dodgy. I don't want to see some wanker who won't use his or her name leading you astray on your first case."

Is that what Beat and Delaney are doing to me? Leading

me down some false path? Keeping me off the scent? Here I am feeling like I am *finally* getting the hang of this, finally moving beyond my own past, but then I'm back where I started, grasping for something to hold on to.

It's like I'm looking into a steamed-up mirror and can see only parts of my face.

I need to talk to Amy. "I'll catch you later, Maia."

"I'm leaving too. I have to meet the team for practice," Maia says, and we walk out together. "I'll see if I can sniff out the perp for you."

I say good-bye to her in the stairwell, then head down to the second floor of my dorm, where Amy lives.

I hear her voice as I near her room: "Oh no! We so schooled you on Aerosmith!"

Her door is open wide, but I knock anyway. Amy smiles brightly, then nods me in. She's wearing a black plastic guitar slung across her shoulder and she's surrounded by three other girls.

"Alex, meet my Rock Band teammate Jess. We totally slaughtered these bitches in the hard round," she says, gesturing first to Jess, then to the two other girls. "That's Lena and Vania."

"Cool," I say.

"Oh! I just had a brilliant idea! You should play with us. You're a musician. You'd totally kill," Amy says. She turns to the other girls. "Alex is this kick-ass piano player. She's going to get into Juilliard and then be the next Leonard Bernstein."

"Hate to break it to you, but Leonard Bernstein was a conductor," I say.

"Then you can conduct us," Jess says, and gives me a wink.

It's weird seeing Amy in her element, with her friend, maybe even her girlfriend. I've only known Amy as the leader of the Mockingbirds, leader emeritus now, because she passed the torch on to me when her term ended last year. I've never known about the rest of her life. But to see her here in her room hanging with her girls is kind of like running into a teacher at the supermarket and seeing her buy Cocoa Puffs. Like, *Wow, didn't know you liked Cocoa Puffs*. And yes, I knew Amy liked girls. But it's just that Amy's life has always been Amy's life, and her predilection for Rock Band or the way she talks when her friends are around are things I never knew.

"All right, chickadees, get your asses out of here," Amy says, and makes a quick *get out of here* gesture with her hands. She takes the guitar off and dumps it on her bed. Jess grabs a satchel-type bag, slings it on her shoulder, and then swoops in and gives Amy a kiss on the lips. I notice Amy close her eyes ever so briefly, and then I hear Jess whisper, "See you later, baby."

Then they're gone.

"Sorry, I didn't mean to interrupt. I should have called first," I say as Amy shuts the door.

"You are always welcome here," Amy says, and now she's shifted back to the Amy I know. She's even dressed the same as last year—skinny jeans, T-shirt, black Converse high-tops. She sits down on her bed, and I take the chair at her desk, pulling it out to the center of the room. On the wall above her bed, she's tacked up several drawings on white paper, all variations on the same theme—hearts, strangely misshapen hearts. One is red and blue with one of the halves drooping over, like a slumped-down, passed-out man. Another is elongated, stretched from the bottom tip all the way up the other side, a pair of hands on each end doing the pulling.

"So what's the latest on your big case?" Amy asks.

I give her the details. When I finish I say, "It's like there are all these little pieces—Delaney says Theo's part of it; Beat says Theo's not. Beat says half the Debate Club is using to win; Maia says no one is."

"Yeah, I feel for you," she says. "Most of the cases I dealt with were much more black-and-white."

"Right! That's my point," I say, and even though she's not telling me what to do, at least she's agreeing with me.

I look at the two hands on the heart and feel for a second like mine is being pulled too. On the one hand are my friends. On the other are the people I am helping.

"I don't know, Amy. Maybe it's not a big deal. But I just think being the head of the Mockingbirds puts you in this weird position where you're not just this normal person or friend anymore. T.S. and I had this silly fight yesterday over whether she could see a tip that came into the mailbox. And then I felt like I was questioning Maia back there. And then she was questioning me. She asked a few times why I was protecting all these unnamed sources. Did you ever feel this way?"

"Of course," she says.

"How do you mean?"

"Well, take just now. With Jess. We were together last year too, but I didn't say a word about you until you filed charges. I couldn't. But she knew I was super involved in a case—meeting with you, meeting with the board, the vote we took to revise the code of conduct to include date rape. She'd ask what I was working on, but I couldn't tell her. Because it was my job to protect *you*," Amy says.

"You put *me* ahead of your girlfriend?" I ask, feeling like Amy just rubbed her hand over the blurry mirror and now I'm seeing things I wasn't able to see before. Like how she took care of me. Like how taking care of me stretched her. "But people knew it was me. They knew I was pressing charges."

"*Some* did. But it was never publicly posted anywhere. We didn't hang a banner and say *Alex is talking to us.* So I couldn't say anything to Jess. It's the same here. No one has pressed charges yet. No one has asked you to serve notice. So you *can't* reveal names."

"And Jess understood?"

"She didn't like it. But she knew it was the way it is."

Then I blurt out, "Carter has a girlfriend."

Amy raises her eyebrows. "Really?"

"Well, I don't know if they're boyfriend-girlfriend, but they were kissing on the quad."

"I guess she hasn't learned the truth yet."

"Which makes me think—do we really do any good? I mean, the point was to take a stand and be the one to say *no means no* and *you can't get away with it* and look what happened. Here he is hooking up with some freshman, probably."

"Was that the point?" she asks.

"What do you mean?"

"Was the point of your case to stop him from dating or for you to get yourself back?"

Did I press charges to punish him or to retrieve me? I'd like to think the latter. I'm not afraid anymore, like I was. But I *am* defined by it.

"But how do you even get yourself back? I feel that *me* is gone. Who I was is gone," I say, and my throat catches as I finally—*finally*—say out loud that a ghost is haunting me and that ghost is me. Tears prick my eyes, so I cover my face with my hands. I hate crying in front of anyone. I blink, trying to hold the tears in. It works, so I take my hands away and continue. "I mean, how can you be so calm and normal and wise about everything? I'm not even remotely close to being over what happened. Are you?"

"Well, I don't have to see the girl who did it every day, and that helps. But you're right. I'm not the same as I was."

"How? How are you different?"

"I'm better," she says, and smiles, straightens up her back. "I'm stronger. Tougher."

Like a broken bone that's stronger when it heals. That's what I can be.

"Besides," Amy says, "I think life is about how you respond to the crap that happens. I was just your average girl before. I did my own thing, had my friends, and beat anyone who took me on in Rock Band. Then Ellery did this," Amy says, tapping her back with her hand, narrowing her eyes, the latent anger that will always be there stirring. "And I *was* different. I couldn't go back. There was no going back. So I learned who I could be. I learned I could be someone who could stand up to bullies. And then I could be someone who'd stand up to anyone, for anyone. I'm not afraid of anything now, Alex. What can anyone do to me now? I've already had someone slice my back open with a knife. What more can they do to me?" she says, holding her arms open wide as if to say *bring it on.* "The same goes for you, Alex. You're not the same. You're not *supposed* to be the same. You're supposed to be different. This isn't something you will ever forget. Twenty years from now, you'll still remember what it felt like to be exposed. And you'll remember too what it felt like to take a stand. You'll probably remember that more."

I know she's right. I know it not just because the tears are now rolling down my face, but because she's the only other person here who can remotely understand how I feel.

I wipe my tears and glance up at Amy's wall, scanning her heart drawings, seeing one I didn't notice before. A rudimentary sketch of a girl wearing a triangle-shaped dress, her legs nearly buckling under the weight of this gigantic heart she's carrying that's ten times her size. She's about to toss the heart to another girl, and the caption reads *Take it.*

I look back at Amy, who's carried the burdens for others, who's carried their hearts when they needed her to, who carried *me* when I needed her last year. Back then I was the girl no one knew. I still *want* to be the girl no one knows.

But there is no going back. I am not the same, and I never

will be. I have to let go of what other people think of me. I have to stop worrying about whether they see me as the girl who was raped. I *am* the girl who was raped.

And I can take my past and declare it mine. I can make it my own.

It no longer has to be my shame. It no longer has to be the thing I have to live down.

So what if the whole school knows my history? I can make a choice to be stronger for it, tougher for it, better for it. I can choose to be on the other side, to be someone who takes a stand not just for herself but for others.

"As they say, there's no turning back."

"No, there's not," Amy says, and her smile is as wide as the sea. And now I'm smiling too, and I'm still kind of crying, and I still kind of hate it because I definitely still hate crying. But I'm not crying because I'm sad; I'm crying because I'm letting go of who I was. I'm stepping into my new self.

I stand up and reach for Amy's black plastic guitar. "One song. We play for bragging rights."

"No fair! You're a musician."

"All's fair in love and music," I say, and turn on her Rock Band, where I proceed to demolish her in Nirvana, Radiohead, the Who, and more because she can't stop asking for just one more song, just one more song.

Maybe it's from all my piano training, or maybe it's just because I'm feeling pretty kick-ass right now.

Chapter Eleven

WILD WEST

After I make Amy beg for mercy, she gives me a suggestion for the case.

"You need the runners to step up their game. Here's what I would do: I would ask a couple of the runners to help out with the investigation. The three of you on the board won't be enough." Amy gives me a wink. "I know who you want to ask."

"Anjali," I say with a smile, because Anjali is one of thirteen runners this year. Council members who aren't selected for the board can choose to stay on as runners. They have to repeat some of the more menial runner tasks like attendance mistakes, but these "tier-two runners"—like Anjali—have more seniority; they manage many of the on-the-ground assignments, and they often assist the board with investigations.

I stop by Anjali's room on the first floor. I ask her to help. She says yes immediately.

"I loved being on the council last year, and I so wanted to help out more," she says.

"I'm really psyched too, because I wanted to work with you in the first place and now we can," I say.

"Totally up for anything," she says, and gives me a crisp salute, then tucks her wispy blond hair behind her ears. She's taller than me by a few inches, maybe five nine, five ten. She stands barefoot and is wearing a short purple skirt with a red tank top and a blue tank top layered over each other. Today's scarf: thin and emerald green with silver streaks. I love how she wears scarves every day, even when it's hot out. I love how they're random and don't match her outfits either.

We discuss the Mockingbirds assignment for a few minutes, then we shift to English class and Mr. Baumann's boarding-school assignments, then to chess.

"I'm having a chess party tonight. Do you want to come?" Her voice rises a bit when she asks me, that cocktail of nerves and hope like when you ask someone on a date.

I hate to let her down, but I haven't spent time with my true love—the piano—today. "I would love to, seriously. But I have a meeting and then a date with the music hall."

"It's going to be so much fun, and you could even be on my team," she presses. "Plus we have the best snacks and lavender soda."

"Lavender soda?"

"Oh, it's great! Have you ever had it before?" she asks,

and it's funny because when she's excited like this, the trace of French in her accent is stronger.

"Can't say that I have," I say.

"Plus, Parker's coming," she adds.

"Can I have a rain check? I promise to come to another one. But I've got to get my act together for my Juilliard audition."

"But of course. You are welcome anytime," she says, and clasps her hands together and then tips her head to me, always the gracious hostess. "And I know Jamie is hoping you can make it soon. She's so excited about you maybe being her mentor."

"I didn't realize you were friends with Jamie," I say, surprised. I don't think I've ever seen Anjali hang out with anyone outside of her year before. "Her being a freshman and all."

"McKenna made a *big* production out of introducing me to her. Well, everyone really," Anjali says, then rolls her eyes. "It's like she's the personal welcoming committee for Jamie. But Jamie's just pretty cool, period."

"Have fun, then," I say, and head down to the basement to meet the boys. I texted them earlier today calling this meeting.

"Hey, you," Martin says, and slides his hand into mine when I sit next to him on the mustard-colored couch. The tips of his hair are still wet from getting out of the shower. I want to lean in and kiss him, then maybe even pounce on him, thanks to my newfound confidence. I entertain a brief fantasy of Parker as one of those small high-strung dogs that chase tennis balls all day. I toss one across the room, he zooms after it, while I steal a kiss with Martin.

Then another.

Then maybe I throw a tennis ball so far away that Parker's gone for a long time and Martin and I are all alone and the thought of last year never even crosses my mind. I squeeze Martin's hand tighter as a ribbon of heat runs through me, then I sneak a quick look at him. He gives me a slight grin, then lifts his eyebrows as if to ask, *What's up?* I squeeze his hand again and when I do he traces the inside of my palm with his index finger and I want to melt into him.

I force myself to focus.

"Busy day," I say as I take out my notebook and give them the details—the note, the dressing-room meeting, the Annie show-and-tell, Theo landing a spot on the debate team, and even Amy's advice to get Anjali involved in the investigation.

"Damn. Impressive stuff," Martin says, and gives me a smile. The green flecks in his brown eyes are lit up and I know that means he's excited, happy. He rubs his hands together. "Now we know it's localized to the debate team, so what we'll need to do next is home in on who's the ringleader. Or *ringleaders*, because I have a feeling we're not just talking about one culprit here."

Parker furrows his brow and taps his pen against his infernally present reporter's notebook. He clears his throat, then says, "I don't understand why you went alone to see Beat."

"What do you mean?"

"I don't understand why you didn't bring one of us with you."

"The note said *come alone*."

"But wouldn't it have been better to have backup? A third person to help record the details and hear what Beat had to say," he points out, and bends his head to scribble something in his notebook. I hate that notebook. Why is it that he always seems to be writing in it when he's disagreeing with me? Next time I'm in Martin's room, I think I'll steal that notebook. Then I'll ship it off to Madagascar. A group of lemurs will await its arrival and rip it to shreds while swinging from tall trees. They'll toss the torn pages to the ground like confetti.

"Are you saying I'm not able to report what went down? That I'm not a reliable witness or something?" I ask.

"No," Parker says, holding up his hands like he's been caught. "Of course not. I was just suggesting it might have been useful to have a third person present. Someone else there. But you didn't do that. So let's move on."

"Let's *not* move on," I say, slapping my notebook down next to me. "Let's address this now. You don't think I'm capable of leading, do you?"

Parker's pupils seem to dilate instantly, brimming with surprise. "I'm not saying that. I just want to make sure we are vetting everything according to proper procedures."

"Dude, there's no rule that says she has to bring another board member," Martin says.

Translation: *back off, buddy*.

Then Parker does that thing he does. That self-deprecating shrug followed by a lopsided smile. "I'm sorry, guys," he says, throwing in a quick chuckle for good measure. I bet he learned that from his tax-evading dad, good old example-setting Senator Hume. *Hey, son, when all else fails and you're cornered for having been a dick, just toss in a little laugh. Wins the constituents over every time.*

But then it hits me. Parker only backed down when Martin told him to. Not when I told him to. And I'm not okay with that anymore. Because I am finally figuring out how to do this job. I can see it; I need Parker to see it too. I look directly at him. "Parker, I'm going to need you to start showing some respect."

He coughs and sputters and generally kicks his feet in the air like a cartoon baby picked up by someone much bigger. "But-but-but I do respect you."

"You don't act like it," I point out. "And I'm not asking you to agree with everything I do. And I'm not asking you to stop bringing an opinion to the table. But I am asking you to stop acting as if Martin is the only one you will listen to," I say, and I like this new me, I like this confident me, this girl on the other side. So does Martin, because he squeezes my hand again.

"Of course," Parker mumbles. Then in a louder voice, "I'm really sorry, Alex. I'll do better."

"Thank you. So let's figure out who we should zero in on," I say, shifting gears. I let go of Martin's hand, reach for my own notebook, and flip it open to list possible suspects.

"I'd say Beat," Martin says quickly.

"What?" I spit out. I couldn't be more shocked if he said me.

"Hell yeah," he says. "He's an actor. He probably even wrote out a script for his meeting with you earlier today."

"You're totally wrong," I say. But I'm not defensive; I'm not angry. I say the words like I'm answering a question in a class and I'm sure of the answer. Because I am sure. I know Beat was telling the truth; I know the *Evita* incident is behind him. "You didn't see him. You didn't see what he was like," I say, but then I hear myself and I'm proving Parker's point. I'm proving that it would have been smart to have brought someone else along.

"What was he like?" Martin asks.

I straighten my back, sitting tall, and now I do feel like I have to prove something, so I am precise and deliberate as I describe the meeting, the pained look in his eyes, the way he implored me to help, his earnestness. I leave out the part about my finding him insanely good-looking.

"Well, he *is* an actor, Alex," Martin says softly.

I press my lips tightly together. The suggestion that I was somehow duped makes me want to erect a wall, put up a shield. "So you think he was just putting me on?"

"It's possible. He copped to drugging those seniors last year, so it's not like he's squeaky-clean."

"Are we judging him guilty already just because he has a

record?" Parker asks Martin, directing his stickler rules at someone else for a change.

"No. I'm just saying let's not rule him out," Martin says coolly. He is not rattled easily, certainly not by someone like Parker.

"I already ruled him out. I offered him immunity for now," I say, standing firm, holding my ground.

"Immunity?" Martin says, and for the first time ever his voice shoots higher. "You can't just offer him immunity. Or anyone."

"Why not?"

"We don't offer immunity."

"Where does it say that?"

"Alex, this isn't like a grand jury here," he says.

"Right, but *I* believe him. He may not have a perfect record, but who does in any criminal-justice system? Everyone has a motive for sharing info. He wants to stay out of more trouble. He's terrified of being pulled into this, just like Delaney. And we're not investigating her. Plus he showed me his Annie scrip. It was totally legit. So he may be an actor, but I don't think he's a drug dealer."

"He might not be a dealer, but I really don't think we should just be doling out promises of immunity," Martin says, and he sounds irritated.

"This isn't some Wild West law and order, Martin. This was a measured, deliberate decision I made. Given the circumstances and given what he shared, I believe there were grounds to justify granting him immunity," I say, like a well-trained lawyer, a veteran of the courtroom. "If it turns out he's the culprit, obviously the immunity goes away. Let's move on to other suspects."

Martin nods and moves on. "So let's get into it. Clearly we're moving beyond the early investigation phase. Theo's obviously a key suspect still. We have to deepen our investigation into him. We have enough concrete info to keep closer watch. We already know he's on Annie. We know the debate team is potentially cheating, so now it's time to figure out if he's the one dealing and supplying to the team. We need to look for forged prescription pads, additional pill bottles, and most of all, signs of him dealing. Plus it adds up that it's him. He has the motive. He can't dance anymore, but he wants to compete still. He has the ability to debate. He's a smart guy. He can hold his own with politics, issues, that sort of stuff. So debate is a natural *sport* for him to slide into—not as the team captain, not even as their best debater, but as someone who's good enough to make the team. Only, he can't win the Elite on his own, because it's a team victory. So he devises a game plan to ensure the whole team can win. He starts using Annie. It ups his game. He realizes if it works for him, why not spread a little good cheer around the team? That's just my theory, at least," he says.

"And it's a good one," I say, ready to give praise where it's due, to keep a strong front as the board.

Then Martin adds, "There's one more reason it may be Theo. Access. If he had a knee injury so bad that it knocked him out of dancing, then he was probably on PKs for a while.

Let's say he gets started with a painkiller, maybe a little Vicodin. He likes the way it makes him feel. He goes back to the doc and gets more. Vicodin's his summer-vacation drug, but Annie's a much better fit for the school year. So he goes back to the doc, does a whole song and dance about how he can't concentrate, can't focus on schoolwork. Boom. He gets his Annie scrip."

"I have another suggestion," Parker says, and glances down at his notebook before clearing his throat and pushing his glasses higher up on his nose. He pauses, like he's about to say something difficult. He breathes out, long and slow. "I hate to say it, since she's your friend. But I think we should investigate Maia."

I answer Parker quickly, glad that I had the foresight to already vet the accusation with my roommate. "She says they're just rumors. And she doesn't know anything about it."

"What else would she say?" he says, and taps his notebook like there's proof in it of Maia's alleged culpability. "Let's face it. She has the most to gain from the team's success. Everyone knows she would pretty much give her firstborn to win the Elite and get into Harvard early. And she is notoriously ambitious."

"Did she nab the only A in some class where you thought it was yours, Parker?" I ask.

"I have straight As in every class and have since I got here," he shoots back.

"Well, Perfect Four-Point-Oh, we don't prosecute people

based on hunches. And all of that is extremely circumstantial evidence. In fact, it's not even evidence at all," I say, and now I'm pissed and I don't bother to hide my anger. I've done things the right way; I've asked the right questions; I've made the right choices.

"All we have is circumstantial evidence," Parker continues. "All we had was circumstantial evidence on Theo, and we started watching him. I'm just saying I think we should leave no stone unturned."

"I already talked to her about this. She was reasonable and totally cool about everything. She didn't flip out. She wasn't defensive. Someone supplying drugs, someone setting up some massive drug ring isn't like that. So, we're not going to investigate her," I repeat. Then I look to Martin. "Right?"

Martin holds my gaze, his brown eyes locked on mine. The flecks are quiet, his eyes solid brown.

"I don't think Maia is involved," he says heavily. "But I think we should keep our eyes and ears open in case it turns out she is connected."

"How can you even suggest that?" I say, and now it's my voice soaring into the stratosphere; now it's me who's shocked.

"I said I don't think she's involved. But the fact is, there is some serious shit going down on her team. And she is the captain. If it were another team, we'd have to consider the captain too, just by virtue of being the captain."

Then there's silence in the laundry room so thick you

could bottle it. Parker breaks it. "We need to investigate her," he says, and the majority wins. Maia is now under investigation.

Then he clears his throat and continues. "I have another suggestion. I think Anjali should be tasked with looking into Maia's activities. After all, I think the three of us might be too close to it. And we did bring Anjali on to help with the investigation."

I bet he never cuts in line. I bet he returns his library books on time. I bet he holds the chess rule book at Anjali's parties and checks it before every move. He is so by the book, so in love with the letter of the law.

He is also completely right, and I hate it. I hate it because back there in the theater with Beat I felt like the leader of the Mockingbirds for the first time. It's as if I had left last year behind me; the potholes and crags in the road had been filled in, leaving only a smooth, easy ride. But now it's bumpy and jarring and my hands are gripped tight on the wheel, just trying to hold on again.

I exhale and look away. "Fine. I will let Anjali know. Martin, you want to look into Beat?"

He nods.

"Parker. You want Theo?"

Parker nods.

I stuff my notebook into my backpack, zipping it up tightly. "I'll look into other angles," I say, and I'm hoping the other angles are the ones that pan out. I don't want it to be my roommate, I don't want it to be the guy who's like me, and I don't even want it to be the person I just gave immunity to. I want it to be someone else.

But the truth is, I don't want it to be anyone. Because if what Beat is saying is true, if what Delaney is saying is true, then Maia is hurtling headfirst into something that cannot possibly end the way she wants.

This can end only one way.

Badly.

Now I know who I am fighting for, and it's my roommate.

Chapter Twelve

STRATOCASTER BET

Hours later, I am fuming at Parker's suggestion as I slip into my *Science Rules* T-shirt.

Maia, who's already under the covers and sound asleep, would never be involved in something like this, I tell myself as I get into bed.

Maia, hard-edged Maia. Ambitious, tough-as-nails, do-the-right-thing Maia. She's got a soft side too, a side she lets very few people see. Like how she has a thing for hats. And I don't just mean her Manchester United cap. I mean wide-brimmed, ladies-who-lunch hats that you buy at a milliner's. She'd never wear them here, but she and her mom put on their proper dresses and their proper shoes and their proper hats every Saturday afternoon in the summers in London and go out for high tea. Or how she has a pet bunny rabbit back home. He's black-and-white, and they named him Silvio. "I don't know why we picked that name, but it's just funny to have a bunny named Silvio, don't you think?" she told us one night last year.

"Dude, you are such an only child," T.S. remarked. "Only only children have bunnies."

"I suppose when you have brothers you have dogs?" Maia asked T.S., who is the youngest of four and the only girl.

"Yes, we have dogs. Mutts. They chase Frisbees and catch sticks in the Pacific Ocean. And we give them dog names like Fred and Susie," T.S. said, then started laughing.

Maia tossed a pillow at her and cracked up too. "Your dogs aren't named Fred and Susie."

"Okay. Archibald and Fiona. We gave them British names," T.S. teased again.

Maia hopped out of bed then and pretended to stare down T.S. "Wait till I get my own dog someday. I'm going to name him T.S."

"I would love to be your dog's namesake," T.S. said. "Just not a bunny's!"

"It could be worse, guys. You could have cats for pets," I said. "My mom got these Maine coon cats, and they spend the entire day in the linen closet. They only come out at night, and when they do they meow while pacing back and forth on the kitchen counters. You wonder why I had to get away from home. And you want to know what they're named? Raoul and Aurelia."

"You so totally win," T.S. declared.

Maia hopped back into her own bed and pulled up her

covers. "Silvio sleeps on my bed sometimes. I don't know when he shows up, but sometimes I wake up and he's sleeping on my feet."

Now I flip over to my other side and picture Maia's pet rabbit, Silvio, curling up at her feet. Then I hear Maia flip over too.

Weird.

Maia doesn't toss and turn.

Maia's made an art form of conking out the second she hits the pillow. But right now she's not operating at the only two speeds she knows: all-out or dead to the world. Instead she's lying in bed wide awake, and she's breathing like she's pretending to be asleep.

I fall asleep, then wake up later to the sound of a door creaking. It's probably T.S., tiptoeing in after another late night with Sandeep. I open my eyes, but T.S. must have slipped in earlier because she's zonked out on top of her covers. It's Maia making the noise, sliding the closet door closed, then slinking back over to her bed, holding something in her hands. I can't entirely make out what it is, but I see a small brown paper bag and near the top a fat white cap.

Like a pill bottle.

For a moment the blood stops pumping inside me, the air ceases to fill my lungs. I've seen something I don't want to see; I know something I don't want to know.

Only, it's not about her.

It's about me.

It's about me being duped, being played, being stupid again.

I don't move, don't let on that I heard her, that I'm now the one pretending to be asleep as I watch her with my eyes like slits. She slides open the side zipper on her black messenger bag, then places the thing she doesn't want me to see inside gingerly, like when you try to open a bag of chips without it making a sound. Something crinkles for a second, and the sound of it splits open the dark silence so completely that I shut my eyes tight and I hear Maia hold in her breath. I peer out again as she completes her mission, zipping the side pocket back up and stuffing the bag at the foot of her bed, where Silvio would be sleeping if she were back in England.

Her behavior is a bit dodgy, if you ask me.

◆ ◆ ◆

A hard coldness fills me overnight, like I've slept in an igloo, like I've cuddled blocks of ice. I'm not shivering, though. I'm one with the ice because now I'm determined to unearth the truth, especially as that messenger bag becomes a part of her, it seems. She's like a toddler clutching a worn little doll everywhere she goes. It goes to class with her, to the caf with her, to bed with her.

As Mr. Baumann launches into his discussion of *Jane Eyre* in our next English class, I shift my eyes down to Maia's black messenger bag, the strap looped around her ankle. I zero in on it, that side pocket, my eyes like lasers, and everything else in the room becomes fuzzy. It's as if I'm the only one in the class. Other students fade away; Mr. Baumann's voice mutes. It's just the bag and me, and I have to find a way to separate her from it.

I have to know what she's protecting. I have to know if I've been played by my very own roommate.

When class ends, Maia darts out, telling me she'll catch up with me later. I leave the classroom and bend down at the white marble water fountain for a sip. When I straighten up, Anjali is waiting for me, her blue eyes lit up with excitement.

"I have news for you on *other angles*," she says.

I glance up and down the long, carpeted hallway of Morgan-Young Hall. We're surrounded by other students. I shake my head and gesture with my eyes to the others. We walk outside, where we can talk about *other angles*, because that's what I actually asked her to investigate instead. I decided not to assign her Maia, because whatever Maia is hiding is mine to figure out. I'm not going to farm out that assignment, no matter what Parker thinks. If Maia's playing me, I'll be the one who'll figure out the truth. If she's not, I'll be the one to clear her name with the board.

"Freshmen are involved," Anjali proclaims in a low whisper.

"Freshmen?" I repeat.

Anjali nods firmly. "That's what I hear. I'm going to do some more digging, though. See if they'll name names."

"Who's *they*?"

"Some other freshmen who saw it going down."

"Are they in the Debate Club?" I ask, wondering if these freshmen are Theo's suppliers.

Anjali shakes her head. "I think they're just opportunists. Besides, they heard Ms. Merritt going on and on about the Elite at D-Day, so I think they jumped at the opportunity to become the team's suppliers."

"Figures it'd be her *tip-off* in some way," I say, shaking my head.

Then we both spot Parker walking toward us. Anjali gives him a broad wave and turns up the wattage on her smile. Before he reaches us, I whisper, "Let's keep this between us until we know more, okay?"

She nods and winks. "Of course."

"Hi, Anjali," Parker says, a little breathy, and I can tell from the way he says her name that he has a crush on her.

"Hi, Parker," she says, and then leans in to air kiss him on each cheek.

Parker's eyes turn into saucers, moons even, as his face lights up. Next he'll probably press his palm against his cheek and try to capture the almost-touch of her lips.

Then he realizes his tail is wagging and his tongue is hanging out and he might as well be a dog greeting his master after a week's absence, so he hastily tries to unscrew the happiness from his face.

"How's it going?" he asks her, assuming his best all-business tone. "Find out anything good on Maia?"

Great. Now Anjali knows Maia is under investigation, and I don't want anyone to know that. I'd like to kick Parker under the table and shoot him a hard stare. But I can't, because then he'd know I'm lying to him about who's tracking who.

"Not yet, but I'll be sure to let Alex know what I find out," Anjali says, without skipping a beat. She's got a great poker face.

The bell rings for my next class: French. "We'll talk *plus tard, d'accord*?" I say to Anjali.

"*Bien sûr*," she says, and gives me that salute again. "You know where to find me," she says to me, then blows a kiss to Parker before she swivels around and heads off to her class, her flower-patterned scarf trailing down her back.

I turn to Parker, who's floating again. "I don't think we should be talking about the case so freely out in public, okay?"

"Well, weren't you talking to her about it?"

"No," I say, lying again. "We were talking about"—I pause for the briefest of seconds, cycling through innocuous cover-ups—"shoes."

Parker glances at my Vans. "I didn't know you were a shoe person."

"Yeah, it's the one thing I don't wear on my sleeve. Anyway, did you learn anything related to *your* assignment?" I ask pointedly.

"Not yet," he says.

"Let's focus on that, then," I say, without breathing Theo's name, in a feeble attempt to set some sort of example on how to lead. But really, I'm not so sure I'm setting an example anymore.

◆ ◆ ◆

I arrive early for music class. Miss Damata greets me with a smile. "Good to see you, Alex."

Her blond hair is piled up on her head in a bun. Loose strands fall around her face. Like Ms. Merritt, she's pretty— but she doesn't try to disguise it. Miss Damata is the *only* teacher here who's a verifiable human being. At least as far as I know. She was instrumental in me having the guts to stand up to Carter last year in our secret underground court. Not that she knows about the student courtroom. But she knows what happened to me. And she also knows I wasn't *culpable* in any way, shape, or form. I think I love her.

"Miss Damata, I was wondering if you had assigned mentors yet for the freshmen, because if you haven't, I would like to request Jamie Foster," I say, making good on the promise I made McKenna in the student-activities office.

"Any particular reason why you want to work with her?" Miss Damata asks.

I'm guessing *because her sister wants me to* isn't going to cut it. "Because she rocked the Vivaldi," I say, referring to the flute concerto she played last week in orchestra practice. "And because I think she could benefit from learning to work in concert more with other musicians. I think I can help her with that."

Miss Damata nods approvingly. It's a far better answer than the one I don't say about her sister, and it also happens to be true. When Jamie enters the music hall, Miss Damata shares the news. I watch Jamie's eyes light up, and then she actually claps her hands together. She grabs my arm and tells me how excited she is to be my *protégé*. I laugh at the word because it's so silly-sounding, but even so I tell her I'm happy to be her *senior mentor*.

"Maybe we can practice later today," she suggests, a hopeful sound to her request. I think back to the first time I met her, before D-Day, and how confident and poised she seemed. Now she's more like a normal fourteen-year-old freshman, awkward and youngish. I wonder if she's different around McKenna, always trying to impress her or something.

"Sure," I say. "That'd be fun. And do you want to have dinner together sometime?"

"Yes!"

After music class, Miss Damata calls Jones and me aside.

"As you probably know, I have a few friends at Juilliard still," Miss Damata begins, and the mere mention of the word *Juilliard* causes an involuntary reaction in me—I stand straighter, taller. She went there, and she taught there. I'll be there too for my weekend visit in just a few weeks. "And a group of us has this tradition every October, where we have a kind of mash-up performance slash jam fest at a local coffee shop," she continues, and I wonder if she means local as in New York or local as in Providence. "It's in the Village. We'll often invite some of our top students to play with us. The only catch is it's in New York."

"Catch? That doesn't sound like a catch. It sounds cool!" I say, then I stop myself because she hasn't technically invited us.

"And since our get-together happens to be the weekend of your Juilliard visit, Alex, I thought you might want to play with us," she says, and all I can think is *yes yes yes*, and that's all I can say too.

Then she turns to Jones. "Our best guitarist is eight months pregnant, so she is going to be out of commission. Would you like to take her place? I know you'd rather be on the guitar than the violin, anyway."

"So it's basically like a gig in New York City?" Jones asks.

"I suppose you could call it that," Miss Damata says.

He nods approvingly. "I just booked my first gig in New York," he says to me, and holds up a hand in the air. I high-five him.

"Your parents are in the city, right? Will you stay with them, or do you want me to make arrangements for you to stay in one of the dorm rooms at Juilliard for the night, like Alex is doing?" she asks Jones. I notice him tense for just the tiniest sliver of a second when she asks about staying with his parents. Jones and his dad aren't exactly having warm family reunions these days. *Standoffs* is more like it.

"My brother's in Brooklyn, so I'm all good. And Miss Damata?"

"Yes?"

"You rock," he says.

She smiles, then says, "If I were you, I'd brush up on Handel, Haydn, and Hendrix."

We thank her again and then head to the caf. "Are you even going to tell your parents you're in town?"

"Hell no," Jones says. "My dad knows the score. I'm not staying with them as long as he's still spinning lies to the press. He was in the paper again yesterday."

"Same thing?"

134

Jones nods. "Yup. His usual denial. *We had no prior knowledge of the complications caused by this product, and we are working hard to rectify the situation.* That's his standard line."

Jones's dad is this big-deal corporate strategist in New York, the kind of crisis-communications guy that car companies call when their tires explode and kill families, that energy companies call when they spill tons of oil in the ocean. This summer a pharmaceutical company phoned up Jones's dad when some of its researchers discovered that—*oops!*—its new brand of children's aspirin actually caused some serious health problems in babies. Jones's dad hired teams of people from the ranks of the unemployed to buy up every last aspirin bottle in every store in every city all across the country and dispose of them.

Jones overheard his dad's conversations and confronted him, telling him to just own up to it. His dad didn't.

Now the company's being investigated by some government agency, and it's his dad's job to keep the real story—the prior knowledge of the complication—from getting out.

"He called last night acting all casual and interested in how school was going. I said, 'Dad, don't think we're going to talk like we used to while you're still lying to everyone.'"

"Good for you. What did he say?"

"That someday he hoped I'd understand that the grown-up world isn't quite so black-and-white," Jones says, sketching air quotes as he imitates his father.

I scoff. "Right. Because here in the *kid* world, everything is crystal clear and there are no shades of gray."

"Anyway, don't tell Martin, okay? It's totally embarrassing what my dad is doing."

My chest tightens for a second, because even though I haven't told anyone, I kind of wish he hadn't singled out Martin. Still, I reassure him. "Jones, you know I don't tell anyone what we talk about. Ever. I told you that this summer," I say, reminding him of my promise to keep this secret way back when he first told me about it.

"I know. I just don't want anyone knowing my stuff," he says.

"You don't have to worry about that," I say.

"So what's the latest with the Annie case? Have you figured out yet who's supplying to the Debate Club?"

I stop in my tracks and stare at him.

"See! You're shocked I know it's the Debate Club. But your old friend Jones keeps his ear to the ground."

I shake my head but still say nothing.

"Alex," he says, all serious now, "you can cut it with the whole act. I *know* you're investigating the Debate Club. I hear the same crap you hear."

I feel stretched and pulled again, like Amy felt like last year when Jess asked about me. I breathe out hard. "Jones," I say.

"Oh, c'mon, Alex. Enough. I tell you all my stuff."

"This isn't mine to tell."

"Do you think you're maybe taking this a little too seriously?"

"No," I say quickly, because I have to take this seriously, especially when I am already bending some of the rules, when I am already doling out little white lies to the board.

"Well, since you're so serious about it, does that mean you're spying on your roomie too? Because Maia's on Anderin "

I place my finger on my lips and shush him. Then I grab his arm and pull him by the side of one of the buildings, down a quiet path.

"How do you know that? Do you know that for sure?" I whisper, thinking of the white cap I saw the other night and of what might lie beneath it.

"She has all the signs of being on Annie," Jones says. "Have you seen a more productive person than Maia? She goes without stopping. She never needs breaks. She could power a small city with her energy. You think that's all-natural energy?"

I shake my head and hold up a hand. "You're saying Maia is the way she is from Anderin?"

"I'm sure she needs the meds, unlike those scumbags who are taking it to cheat or whatever. But I'm also saying her natural intensity is amplified by the drug. You didn't really know her well freshman year. But she struggled then. She was so scattered. Distracted in class. Trouble focusing. She came back sophomore year like a well-oiled machine. I bet that summer she was diagnosed with ADHD and went on meds."

"How could you know this and I knew nothing? Did she tell you?" I ask, feeling stung that Maia would never tell me.

"No. She didn't tell me. I'm just saying it all adds up. And, look, I never rooted around in her bag or whatever. But I'd bet my Stratocaster I'm right."

That's a bet I'm going to have to take.

"Can you do me a favor?"

"Of course. What is it?"

"Please don't tell anyone about what you just said."

He tilts his head to the side and studies my face, like he can find the answer in my eyes or my cheeks or my nose. But there's no answer. Just questions—questions about my roommate that I don't want anyone else asking yet.

"You keep my secrets. I keep yours," he says, then slings his arm around my shoulder.

We make our way to the caf like that, and as I walk in with Jones I realize I was supposed to meet Martin here ten minutes ago. He's seated with Sandeep and T.S. at our usual table, but when he sees me with Jones, he has this strange look in his eyes.

Then he looks away.

I glance briefly at Jones, then at Martin, and in an instant, their roles have been reversed. Jones is the one who knows more about the case than Martin. And for now I have to keep it that way.

I do, however, step ahead of Jones in line so his arm is no longer around me.

Chapter Thirteen

TWO HALVES

I do my best to finish *Jane Eyre*, but the words are scribbles levitating off the page. Black letters that make no sense mutate in front of my eyes. As I stare at the page that might as well be blank, I shoot glances at Maia, over at her desk, typing away on her laptop as the Smiths blasts through her headphones. Twists and knots dig into my sides as my stomach nose-dives ceaselessly. Maybe I saw the pill bottle wrong in the dark. Maybe it's something else. Maybe Jones got it wrong and is just being Jones—suspicious, on-alert Jones. Maia wouldn't hide drugs, because she wouldn't supply drugs, she wouldn't engineer a cheating ring, and she definitely wouldn't deceive me about any of it. Especially not after last year and what we all went through. She defended me last year, stood by me every step of the way. She wouldn't lie to me.

So how can I root around in her bag? How can I spy on one of my best friends?

Because she wouldn't tell me the truth.

I put my head down on the desk, taking a deep breath, knowing I have to do this, knowing this is the choice I made that day in Amy's room. This isn't just about me anymore. I remind myself of Delaney, of what she stands to lose. Of Beat and what he stands to lose. Of my job: to be the one who helps them, who listens, who gives everyone a fair shot.

The one who has to spy on her roommate to be fair.

My stomach spins again, making cruel loops inside me.

A chair scrapes across the floor.

"Going to the loo," she says. As soon as I hear the bathroom door down the hall slam shut, I pounce on her bag. I don't let myself give it a second thought. I don't drag my feet or peer around the corner. I just lunge. It takes all of five seconds for me to unzip the side pocket, open up the brown paper bag, and confirm my suspicions, to verify what Jones had surmised. Because inside that bag are three ridiculously large bottles full of little orange pills. There are prescription labels on them, with the name of a doctor and a pharmacy in London.

I stuff them in the pocket, zip the bag, and return to my desk. I even manage to pretend-read two full pages before Maia returns, settles at her desk, and pops her headphones on.

But as she plunges back into her music, I feel bruised all over, little tender black-and-blue marks spread across my skin because my own roommate wouldn't tell me she's on Anderin. She knows everything about me. The whole school knows everything about me. I'm public record. So why wouldn't Maia tell me about a freaking prescription for ADHD meds?

The only reason I can figure is because they're not just for her. They're for the team.

I steal a glance at the back of her head, bopping to Morrissey's lyrics of self-loathing.

I leave without a word. Down the hall, down the steps, out the door. I walk around the perimeter of the campus trying to sort out what's going on, trying to understand how Maia could be a pill pusher. I make three loops around campus before it hits me. It hits me so hard, I laugh.

Just because she has the pills doesn't mean she's supplying. She's worried she'll be implicated, same as Beat, simply because she has a legit scrip. So she hid her meds. It's that simple. She's just a girl with ADHD, not a drug dealer, not a cheater who'd do anything to win the Elite.

Right?

I return to the room and I don't prep, I don't practice, I just go for it.

"Maia, why didn't you tell me you have ADHD?" I ask.

"What?" she says.

"I saw your pills."

She cocks her head to the side, raises her eyebrows, and says, "You looked through my bag."

"Well, why were you hiding them?"

"Why are you spying?"

"Why didn't you tell me you've been on meds? You never once mentioned it, and we've roomed together for two years now."

"Why is it your concern?"

"Because I'm your friend," I say, as if it's obvious. It's obvious to me at least. Why isn't it obvious to her?

"But that has nothing to do with why you were snooping, does it? Were you snooping because you're my friend or because you're a Mockingbird?"

"Maia! Me being a Mockingbird has nothing to do with this conversation," I say, and I'm verging on shouting. How can she not get this?

"Hardly. Whether or not I'm on Anderin has never been an issue in two years of rooming together, and now suddenly it's an issue simply because the Mockingbirds are investigating an Anderin case. It absolutely seems like this conversation has everything to do with the Mockingbirds and nothing to do with us," she says coolly, like I'm the latest opponent in a debate match and she's going to mow me down with her calm demeanor, with her headfake. Then she adds, "Which makes me wonder if I'm going to need to request my attorney to talk to you? Do you want to read me my Miranda rights?"

"I'm not talking about the Mockingbirds right now, Maia. I'm asking you personally. I'm trying to talk to you as a friend."

"But this would never have mattered to the old Alex. The old Alex respected privacy."

It's like she lit a torch and set the room on fire and now I'm burning white-hot. "Do not even go there with me when it comes to privacy. I have had my entire freaking past plastered all over this school. So don't give me crap about privacy."

"Then you of all people should respect my need for it."

I cut through her words, her rhetoric, and ask her again, the words coming out hard and coarse. "Are you on Anderin, Maia? Do you have ADHD?"

She remains unruffled. "I'm going to need to know if you're asking me on the record for your case or as my friend."

"As your friend. As the girl you represented in the laundry room last year," I say, playing the rape card for sympathy for the first time. Then my voice breaks, and tears start to well up in my eyes. I say softly, "This isn't about the case right now. This is about us. Why would you keep it a secret? We talk about everything."

"Because it's personal," she says softly, and her throat catches on the last word. Her cheeks turn the faintest color of red and she looks away, swallowing quickly, sucking in her almost tears. She is no longer the girl at the podium plowing down challengers. She's the girl who likes hats, the girl who has a pet bunny, the girl who has a secret she didn't want anyone to know. I feel like the worst friend in the world, because now I've forced my roommate to admit something she wanted to keep private.

"I never would have judged you for having ADHD," I

say gently. "I want to be here for you. I want to support you."

She turns back to me, steely-eyed again, tough again. "Thank you. But I don't need any support. I am fine. I take them for me, only me, and only as prescribed. I didn't tell you, because it's not something that needs to be shared. It's not something that needs to be supported. And it's not something that needs to be investigated. Because I'm not the one supplying the team. I would never do that. I don't cheat. I don't need to. And I would never ever encourage or suggest or condone it. And if you really are Alex my friend, then you better believe it's not me."

"I know it's not you," I say, wanting to get down on my knees and beg and plead and prove.

"Then please act like it."

♦ ♦ ♦

I am now a snoop.

It doesn't happen over several agonizing, painstaking months of transformation. It happens in a heartbeat. You make a choice, you make the wrong choice, you root through your friend's stuff, and you become someone you're not, someone you never wanted to be.

Someone your friend doesn't trust.

Someone who violates privacy.

Someone who breaks the rules. Because digging through my roomie's bag surely goes beyond the Mockingbirds' *keep your eyes and ears open for clues* guideline. So does lying by omission to the board, another thing I've been doing.

The next morning Maia grabs her shower basket from the closet and then turns to me, since T.S. is off at soccer practice. "I'm going to the shower now, Alex," she says. "Just in case you're keeping a log of all my activities."

"I'm not, Maia," I say.

"And after I shower I'll be brushing my teeth, then blow-drying my hair, then getting dressed. Feel free to let all your Mockingbirds friends know. I think I may have breakfast after that. Perhaps tea and jam. And I'll be sure to submit a diary to you later today of my schedule."

"I'm sorry," I mutter, but I know it won't cut it for her right now, not when she's fuming.

"Or you can just follow me if that's easier," she says, then walks out.

I grab a brush from my desk, run it through my hair, then decide I'd much rather toss it against the wall. I chuck it halfway across the room and watch as it bangs the brick wall, then falls to the carpet with a dull thud. I wish it had shattered. I wish it had broken into a hundred satisfying pieces on the floor. I would have relished cleaning up the pieces. And the whole time as I filled one hand with the bits of my hairbrush, I'd think what I'm thinking now—that I wish someone would have told me what this was like. That I wish someone would have warned me that the Mockingbirds can save you in one breath, then slash your heart in the next. That being part of this group means being separate from other people, from the people we're trying to help, from the people who are being hurt, and definitely from our friends.

But is this worth my friendships? They're *my* moral code. My friends stood by me last year, no questions asked. Now I feel like I'm pitted against them, and this just isn't worth it. It's not fair that I have to do this. It's not fair that any student has to do this. We shouldn't be policing one another. We shouldn't be spying on one another. We should only be helping one another, laughing with one another, goofing off with one another.

There is *only* one person who should be dealing with this, and her name is Ms. Merritt.

The woman who has an open-door policy.

She said I could trust her. She said I could come to her for anything. She said I should have come to her last year. Let's see what she'll do this year.

When I leave my dorm, I head straight to the administration building, my jaw set, my muscles tight, as I push open the door so hard, it smacks the inside wall. I pinpoint my destination at the far end of the hall, never wavering, never taking my eyes off the open door to the dean's office. When I reach it, I knock once and step inside, the cushy chocolate brown carpet sinking beneath my red-and-white Vans.

Her secretary glances up from the computer and turns to me. "Hello. How may I help you?"

"I'm looking for Ms. Merritt. I need to see her, please," I say.

"She's not available right now. May I have her get back to you?"

"She's not available?" I repeat, as if the words don't compute.

She smiles and shakes her head. "That is correct. She is not available."

"I'm sorry, I don't understand. I thought she had an open-door policy. I thought students were allowed to come see her and talk to her. She said we could come see her anytime."

"I understand that," the secretary says robotically but sweetly, like this is how she was programmed by her maker. "But she is not available right now."

"Well, when do you think she'll be available?"

"When she frees up."

"When will that be? This is important. This is really important. I guarantee this will be the most important thing she has to deal with all day, all semester."

"She's simply not available."

I place my hands on the edge of the desk, not sure if I am coming across as crazed or desperate but not caring. "Why? Where is she?" I ask.

"I think it would be best if I give her a message and have her get back to you."

"How? How will she get back to me?" I ask, holding my hands up in the air. "Does that mean she'll call me? Does that mean she'll set an appointment for me to come back? What will she do? How will I hear from her? Is she going to text me or something? Maybe with a smiley face and an OMG too?"

"I think I would feel more comfortable if you didn't stand quite so close to my desk," the secretary says, and makes a gentle shooing motion.

"I would feel more comfortable if I could talk to Ms. Merritt right now," I say.

The secretary casts her eyes a few feet from me, making it clear I am to back up before she speaks again. I step back and fold my arms over my chest.

"Now, what is the message?" she asks.

I close my eyes for a second and the recklessness of what I am about to do almost overcomes me. But I have to be brash; I have to test the positive-reinforcement-only philosophy for myself. I've only known of it from reading our records of past cases. But I *need* to know firsthand if she really will turn a blind eye.

I consider my words carefully, giving only enough info to cause concern, not enough to implicate, but punctuating each word so nothing is lost in the translation, so the honor pledge we all took is underlined, as I say, "Please tell her it is about Anderin abuse."

The secretary smiles at me without showing any teeth.

"And please tell her I need to talk to her right away," I add, giving her my name, my e-mail address, and my phone number.

"Of course," she says, and I watch as the secretary writes the message down in her pristine, crisp handwriting. "Is there anything else?"

"No," I say, and as I leave I catch a glimpse of Ms. Merritt's office and the empty spot on her shelves for that dumb trophy.

◆ ◆ ◆

I'm in my room later, pacing, waiting, checking my phone, checking my e-mail. It's as if Juilliard itself is going to get in touch with me, that's how much I want to hear from Ms. Merritt, and not because I *want* to hear from her. Not because I want her to solve this really big freaking problem at her school. But because I want to know if she even will.

I flip open my phone again, just in case there is a message I missed. None. I shut it just as Maia walks in.

She nods curtly, straightens up, and walks to her desk, where she sits down.

"What's going on, Maia?" I ask casually, the way I would have asked before our friendship turned to tundra this morning.

"Why are you asking?"

"I'm just curious," I say, wishing we could go back to the way we were before, wishing I knew how to navigate that route. But the map has been lost somewhere, several miles ago, under the passenger seat, next to crumbs and food wrappers, and the driver doesn't have a clue where to find it.

"I'm studying for a debate tournament coming up in Miami. You can see the proof of my hard work there in my bag where I keep all my *uppers* that I share with the team."

"Can we just move on from here, please? I said I was sorry."

"I don't know. Can we?" she asks pointedly. "Are you *really* sorry or just sorry I know you were snooping?"

But before I can say anything, I hear a sound, like a slight *whoosh*. I look in the direction of the door and see a slim white envelope that's been slipped underneath. My name is on it, so I grab it. I open it and there's a brochure inside. It's on Anderin abuse, the warning signs, the dangers, the symptoms, and a phone number for a hotline for help. Paper-clipped to it is a note on plain white paper:

I'm so very glad you came to me about this, Alex. I do hope this information helps, and please don't hesitate to let me know if there is anything else I can assist with. Can't wait for your Faculty Club performance. It's going to be great! —Ms. M.

In pristine, crisp handwriting.

I squeeze my eyes shut and breathe out, a hard breath, deep, full of the kind of anger that could fuel a small city if you channeled me to a power plant right now. I open my eyes and crush the brochure and the note into a ball, the note the dean couldn't even bother to write herself.

She treats us just like her dogs.

Maia is looking at me, waiting for me to tell her what the note is.

"It's from the dean and I hate her," I say, and then I do

something rash. Totally and utterly stupid and dumb. I slam my fist against the brick wall. And it hurts like hell. I shake my hand out and see Maia staring at me like I've gone crazy.

"Sorry," I say, but it comes out like a hiss, so I just leave. I head to the music hall, where I'm alone, just like I am with this case, just like we all are at this school.

All I can do now is find a way to clear Maia's name. Because no one else—no adult in charge—is going to help me.

Chapter Fourteen

THE GRAND ILLUSION

Ms. Merritt waits outside the administration building, holding the door open, a smile of epic proportions plastered across her face. She's happy; of course she's happy. We're about to perform and she loves a good show. I picture reaching out and peeling that stupid grin off her like a Band-Aid. I bet it'd hurt and be all raw and red underneath.

"Good morning, Martin. Good morning, Anjali. Good morning, T.S. Good morning, Parker. Good morning, Delaney. Good morning, Alex," she says, then says hello to a few runners who are also singing with us today. Then she shuts the door with them inside, separating me from my merry band of Mockingbirds.

"Alex, is everything all right? I was so concerned when I learned you had dropped by and I couldn't be there in person to help you. I do hope everything has been sorted out since then?"

"Sorted out?" I ask, shocked at the ridiculousness of the question. "No. Nothing's been sorted out."

She sighs heavily, then pushes her glasses against her nose. "I'm sorry to hear that. I do hope this isn't distracting you from your goals this semester."

"I assume those would be our shared goals," I say sarcastically.

"But of course. Are you able to focus on your music? On your application to Juilliard? Do you need any extra help from myself, or perhaps even from Miss Damata, because I could certainly arrange that. I know how very hard it is to be a student here."

"You have no idea what it's like to be a student here these days," I say, and then take a step back because it's as if I just discovered a superpower I didn't know I had, like I've just learned I could fly or lift cars with one hand. Because I can't believe I have it in me to talk back to the dean herself.

"Excuse me?" she says, arching an eyebrow. I watch as it rises above her hideous glasses. Her face looks pinched, pulled back tight by her French braid.

"Nothing," I say.

She nods several times, as if she's forgiving my impudence. "I understand what you're going through, Alex. It's not an easy time. Senior year is particularly tough," she says, then gestures to the doors. "So let's enjoy the rest of the day. Because I am certainly eager to see why the Mockingbirds are indeed the finest singers in the school."

Then she walks ahead of me, and I hear a voice, loud and booming, behind me.

"Still room for one more?"

It's Jones, and he has his guitar with him, the sleek, silver Stratocaster.

"Jones! You didn't tell me you were coming!"

"I like surprises. I like surprising you."

"I am definitely surprised in more ways than one. And so you're not," I say, reaching into my back pocket for a sheet of paper, "here are the lyrics."

As we walk into the Faculty Club, I inhale deeply, imagining the air filling my lungs, giving me strength, guts, sinew to face the one real enemy we all have. Martin is taken aback when he sees Jones and shoots me another curious look like that day in the caf when Jones and I walked in late. So is Parker, who leans in to whisper, "But he's not a Mockingbird."

"Neither is Delaney," I whisper back.

"Right. But I thought she was an unofficial one?"

"Like a mascot?" I joke.

That eases things with Parker, the stickler. But he feels even better when I remind him of *why* we need ringers. "The more believable we are, the less likely Senator Hume is to find out," I whisper.

I take a step forward, the rest of the Mockingbirds, real and fake, forming a line behind me. I bow to the faculty members who have gathered for our performance. They're all here—Miss Damata; Mr. Baumann; the French teacher,

Ms. Dumas; the Spanish teacher, Mr. Bandoro; my former history teacher Mr. Christie; and even the headmistress herself is back for this performance. I guess Ms. Vartan is taking a break from her Prep Schools of the World Tour. How very lovely for her to return for the show.

Some faculty members are seated in the high-backed leather chairs; some are standing casually next to the floor-to-ceiling bookshelves, lined with leather-bound first editions. A nearby table is packed with fresh fruit and bakery breads that look like they rose in the oven this very morning. Then I notice another table—this one is manned by a gentleman in a white chef hat and jacket. He's presiding over a skillet, and next to the skillet are sliced mushrooms, shredded cheeses, delicately cut tomatoes. Ms. Merritt hired a caterer.

She's going to serve omelets after we perform.

She's going to maintain her grand illusion.

I fix my eyes on her, because if I look at Miss Damata, if I look at someone I respect, I might break, I might laugh, I might run. Instead, I lock Ms. Merritt into my crosshairs. Then I speak.

"Let me begin by thanking you, Ms. Merritt, for bestowing the honor of the very first Faculty Club performance of the new school year on the Mockingbirds. Thank you, Ms. Vartan, for being here as well. I speak for all of us when I say we are deeply flattered and humbled," I say, then gesture to my merry band of Mockingbirds. They bow before the faculty. "And because this is Themis and because we believe in excellence in all endeavors—we wrote you a song. Actually it's kind of like a mash-up of some tunes we all know from childhood. *Early* childhood. Because who doesn't want to reconnect with their inner child while here in high school?"

Miss Damata shoots me a curious look, but I go on. "I'm presuming you've all heard 'Pussycat, Pussycat, Where Have You Been?'"

Many of the teachers nod, and I gesture for them to join in my recitation. They do. *"I've been to London to visit the queen. Pussycat, Pussycat, what did you there? I frightened a little mouse under the chair."*

I pause as they finish. "It's short and sweet, but so is our version, and I'm going to let Delaney take the lead."

I retreat to the rest of the line while Delaney steps forward. She's in full regalia today—her purple hair is sleek and blown out straight, bangs landing crisply across her forehead, cutting a line just above her navy-blue eye makeup and heavily mascaraed lashes. She wears red vinyl boots, dark jeans that might as well be painted on, and a black T-shirt. I have to say, she looks smoking hot.

The rest of us begin a little doo-woppy sway, snapping our fingers and shaking our hips in time, as we croon out— badly off-key, most of us—a mix of "ooh" and "ahh," like the backup singers we are right now.

The girl with the purple hair begins, her smoky, sexy voice hitting all kinds of notes as she sings a new tune: *"Dirty clothes, dirty clothes, where have you been? We've been down to the laundry room to get ourselves clean. Dirty clothes, dirty clothes, what did you there? We told the dryers all about the affair."*

"And now a mash-up," I say, and nod to Jones, who joins Delaney in front of the line for a duet. We continue to back them up as they sing modified versions of "Hey, Diddle, Diddle" (the teachers jumped over the quad; the little students laughed to see such sport); a reimagined "Mary Had a Little Lamb" (then the students called her names, and the lamb was very sad); and my personal favorite, "I've Been Working on the Railroad" (we've been working on our college apps all the live-long day).

Then we're done, and Ms. Merritt begins the clapping. Because she has to set the agenda for the teachers. She has to let them know she is pleased, and they should be pleased too; they should follow suit with their cheers. They do. And I know on some level she *must* get it—who we really are, what we really do, that our musical choices are not just a roast, not just normal teenage teasing of authority.

As she beams, a smile so wide it nearly reaches her braid, it's the reminder that even if she knows, she just doesn't care. Because what matters to her is that we have excelled, like her Weimaraners, like her twins.

"Would you like an encore?" Jones offers.

We don't have any more songs, so I don't know what he has up his sleeve.

But the approval is unanimous, so he plugs in his guitar to the portable amp he brought and then whispers to Delaney. She nods and smiles at him, then turns to me with a wink.

Jones looks at me and says out loud, "You guys can kick back for this one. We'll take care of it."

Then the two of them launch into a hot, loud, and electrified version of Bob Marley's "I Shot the Sheriff."

I can't think of a more apropos song.

◆ ◆ ◆

"They were amazing, weren't they?" I say to Martin for the fiftieth time as we leave the cafeteria after lunch and head to my room.

"Yep," Martin says.

"And Jones. God, he was great. He really can sing," I say as I bound up the stairs, Martin a step or two behind me. "And he can play. I don't think I've ever heard a better guitarist."

"Yep, like Jimi Hendrix himself descended to the Faculty Club," Martin says, but I ignore the sarcasm in his voice, because in my world Jones is as good as any of the Guitar Gods.

"Exactly," I say. "He is totally going to be a rock star someday." Then I realize now would be the perfect time to tell Martin about the jam fest in New York with Jones. Especially since Martin *can't* go. He's going away with one of his brothers for the weekend—some last mountain-bike ride before the Summers family turns to their snowboards. "Hey, so I wanted to tell you something about Jones—"

"Let me guess. He seduced you with his musical fingers

and silver guitar and now you're leaving me to run away with him and form some piano-guitar-playing hipster duo in Brooklyn."

Maybe now's not the time to mention that weekend after all.

"I'm not leaving you for anyone," I say.

"Good. Let's keep it that way," he says, and drapes an arm over my shoulders. I like it. It feels protective, safe.

When we reach my room, Maia's there, headphones on, Duran Duran blasting through them. Her affection for British bands from way back when runs strong. She looks up, shoots me a cold stare, then pulls off her headphones.

"This must be an official inspection," she says, cutting and cold. "Martin, would you like to root through my things too? Maybe check and see if I have a list of all the alleged users or anonymous sources or spineless bastards you guys want to protect?"

Martin holds his hands up. "Whoa. Chill, Maia."

Maia continues. "What? You didn't know Alex has been spying on me and going through my things?"

My face turns red, and Martin turns to me. Martin's not supposed to know I was investigating Maia. Like Parker, he thinks Anjali's been doing it. I've led them both to believe Anjali's been doing it.

Then Maia laughs and points at me. "Oh, that's cute! He doesn't know you've been looking through my stuff."

"I think we're going to go hang out someplace else," I say, and grab Martin's hand, pulling him out of my room.

As we walk down the hall, Martin asks me what's going on. "I thought Anjali was investigating her, Alex."

"No. I am," I admit.

"Why?"

"Because she's my roommate and she's my friend and she's not guilty, okay?"

"But what did you find when you were looking through her stuff?" he asks carefully.

"Nothing," I say, keeping my eyes fixed straight in front of me as I lie. It's not like I took an oath to put the Mockingbirds before my friends. Right? The board doesn't need to know everything, especially if I was breaking Mockingbirds rules when I found the pills because snooping in someone's bag is definitely verboten. But if I'm going to be protecting people, I've got to protect *my* people too, my friends, even if Maia's mad at me, even if she won't talk to me. I have to maintain some lines, because the slope is slick and oily under my feet, like the muddy hillside after a rain.

But like I snooped on my roommate, now I'm lying to my boyfriend—not to Martin the Mockingbird but to Martin *my* Martin. Because *this* is the kind of thing I'd tell him. And this is what Amy warned me about. The secrets you have to keep, the people you have to protect. You don't get to be this great stand-taker without being yanked in every direction, without having your loyalties tested in every which way.

"I'm surprised, that's all," Martin says.

"Surprised? Like you thought it was her?" I say, snapping at him.

"No. Surprised at *you*. I just thought you were into playing by the rules."

"You must have me confused with Parker. Because there's another set of rules, and those are the ones that say you don't let other people investigate your friends," I say. But even as the words come out, I know I'm already doing the limbo under both sets of rules.

Do the ends justify the means, though? Does protecting Maia's secrets make it okay?

"But what if your friends are doing something wrong?" Martin asks.

I stop on the landing and look at him, my eyes blazing. "My friend isn't doing anything wrong."

We walk down the steps in silence. I realize I'm shaking, like I've had way too much caffeine. There's only one thing I need right now, and it's not Martin.

Chapter Fifteen

ADMISSIONS SWOON

The piano waits for me in the music hall. It's like a well-worn blanket and I want to nuzzle it, cuddle it, bury my face in it.

I close the door behind me and walk to the beautiful thing I love, dropping my backpack on the floor. I run my hands along the black lacquer, smooth as glass underneath my skin. I close my eyes, spread my arms as far as they can go, palms pressed on the instrument as I take a deep breath. Nothing is complicated here. Nothing is confusing here. There are no friends against friends, no boyfriends you lie to, no dean who just smiles and waves.

The piano asks no questions. The piano tells no lies.

I sink down onto the bench and at once I feel calm, quiet. This is my haven and the only one I share it with tonight is the French composer Maurice Ravel. I could play his most famous piece, *Boléro*, for my Juilliard audition CD. But everyone else will play *Boléro*. It's famous for a reason. It's sex in music form. The whole thing is foreplay. It's one long build. That's why everyone picks it. They think they can send Juilliard admissions officers into a swoon by playing *Boléro*.

Sure, there's no question it is quite possibly the most visceral, most sensual piece of music ever written. But it has to be played by the *whole orchestra* to work. The turn-on comes from every instrument having its say as the melody rides from flute to clarinet to bassoon and on and on and on. Then there's that snare drum, that delicious, tingly snare drum a constant throughout, keeping score of the desire that can't stop itself, that lasts and lasts until . . . a burst of sound, then it's over.

Let all the others try to seduce Juilliard with *Boléro*.

I will seduce them with prowess, because I have chosen a piece you play with only one hand—a concerto Ravel wrote for the left hand only. He composed it for a classical pianist who'd lost his right arm in the first world war. Ravel's goal? To create a piece to play one-handed that was as challenging, as complex, as virtuosic as something you need all ten fingers for. It's a crazy-hard piece, since you have to cruise through several speeds and several keys without a pause. I've mastered it technically. Note for note, I can breeze through it and wring all the gorgeousness out of it with four fingers and a thumb. But sometimes it feels as if something is missing, and I don't just mean another hand. Something deeper, like a secret in the piece that needs to be mined.

I begin the excavation.

I play and I play and I play. Without stopping, without breaking, without thinking. This is the blissful emptiness of a world that makes no more demands of me than I make of it.

When I finally stop hours later, I don't know that I find what I'm looking for, but I do find a temporary peace. I stretch out my neck, shifting to the left, then the right. I feel a buzzing in my pocket and I take out my cell phone, noticing that it's almost nine and I've been playing since the middle of the afternoon.

Would you like a visitor?

I remember how I disappointed Martin. I remember how he pissed me off. But for all intents and purposes, I've just been to the spa, getting a massage for the last few hours.

Sure. Leaving soon, though...

Three minutes later he's here and I let him in.

"Hey," he says.

"Hey," I say.

Then there's silence, the awkward silence of a fight still lingering between us.

"Just because I don't always agree with you doesn't mean I don't respect your point of view," he says, going first with the apology. As he says he's sorry I am struck by how it's not what most guys would say. Most guys would say, *Just because I don't agree with you doesn't mean I don't want to be with you.* But Martin, he knows this isn't about whether we like each other after a disagreement. Martin knows I would never be that girl who thought he didn't like me because we didn't see eye to eye. Martin would never be that guy either.

And because he puts himself out there like that, because he opens himself up to me, I'm disarmed. And I like it.

"I guess I feel the same," I admit.

"I just want us, the group, to do things the right way, even if the right way sometimes really sucks."

"Yeah, the right way totally sucks."

"So do we agree to disagree, then?"

I smile. "What choice do we have?"

"We could arm wrestle."

"I think you'd win."

"I hear you have pretty strong hands, though," he says.

"They are powerful," I say, holding up my hands like they're claws.

"Show me how powerful," he says, reaching for my hands, linking his fingers through mine. But rather than pull me close, he spins me around so I'm facing the piano. "Will you play something for me, Alex?" he asks.

With his hands on my shoulders, he sits me down at the piano bench. "What do you want to hear?"

"Ravel," he says. "You've only been telling me about his left-handed piece for the last three months."

"Oh, ha-ha."

"But I want to hear the one you're *not* going to play. I want to hear the one you think is too sexy for them."

"I didn't say it was too sexy! I said it doesn't sound right just on the piano. You need a whole orchestra for the piece to be sexy."

"Hmm...," he says. "That is a dilemma. But I'm willing

to let my ears be a guinea pig and tell you if it's a turn-on without all those other instruments." Then he moves in behind me, crowding me forward a bit, a leg on each side of me, his chest against my back. His hands slide down my arms as he rests them just above my wrists.

"That's a bit distracting," I say softly.

"Maybe like this you can get the piece just right," he whispers.

"Close your eyes."

"Oh, they're closed, all right," he says, his warm breath next to my ear.

So I begin. I glide through each of the repeating sections, naming the instruments that we're supposed to be hearing as I go. "This would be the flute," I say.

"Flute," he repeats, brushing his lips against my neck.

"Clarinet," I tell him.

"Clarinet," he echoes, finding this spot just beneath my ear.

"Now the bassoon."

"Mmm...bassoon."

"Oboe."

"Oboe," he says, low and soft.

"Clarinet again."

"Clarinet."

"Now trumpet."

"Trumpet," he says, and traces his fingers up my right arm.

I shiver, then say, "Saxophone."

"Saxophone," he repeats.

Then there's another saxophone, then piccolos, then his hands. Then more oboe, more clarinets, then his lips. Then more instruments, they all play together, those same eighteen bars, building, onward, further, over and over, hands on my arms, lips on my neck, breath in my ear, music all around.

Then it all just ends in a loud, very loud, finale.

And now silence.

The fabric of my T-shirt is burning, almost wet, with the pressure of his chest on me. I feel his heart beating against my back, his breathing, slow and steady, in the space between my neck and shoulder blade.

"You're right," he says quietly.

"About what?"

"You can't play that for them."

"Why?"

"Because then they'd want you as much as I do right now."

Heat floods me as his arms fold around me. I have never wanted him more. I have never wanted to be closer to him, to anyone, than I do right now. Here with the boy I love wrapped around me, all I can think about is him. And me. And him and me together.

In every way.

"Martin," I say.

"Yes?"

"Are your roommates in your room right now?"

"Yes. But I can kick them out in a heartbeat."

"I would like that."

Chapter Sixteen

SECRET KEEPER

I always thought I'd tell T.S. right away.

Or T.S. and Maia at the same time.

But now that it's happened, I don't actually want to tell anyone. I want to keep it to myself. I like nobody knowing what I did last night.

Because even though I wasn't a virgin, it felt like the first time. The real first time. The way I always wanted my first time to be. Soft, and slow, and under the covers, with just a sliver of moonlight shining through the windows. Looking into his eyes, seeing my own nervousness reflected back, knowing he was the one worth waiting for.

And he was.

Because it was just us. There were no harsh memories slamming between us, no images crashing into me. And maybe, just maybe, that means I've managed to banish them for good. My heart soars at the thought, at the possibility that somehow, at some point, I crossed this hurdle, and this part of last year is behind me, where it should be.

That's why all day Sunday I find myself keeping my mouth shut, just smiling goofy smiles at Martin when we sit together in the caf for breakfast, then again for lunch, then again when he comes to visit me in the afternoon and we go outside and walk around the quad holding hands, squeezing back and forth like we're sending secret signals to each other.

Which we are, I suppose. Every time I look at Martin, he gives me an *I-have-a-secret* look back.

"Stop it!" I say playfully as we stand under a tree.

"I can't help myself," he says, and puts his arms around my waist. "You just seduced me there at the piano last night. You seduced me with your piano playing."

"I'm a seductress," I say, trailing my fingers across the front of his shirt as I laugh, because I couldn't be happier that he finds my music sexy.

"And I'm just smiling because I'm so in love with you," he adds.

It's not the first time he's said it. I've said it too. Nor is it the first time he's said he's *so in love with me*. Because, really, if you're going to be in love, *so* is the kind of *in love* you want. But hearing him say it now, again and again, *after* the fact, makes me feel like all is right with the world, or at least my own little corner of the universe, perfect as it is in this moment.

So I keep my own secrets, keeping last night all to myself. This is my new history, the history I get to record. This is the way it should be between a boy and a girl. Then I say good-bye to him because I have a new dinner companion tonight, and it's Jamie. We practiced together the other day and then made plans for dinner too, because that's part of the whole mentor-mentee thing. I can't say *protégé*. It's too pretentious.

"I'm going to do my first duet soon!" Jamie tells me when we sit down to eat. "The captain of the VoiceOvers said he was super impressed with my singing, so he's going to assign me a duet. I can't wait."

"That's awesome," I say. Jamie's a true musical prodigy—not only is she a rising star in orchestra, she is also a singer, and she nabbed a spot in the VoiceOvers, Themis's real a cappella singing group.

"So, if you had to pick flute or singing, which is your favorite?" I ask as I take a bite of my pasta.

"Am I going to get in trouble if I say singing?" Jamie asks, a touch of nerves in her question.

"Of course not."

"I mean, I'm *so* glad you're my mentor, and I totally want to get better at the orchestra and performing, but singing is my first love, know what I mean?"

I nod as I chew my food. Then I say, "Totally. I get it. And I wish I could sing too. But sadly, I can't sing to save my life."

Jamie laughs. "I highly doubt you could do anything wrong musically."

"Ha," I say. "Trust me on this one."

Then I feel a finger tapping my shoulder. It's the girl sitting next to me. I turn to face her. She has honey-blond hair, pulled back in a loose ponytail. "What's up?" I ask.

Her eyes dart back and forth, then she asks, "Is it too late to still try out for the council? For the Mockingbirds? Because you're the leader, right?"

I nod. "I am."

"I saw the posters earlier and wanted to try out for the *New Nine*," she says, using our secret code.

"That's great. But we actually picked the New Nine already. Were you a runner last year?" I ask, because while I know the names of the runners, I don't know all their faces.

Her face falls and she shakes her head. "No," she says.

"But that's okay! You can be a runner next semester. That's how you start," I explain. "Mockingbirds start as runners, then move to the council, and then some to the board."

"And you're on the board, right?"

I nod proudly. I want her to feel proud too to be a Mockingbird if she decides to try out.

"So you must have been a runner, then? And a council member too?"

I flash back to Amy's room, to the decision I made there to *own* my past. I straighten my shoulders and answer her. "It was different for me. The leader is always someone who's been helped. The Mockingbirds helped me last year when I was date-raped by another student," I say, and it's like I've stripped down and I'm standing naked before this girl. But

I'm not ashamed of my body or my past. I stand here without any clothes on and I don't hide and I don't cover up and I am vulnerable, exceedingly vulnerable, but I am also choosing to be okay with this moment, all of it.

"Holy crap," the girl says, covering her mouth with her hand. "Are you okay?"

"I am," I say, nodding. "Thank you for asking."

She shakes her head like she's trying to shake away the shock. "I had no idea," she answers. "But that's pretty courageous."

"Thank you. I hope you'll try out to be a runner next semester."

"I will."

I turn back to Jamie, and she's frozen in place, holding her fork in midair, her mouth hanging open. When my eyes meet hers, she speaks. "That was, like, the bravest thing I've ever seen anyone do."

Then McKenna drops by, sliding in next to us. "Yay!" she says, clapping. "I am so glad that it all worked out and you are Jamie's mentor."

"Me too," I tell McKenna.

"Soooo," McKenna says, raising her eyebrows and looking at her sister. "Everything fabulous?"

Jamie nods and says yes, but her voice sounds barren, empty. I watch as they lock eyes and something passes between them. Maybe a secret between sisters. God knows I have my fair share of secrets now.

◆ ◆ ◆

I spend the next day entirely distracted in all my classes. It's not just that I'm replaying Saturday night with Martin—my stomach flips every time I think back on it and every time I think about how much I want to do it again—but I am also wracking my brain to figure out how to prove Maia innocent.

I want to prove it to the board. I need Parker and Martin to *know* that she's not the dealer. And I need to do it in a way that doesn't reveal her secret—that she has the prescription, only she needs it for the right reasons. Most of all, I want this case behind me. I want my friendships back. I want to return to when T.S., Maia, and I could talk about silly names for pets, and mock our teachers, and, yes, talk about boys and kisses and sex. I want to tell them about my real first time and how I now have new memories, *good* memories, toe-curling memories to replace the bad ones.

But I can't right now.

During my history class I study the Debate Club roster. I recognize some of the names, and one in particular stands out to me: Vanessa Waterman. She's kind of scatterbrained and always dropping her books and leaving a trail of papers behind her, but from what I've heard from Maia, she's one of the top performers on the team. She's also sitting two desks in front of me right now. Vanessa and I have been in the same history class every year since we started here, and we were also paired up on special projects each of our first three years.

Here's hoping that shared history will count for something.

When class ends, I stop at her desk. "Hey, Vanessa," I say. Her desk is like a smorgasbord. Stuff is spread everywhere—notebooks, papers, textbooks, even some barrettes. She's jamming it all into her backpack, her frizzy brown hair piled up high on her head.

"Hi, Alex."

"Can I talk to you for a sec?" I say in my library voice.

She tenses, and tilts her head to the side. "About what?" she asks as she pushes some papers into the bottom of her bag.

The rest of the class filters out, including our teacher, so it's just us now.

I crouch down next to her. "So, listen, I wanted to ask you something. And this'll be totally, one hundred percent confidential. But we've been hearing about some stuff going down in the Debate Club and—"

"What sort of stuff?"

"Well, basically that there's some sort of widespread Anderin use, sharing, snorting, selling."

Vanessa gives a coarse laugh. "Oh. That's all?" she asks sarcastically.

"Yeah. I know, right? Crazy stuff. So I was just wondering if you had heard anything or might know anything about it, because we were asked to look into it. You know, the Mockingbirds."

"So you want to know who's involved?" she asks in this

conspiratorial way, like I've come to just the right person. *Score*, Alex!

"Definitely," I say, my eyes glowing as I wait for the goods.

"I. Don't. Have. A. Clue."

Then she walks out, and I feel like I've been slapped. I put my hand on my cheek briefly, as if my face is still stinging from where she smacked me. Maybe it's red too.

But then I look down at the floor, and I see that Vanessa left behind a lot of stuff: a bunch of hair clips, a notebook, and something else. Something better. Her cell phone. I stare at it for a second like it has a heartbeat, like it's beating loud and seductively, wooing me to lean down, wrap my hands around it, touch it, scroll through all its contents. I glance around. No one's here.

The way she shoved my question back in my face tells me she knows something.

And maybe that something is on her phone.

The room is so quiet that the silence in here feels like a life force, like another person standing next to me, urging me to look. I'm burning up inside; this hot, racy feeling of danger slams through me. Then I just do it. I grab the phone, swipe my finger across the screen to bring up her messages, and click on her e-mail.

I hold my breath the whole time as I flick through her messages. *C'mon, there must be something here.*

Then I see it. A note from Theo. A group e-mail. Thank God I have steady hands, because inside I'm so jumpy, my nerves are about to boomerang out of my body and bounce across the room.

Got more of the good stuff. I'll spread the love as usual. Same Bat-time, same Bat-channel.

Then I hear footsteps heading toward me, clicking closer and closer. I grab my phone from my back pocket, snap a picture of her screen, then swipe her phone back to its home screen. I lay it on her notebooks, right next to a red barrette.

Then I walk out of the room, keeping my own phone in my hands as if I'm deeply engrossed in a salacious text-message conversation, affixing a silly grin on my face because this message from T.S. is so freaking raunchy that I nearly bump shoulders with Vanessa on her way back in.

I spend the rest of the day staring at the picture I took like it's a note from a lover.

But that heady feeling slips away at night when I show the picture to Martin and Parker in the laundry room. They ask me how I got it, and I'm pretty sure digging around in someone's phone, checking e-mail after e-mail, won't pass muster as an ethical investigation technique.

So I cloak myself in a new layer of gray as I make it seem like Vanessa's phone was just a gleaming twenty-dollar bill I found on the sidewalk and happened to pick up and, lo and behold, the message was right there on the home screen *that very second*. Naturally, I had to snap a photo.

As I tell the tale I feel like I'm swallowing my grandma's badly cooked pot roast and pretending it tastes good. I stick to my story, figuring the ends for now *have* to justify the means. Besides, I'm one step closer to clearing Maia's name, to returning to the way we were.

We all agree that Parker needs to tail Theo more closely now, to try to figure out where and when these deals are going down. Amy had said in our phone call at the start of the case to be cautious about following students. But we have enough clues now to track him more closely.

Martin and I will keep our eyes on the others in the e-mail thread.

Later that night in the library as Martin studies inorganic chemistry, I think back to what Anjali said—*freshmen are involved*. I wonder if I should spend some time in the freshman dorms too, maybe pay some calls to first-years along with Anjali. Then I feel Martin brush his lips against my neck. I shiver at his touch, then whisper, "More." He moves in closer to me, lingering this time, his soft lips leaving a trail of warmth across my skin. I am suddenly more daring than I have ever been in public, even though we're tucked in a quiet corner where no one can see us. I move still closer to him, placing a hand against his T-shirt, feeling the smooth lines of his stomach even through the gray fabric. A small sigh escapes his lips, and I press my palm harder against his shirt, against him, feeling a zing shoot through me as I touch him.

Then his voice is low in my ear. "I'm going to spend one hour with Johns Hopkins, MIT, and Stanford, and then I'd really like to take you to the science lab." He takes out a key from his front jeans pocket and dangles it in front of me. "I have a key."

"Then we really should experiment."

As we're packing up our books an hour later, Martin tells me about kangaroos. "Did you know they're not really from Australia?"

"I have to say I did not know that at all, Mr. Summers," I say, and give him a grin, because this is yet another reason why I am crazy about him. He is fascinated with biology and he loves to share what he learns. He'll get this excited look in his eyes; I've seen it many times when he talks about biology and science and animal behavior. This is music to him; this is his Beethoven and Chopin.

"They've been fooling everyone, those sneaky marsupials. Now there's evidence they're really from South America," he says, and begins telling me about jumping genes and junk DNA, but then I get a text I can't ignore. It's from Jones, so I flip open my phone to read it as Martin talks.

Dad just called. So pissed. Come visit?

I turn back to Martin and he's no longer talking and there's this look in his eyes now. Retreat, maybe. Because maybe he thinks I'm like the girl who says she loves football when she dates the quarterback but is just faking her affection for punts and plays and handoffs.

"I'm sorry," I say, because I don't want to be that girl. I'm not that girl. I'm not faking it. I'm not faking anything with Martin.

"No worries," he says, and looks away as he jams a book in his backpack.

"Can I take a rain check?" I ask.

Martin gives me a curious look.

"It's Jones," I explain, and I feel my cheeks go red.

"You guys going to go practice or something?"

"Uh, no," I say.

"Okay," he says slowly, waiting for me to explain why I'm dissing him for another boy.

"It's just . . . I need to see him," I say. I'm guessing now would be another bad time to mention that weekend trip to New York.

"You need to see him," Martin repeats, and it's not the words he's saying that matter, it's the surprise in his voice; it's the way he knows I'm not telling him everything. But I can't. I've sworn to Jones I won't tell anyone about his dad, not even Martin. "I thought we were going to . . ."

"I know and, trust me, I want to. I would much rather be experimenting with you. But it's just he's going through some stuff, okay?"

Martin holds up his hands and now he's the one backing off. "Then *stuff* should take precedence, especially with the soon-to-be rock star."

"Martin," I say, protesting, "that's not fair."

"I'm not going to apologize for wanting to be with you," he says. "Especially after the other night."

And there's that stretching, tearing feeling again. Only this time I feel like I'm being ripped in half and it hurts like a son of a bitch.

♦ ♦ ♦

Jones is alone in his room because Jones has a single. He requested it, made a case for it, saying he'd hate to disturb roommates with late-night violin playing. He is now one of the few seniors who lives roomie-free, though his late-night playing is of the guitar variety only.

"Come in," he says after I knock.

His hands are wrapped around the silver body of his guitar, and he leans back on his bed.

"Feeling up your girlfriend?"

"Oh yeah. Problem is she's a cold fish."

I pull out a chair and sit down. "So, what's going on?"

Jones rolls his eyes and pushes his guitar to the side of his bed. He puts his hands behind his head and closes his eyes. "He's such a dick. Now he said if I'm going to keep up my cold front with him, he's going to rethink whether he'll pay for college."

"Wow. He's hard core."

"Yeah, tell me about it. This is obviously why companies call him to clean up their messes. He hasn't met a line he won't cross."

I bristle for a moment, thinking of all the lines I've been crossing—snooping, spying, little-white-lying. Am I like Jones's father, playing both sides, justifying every action and inaction if I can get what I want in the end?

"Do you think he'll really cut you off, Jones?"

Jones sits up, pushes a hand through his long dark hair. "I don't know. He might be bluffing. He might not be. But the fact is, this is what he does. This is how he operates. You'll never know what the truth is with him, just the strategy."

"What did you tell him?"

"I told him I would gladly go to community college. I'm not going to beg him for money."

"Dude. You are a rock star," I say, admiring my gutsy friend for standing firm on his own moral ground, for wanting his dad to be a man of conviction too.

What's my moral ground, though? Have I somehow become more like the father than the son?

Chapter Seventeen

BROKEN BOY

I haven't been in one of the freshman dorms since I was a freshman. But here I am now with Anjali. As we visit some of the first-years and ask them questions, I feel a bit like we're door-to-door salesmen. I tell her that, and she laughs. Her laugh even sounds French.

"I wish I sounded cool like you. You must be able to get away with anything with an accent like that," I tease as we walk down the hall.

She raises an eyebrow playfully, then whispers, "The best part is how it works on the boys. They'll do pretty much anything when I unleash my Full Euro Woman on them."

I crack up, and so does she.

"I think it already worked on Parker," I say.

She shrugs, then smiles. "He's kind of cute."

I refrain from saying *to each her own,* and instead we visit with some freshmen in the Debate Club who look scared out of their minds to be talking to the head of the Mockingbirds and Full Euro Woman. When we ask about the Annie dealing and the cheating ring, they all shake their heads and say variations on *no* and *nothing* and *I don't know a thing.*

"Maybe we should post some signs in the hallway," Anjali suggests as we make a pit stop in the girls' room. "They might be too nervous to say anything right now. But we could use the signs to encourage them to track us down if they have info."

"That's a brilliant idea," I say. "I really wish you were on the board, Anjali. But I'm superglad you're helping."

"Why don't we make them orange for Annie?"

"Yes!" I say, snapping my fingers. "And we can put lyrics on them since we're a *singing group.* Like to a song with orange in the title. 'Follow me, don't follow me,'" I say, then sing the rest of the chorus to R.E.M.'s "Orange Crush." "It's old school and all, but it's kind of the perfect song in a totally sick way, because if you're snorting Annie, you usually crush it up."

"Ewww!"

Together we make posters and tack them up in the freshman dorm hallways, urging anyone who knows anything about a little "Orange Crush" to come forward.

As we leave I notice a few freshmen glance at the signs, including a short, awkward-looking boy.

◆ ◆ ◆

Call it a sixth sense.

Even though the dancers are done for the day, I can tell the studio's not empty. Even though they left hours ago, I *know* someone's in there. So as I leave the music hall the next evening, I decide to follow my senses. I walk slowly down the hall, tiptoeing until the windows come into view.

He's there, alone. Theo. I stand to the side, just out of sight, watching him. He's wearing black pants and a white T-shirt. His head is tossed back, arms to the side, and he's almost slinking across the floor, a slow, sumptuous sort of glide. Then he leaps, and I find myself crossing my fingers, hoping he lands without pain. When his bare feet meet the hardwood, I can see he's clearly favoring the right knee. The left one is the damaged one. He winces, closes his eyes, opens them, spins once, twice, leaning again to the right. Then he falls, and my heart catches. I open the door to see if he's okay, but as I do he's simply pushing himself back up and I realize, stupidly, he meant to fall.

It was part of the choreography.

But now he's stopped because I'm here.

"Hey," I say, brushing an unseen piece of lint off my shirt. "I was just..."

"Watching me?"

"I thought you fell."

"I did. Then I got up."

"Anyway, sorry."

"It's okay. Do you want to watch? I *miss* having an audience," he says, and I can hear myself in him, in his voice, in the longing, and it's like this quiet hum connecting us, an invisible thread of energy that links us.

"I would feel that way too. It's the same with music. We're meant to play it for an audience. Dancers are meant to dance for others," I say as if I'm in a trance, enchanted by his artistry, and there's no way I can ask him anything about cheating right now. Not when he's been cheated out of what he loves.

"Exactly. It's not dance unless it's seen."

"Your knee's not the same," I say, pointing to his leg, because I can't stop talking to him or asking him questions.

"Never will be," he says, and if I could bottle his voice and sell it as sadness it'd be the perfect recipe. But no one wants to buy that, just like no one wants to watch a broken boy.

"How do you do it? How do you deal? How do you just get through the day?"

"Not well," he says, but then he returns to the dance. I watch him, becoming his audience, his only audience, maybe the only one who'll watch him anymore. He's not the same. He's not even close. But there's still something poetic in the way he moves.

When he's done, I clap, then stand, then bow.

"My last standing ovation," he says wistfully, then returns the bow with a flourish. He runs a hand through his caramel-colored hair, then walks back and stands right in front of me, maybe five, six inches away. He's taller than me, so much taller. I'm used to taller because Martin is easily six feet, but Theo's got a few inches on Martin.

Theo looks down at me and his eyes are harsh now. "Parker's not very good at his job," he says, punctuating every word.

I feel like I've been cruelly woken from a sweet dream. The dance is over; the dancer is gone. "What did you say?"

"He should be more like you. He should try just having a conversation. Maybe if he did, then he'd learn something. Instead he follows me. I know you guys are investigating me," he says. "Remember, I'm not stupid."

"I never thought you were."

"You guys need to butt out."

"Who said we're in?" I say, playing it cool.

"I mean it. You should stay out of it. It doesn't involve you," he says, then grabs his backpack. "But I would expect *you* of all people to understand."

He lets those last words linger. Neither one of us moves, neither one of us makes a break for the hall. We're stuck here in some strange sort of standoff in the dance studio.

I decide to make the first move.

"I *do* understand. But that doesn't make it okay," I say.

"Ah, but that is where we disagree," he says. "And now it's time for me to go. Shall I walk you back to your dorm?"

He's serious. He can shift gears and go back to how we were just seconds ago. I wish I were like that, able to section off parts of myself and my emotions. But every feeling in me spills over, blurring into the next one.

I shake my head and gesture to the music hall. "I'm going to play some more."

"Alex?"

"Yes?"

"You can watch me dance anytime," he says tenderly. He is soft again, sweet again, and I look at him curiously, like I could peel away a layer, then another, then see underneath, see who he really is. Then I realize he is truly two people now. He's the boy who could dance, and he's the boy who can no longer dance.

He is severed in half.

And because I'm not that cruel, I'm not that mean, I tell him yes. "I'll watch you again, Theo."

Then I return to the music hall and I don't stop playing. I play past midnight, I play while the world is inky black and sleeping, I play until the first light of dawn peeks through the windows, I play because I can. And finally, when I am spent, when I am exhausted, I play one last piece before I lay my cheek on the keys.

Chapter Eighteen
SCHOOL PRIDE

September rolls to an end, sweeping the last remains of summer with it as autumn pulls in, bringing my eighteenth birthday, crackling leaves, cooler skies, and a big fat piece of evidence thanks to the orange posters. I find an envelope inside my mailbox one afternoon. A twinge of excitement rushes through me as I slide my finger under the flap. I reach inside and there are two slips of paper. I look at the first one. It's an Anderin prescription, a real one, from a local doctor. I look at the second one. Same prescription, same doctor, same signature, except the *T* and the *R* are much more legible in the second one—the forged one.

And as I make out the last name, I feel like I've just been sucker punched.

But I pull myself together to read the note: *There's more where this came from. I need your help. Can we meet?*

It's signed Calvin Tarkenton, then his year. He's a first-year. Despite my shaky fingers and jittery heart, I call him and tell him to meet us in the basement laundry room at eight. Then I tell him to bring quarters.

Four hours later, I'm playing Trivial Pursuit with Parker and Martin and, I have to say, even though the game is for show, I am kicking their asses. But it only lasts for five minutes because at eight on the dot, Calvin arrives.

Calvin is a small, awkward thing, pale, with cheeks marked by acne scars and an Adam's apple so precariously large, it teeters off his throat. I realize he's the boy I saw checking out the posters we slapped up a few days ago. I introduce myself, then Parker and Martin, and I invite Calvin to start his laundry so the sounds muffle our conversation. Calvin almost trips over his own feet on the way back from the washers.

"Thank you for coming. Do you want to tell us what you know?" I ask gently, because this boy seems to need a soft touch right now.

Calvin says he knows who's behind the drug ring. He knows who's getting the prescriptions. He knows who's selling them to others. And it's not Theo. And it's not Beat. And it's not Maia. It's a girl, though, someone I know.

"How do you know all this?" I ask.

"She wanted me to help her. She wanted a counterpart," Calvin tells us in a squeaky voice that borders on an alto. Strange for a guy, even a freshman. "I'm in the VoiceOvers with her and we're doing a duet. After rehearsal one night in the choir room, she kind of hung behind and when it was just the two of us, she asked me to help her out."

"What did you tell her?"

"No," Calvin says. I make note of the fact that he simply says *no*. He doesn't say *absolutely not* or *God no*. His no is simple.

"Why'd you say no?"

"Look, I don't like the idea of being a narc and ratting out other students, okay? But this thing is spiraling out of control. It's the kind of thing that could take over the school, know what I mean?"

I picture a tiny little rock rolling down a snowy mountainside, adding a little powder here, a little powder there, building speed, building strength, becoming monstrous, and then just burying the ski town at the bottom of the hill in the mother of all avalanches. Some, like Beat, choose to batten down their own hatches. Others, like Calvin, try to save the ski town.

Calvin continues. "I don't want Themis to be the next Miss Coleman's or Waterstone."

Miss Coleman's is an all-girls school in Connecticut. A couple years ago a group of girls formed a secret club whose mission was to push other girls around. They prided themselves on their "water torture technique" because they'd wear all these other girls down with a thousand tiny little instances of bullying. One of the girls withdrew. Her parents turned around and sued the school and *won*. No one wants to go to Miss Coleman's now.

Then there's Waterstone up the road in Massachusetts. It used to be known as a bastion of diversity, a school that attracted students from all over the world, all walks of life, all colors, all creeds, all sexual orientations. It was like Brown University but prep school. Waterstone's gay-straight alliance had even become a model for other prep schools around the country. Until a couple of seniors beat up on the group's leaders, resulting in broken bones and a broken alliance.

"That's not the kind of school I want to go to," Calvin says. "So after she came to me, I collected some evidence."

"How'd you get the evidence?" Martin asks.

"She's not that cautious. All the stuff—it's kind of out and about on her desk. It's weird, but she's not really trying to hide it. I think she wants people to know it's her. So they'll come to her. And she figures she'll never get caught."

"Since it's Themis," I add.

Calvin opens his backpack. He pulls out one of those freezer-size Ziploc bags and offers it to me. "Go ahead. Open it."

I reach for the bag and feel as if I'm in a state of suspended animation, like everything is happening to another Alex, in another city or another life. An Alex who opens Ziploc bags of evidence. An Alex who knows what to do with such evidence. I take out the goods, inspect each one, then pass them on to Parker and Martin in some bizarre form of underground show-and-tell.

There are pill bottles with several different students' names on them. They've been filled at different pharmacies, but all local ones. Then there's a photocopied sheet of paper with a list of names that match the ones on the bottles, then amounts, then the price they paid. A hefty premium is being charged. Finally there is a handful of blank prescriptions. They're waiting to be filled out, but they're all presigned and the *T* and the *R* are crisper than in the original.

Because they've been inked by the daughter of a pair of doctors. A daughter who's been forging her parents' signatures.

Then Calvin says the name out loud, the person who's forging the names, who's peddling the pills.

Jamie Foster.

Chapter Nineteen

MAKE AN OFFER

It doesn't make sense that it's Jamie.

Not when Theo practically admitted it to me. Not when I saw his pills. Not when I saw Vanessa's e-mail. Not when Delaney tipped me off way back when. None of these clues would be *admissible* in a court, but still I know he's part of this.

And yet Calvin never mentions Theo. We even ask him if Theo's involved, but Calvin says no, not that he's aware of. Just like Beat said.

How the hell can the dancer boy be so open with me and so under-the-radar with everyone else? How can he scoot by unscathed, unnamed?

But then there is the evidence. And evidence means we have a case.

We mobilize the runners to start docking points. They're

streaking up and down the classroom hallways, gathering attendance slips and marking a certain alleged drug dealer absent from pretty much every class. Every time the board authorizes another point deduction, my stomach clangs inside me, smashing against my skin. I barely know Jamie, but I do *like* Jamie, and I know Jamie likes me. So I feel nothing but this piling knot of dread in my belly as we take away points without telling her. It makes me think of Carter last year, of how he must have felt when the Mockingbirds started trimming his point totals before he was served. I don't know that I could ever in my whole life feel sympathy for my rapist, but if I could, this would be the one time. Because now we have moved beyond our role as investigators. Now we are practitioners of vigilante justice. This is what it feels like when people use that cliché *the lesser of two evils*. Because that's what vigilante justice is: the lesser of two evils.

I wish there were a better way. I wish I could drop this whole entire case in someone else's lap, where it belongs. I wish an adult could do the dirty work of punishing a girl I like—a girl I thought of as a friend.

By the end of the next week, McKenna's little sister barely has enough points to get a cup of coffee. Jamie waits for me at the end of music class, clutching her backpack. "Alex," she says, then gulps, "did I do something wrong?"

Shoot me. Just shoot me now, please. If I thought it was bad having T.S. ticked off at me, if I thought it sucked having Maia lashing into me, this is even worse. Because Jamie just looks so innocent, especially as she holds on to her white backpack with pink polka dots like it's a lifeline.

Especially when Theo should be the one in her place.

"What do you mean?" I manage to say, but the words catch, like stones in my throat.

She shakes her head quickly, over and over, her long, straight hair moving with her. Then she backs away from me, like she's scared of me. "I'm sorry."

The sound of her words is like a jolt to the heart, an electric shock I didn't see coming. Because we were friends—or at least starting to be—and now we're judge and criminal. As she darts out, her black hair like a sheet behind her, her white and pink polka dots flashing by, I wish someone had told me that being unbiased, being impartial, doesn't stop you from having feelings about a case, about a victim, or even about the accused.

I may be a Mockingbird, but I'm still a human being. It's getting harder to reconcile the two.

◆ ◆ ◆

At our next board meeting, I bring up the nagging issue in this case, the one that's plagued us from the start.

"If we're going to file charges, who are we going to file charges on behalf of? It can't be Calvin. He's a witness, not the wronged party. It can't be Delaney. Or even Beat. They're not the ones pressing charges. This isn't one person against another."

Parker speaks. "It goes back to what we talked about at our very first meeting. That these sorts of victimless crimes are really crimes against society. Against the greater good."

"And in the real justice system, a lot of crimes are actually crimes against the state, let's not forget," Martin points out. "The people of Rhode Island versus John Doe, and so on."

"But we've never tried a case like that before," I say, tapping the notebook. All our past cases have been brought to us by the victims. "And if it's going to be a first case like that, we should take a vote. Like you did last year."

They nod and agree, because the precedent with new types of cases has been set. Mine was the first date-rape case tried, so the Mockingbirds asked the student body to cast their votes on whether date rape should be considered a violation of the students' code of conduct. The students voted yes.

"Let's put it to the students, then, whether a cheating ring is a crime against the whole school," I say.

That keeps us busy for the next week, posting signs in the dark of night about the coming vote, distributing ballots under doors one morning, collecting them in our mailbox, tabulating them, and then announcing the results in our usual fashion—by flyer, in code.

The student body is with us by a strong majority: 73 percent.

None of this makes the next day any easier. Because I have to do my official duty and pay Jamie a visit.

McKenna's there with her, and I feel like a complete jerk.

Jamie barely speaks when I give her the option to settle. She just shakes her head and says, "No, I'll take it to trial."

McKenna gives me a steely glare, then wraps an arm tightly around her little sister. "She didn't do it," McKenna says. Jamie cowers under her sister, her brown eyes like a deer's. "Besides, how can you accuse her? You're supposed to be looking out for her."

I can't do this. I'm not made for police work; I don't have the kind of scorn for the guilty that would make this easy. When I thought about the Mockingbirds this summer, I figured the cases would be like mine—black-and-white, good and bad. This case is all bad.

"We have evidence. A lot of it," I manage, saying it softly, because that whisper of her *sorry* still hangs in the air.

"What kind?" Jamie asks.

"Forged prescriptions taken from your parents. A list of the students buying. Pill bottles."

"Someone planted that. Jamie would never do that."

"It's pretty compelling evidence. It'd probably be easier if you settled. We're willing to settle, and I can make you an offer right now," I say, and nothing about this feels comfortable. Nothing about this feels remotely normal. I might as well be in Turkey trying to translate for the government.

I tell her the settlement terms. Jamie will have to give up VoiceOvers for the rest of the year and consent to regular inspections to make sure she's not still dealing. If found guilty at trial, she'd be out of VoiceOvers for the rest of her time at Themis.

"This is all better than what would happen if the police found out," I say, even though I have no clue what the police would do.

McKenna snaps. "She's fourteen. She's a freaking minor. She's not going to jail. You know why? Because she didn't do it. We're not settling. You accuse my sister, you might as well be accusing me. So I will be the one defending her. I will be her lawyer."

"I understand," I say, and that means we will be filing charges on behalf of the entire student body—the Students of Themis Academy versus Jamie Foster.

The girl with the polka-dot backpack, who also happens to be my *protégé*.

A couple of days later, I wake up before the sun rises and tack sticks of Juicy Fruit gum to the trees in the quad, a sign that a student is about to be served. We serve her, and then later that day as I'm on my way to the library to write Jamie's name in the permanent copy of *To Kill a Mockingbird*, I catch sight of curly red hair. It's that girl Carter was kissing, that girl Carter is dating. She's leaving the caf, and he's right next to her, holding her hand. He leans in to kiss her on the cheek, but then she turns closer, making sure it's a full lip plant. I gag and look away, hurrying into the library, wondering if we do any good at all. Because everywhere I turn, I see wreckage.

I retrieve *To Kill a Mockingbird* from its shelf, flip to the back, and take a deep breath, my right hand suddenly shaking. I exhale, but my hand is still jittery, like it's resisting what it's about to do. I wait a minute, then another till it stops.

In the back of the book, I write the crime: *Pharming Without a License.*

I hesitate for a sliver of a second, wanting to write Theo's name. Except he's somehow skating past us, and I wish I knew how he's pulling it off.

But I don't.

So I add Jamie Foster's name to the Themis Academy list of the accused.

Chapter Twenty

BIG MAN ON CAMPUS

It gnaws at me that Jamie isn't connected to the users. She's not on the debate team, but nearly all the users on the list from her room are debaters. I can't help but feel we're being set up, like we're being led down this path by some unseen, unnamed person.

Someone who doesn't want us to know Theo's really the dealer.

I start following him around, doing the thing he said irked him when Parker did it. But I'm better at this than Parker because I learned how to avoid people last year. I learned how to dart around bushes and duck down hallways and hide out on the sides of buildings. Ironic how avoiding Carter then helps me be a better spy now. Because that's what I do for the next three nights, lurking outside the music hall, waiting for Theo to emerge from the dance studio. Every night I watch him. Every night he goes straight to Debate Club practice or straight to Delaney's.

I look at my watch, and it's almost time to follow Theo again. For now, I'm meeting with the board and Sandeep in Martin's room. We decided to keep the evidence in Martin's room. It seemed safer, less risky than my room, what with the captain of the debate team being my roomie and all.

"So this guy Sam looks like he's been on Anderin for about twelve weeks and two days, which means he started back in the summer," Sandeep says, since we asked him to be the "DA." With a case this far-reaching we couldn't have someone in the group representing the whole student body. Plus, Sandeep is pretty much the definition of un-flappable, which is why he'll be an amazing hand surgeon someday and why he'll be the perfect prosecutor in our courtroom. "And he's consuming triple the recommended dosage," he adds.

I look at the list again and scan for Sam's name. He's a debater, same as Theo.

I glance at Parker and wonder why he never found anything on Theo. Maybe he didn't look hard enough. Maybe he didn't try at all. Maybe he's in cahoots with Theo. The strange, inconsistent details of this case weigh on me more, and I am dying to get to the bottom of this. Even as I close my notebook I can still see the words *be respectful* hanging in front of me like a warning sign, blinking yellow lights. But I don't see how we can do our job by being goody-goody every second.

Besides, I don't think following him is disrespectful.

I think it's absolutely necessary.

"I've got to go," I say as I stand up.

Martin gives me a strange look.

"I have to rehearse. Practice," I explain, going for a quick cover-up.

"Practicing with Jones," Martin says, and there's a distance in his voice I'm not used to.

"Not this time," I say, and give him a look. But I'm not going to say more in front of his roommates, so I leave and head to the music hall, crunching on the crackling leaves on my way. It's early evening; dusk is settling in. When I reach the music hall, I take off my shoes and pad down the hall in my socks. I inch close enough to confirm Theo's alone in the studio again, but not close enough for him to see me.

Then I return outside quietly and hide behind the bushes, slipping my shoes back on. I crouch and I wait. I stay for the next half hour or so, thighs throbbing, knees aching, but I don't care. I will succeed where Parker failed.

The door creaks open, and I hold my breath. I watch Theo walk away. When he's a safe distance out, I follow him. As he walks toward Morgan-Young Hall, he checks his watch. Then, as if he just remembered something, he makes a sharp right into Richardson Hall. I know he lives on the first floor, room 103. I count three windows down and do my best to walk ever so casually, but ever so slowly, past his window. The blinds are half-closed, but I can still see him reaching for something on his desk. I squint to make out what it is, but it's too small to see. Then it looks like he takes out his phone and presses it hard on his desk, pushing the edge of his phone back and forth, back and forth, in one small spot.

Theo bends his face down to the desk, reaches for a pre-rolled piece of paper, a dollar bill or something, and snorts. My breath catches in my throat, and my whole body, the whole night, goes silent and still. I don't want to watch, I want to turn away, but I can't stop looking. It's the wreck on the highway, and the medics are pulling out the body.

I could be him but for one bad landing. That is all that separates us.

When he raises his head, shaking it, twitching his nose, then inhaling deep down throughout the far reaches of his body, filling his tissues, his bones, his sinews, I take a step back, almost stumbling.

My skin is tingling, crawling. I take a deep breath and try to center myself. I don't know why he'd be so careless, so casual, when it's not that hard to look in his window. But maybe this is what happens when you lose everything you love.

You no longer care.

I watch Theo again, and he lifts his shoulders up and down a few times, then reaches both his hands high up in the air, like he's smacking the ceiling in triumph with those long, muscular arms. He stuffs something in his pocket, looks at a sheet of paper on his desk, then turns off the lights and leaves. I walk quickly to the other side of Richardson but peer around the edge so I can see when he walks out. A few seconds later he's walking down the steps and then nodding to someone. I half expect it to be Delaney meeting up with him for another side-of-the-building rendezvous.

But it's Sam.

Sam from the list.

Sophomore Sam, wearing jeans and a hoodie, his hands stuffed into his front pockets, his curly brown hair poking out from under the hood.

Theo reaches into his pocket, hands something to Sam, then Sam digs back into his pocket and gives something to him. They shake hands, laugh, then walk off together.

I want to spring from my hiding post, run across the quad, and tackle Theo. I want to whale on him, beat my fists into his chest, his arms, his face, his stupid injured knee that has turned him into *this*.

But I don't. I stay where I am, tucked against the wall of his dorm.

With Sam beside him, Theo resumes his route to Morgan-Young Hall, where the debate team is meeting for its regular practice. I notice there's a slight change in his walk as he enters Morgan-Young Hall, as if he's more confident, more excited. I count to ten and then head in after him. I'm dangerously close to Maia's territory, so I have to be even more cautious. But I can't turn back now.

I walk past the classroom where the team practices. I glance in and it's as if Theo's a new man here—gregarious, patting students on the back, a beacon of energy. I pace myself, walk to the end of the hall, lean down to the water fountain for a drink, then chance one more peek. I walk past the room again and see Maia, her back to the group, writing something on the board. Theo's next to her, like a lieutenant, ready for duty. Beat's there too, standing at attention as well. Most of them are standing. Most of them are on high alert. Even from the hall, the room is practically buzzing. It's almost as if I could get a contact high just being near that much energy.

"See anything good?"

I jump and make a sound. It's Jones.

Chapter Twenty-One

SPARKS

"You scared me!"

"I can tell," he says, a look of mischief in his dark blue eyes.

I walk toward the doors, motioning for him to come along. "What are you doing here?" I ask.

"I missed English today, so I was picking up the assignment."

"Why did you miss English?"

"My mom called this time. She wanted me to know my dad's being summoned to a hearing tomorrow and that she fully expects me to be on board with whatever he says."

"What do they think? That you were going to call up the *New York Times* or something and say he's lying?"

"Yeah. I think they do think that. And I would never

rat out my own family, but trust me, it's tempting when they give me their whole *be quiet or else* routine. So oddly enough, I didn't feel like going to class. Anyway, why were you checking out Debate Club practice is the more interesting question."

I shrug in return

"Yeah, that's not really going to fly. You're spying."

I hold up my hands in admission.

"What'd you find out?" he asks as we hit the quad.

"Where are you headed right now?" I ask, deflecting.

"Wherever you're going."

"Music hall," I say.

"Cool. I left my guitar there earlier today. So tell me, what'd you learn?"

I don't name names, but as we head into the music hall I do tell him I saw the *real* dealer dealing. We sit down and Jones takes his guitar from its case. The silver gleams, almost like he's polished it. "How can I prove this guy should be on trial too, Jones? God, I wish you were in the Mockingbirds," I add wistfully. "You would be the perfect person to help me get to the bottom of this case."

"I have no doubt you'll figure out how to get this guy on trial, whatever it takes."

"But isn't *whatever it takes* what your dad did?"

Jones laughs deeply. "Well, I'm not suggesting you take advantage of the unemployed and hire teams of them to buy up all the Annie in Rhode Island," he says, then punches me on the shoulder.

207

"Really?" I tease. "Because I was thinking of doing that and then redistributing it to the uninsured."

"Then you are Robin Hood. And it is fine," he says, and holds up his index finger in the air to punctuate his point.

But the wheels are turning and the words *whatever it takes* are clicking. Because now I know the next thing I need to do, the next person I need to see—Beat—and it's a visit I'll make alone tomorrow. Whether it makes me Robin Hood or not, I don't know. But it's what I have to do.

"Jones," I begin, "do you ever think about why your dad did what he did? I mean, I'm not condoning it. I'm totally on your side. But do you ever think what you would do in that situation?"

"I would never *have* to lie at a government hearing because I never would have covered it up in the first place."

"Right. But what *drove* him to that? Why did he feel like hiding the truth was his only option?"

"I think he picked it because it was the *easy* option. Or so he thought at the time."

I close my eyes, wishing there were a right way, a simple *and* honest way, to tie up all the loose ends on this case, but I don't know anymore what that'd be. The whole thing is a haze, a blurry mirage on the horizon. Now you see it. Now you don't.

"Jones, will you play *Adagio for Strings*?" I ask, because music is the only thing that is exactly what it is.

Jones drifts into Samuel Barber's piece, and I just listen to the haunting music, to what many have called the saddest piece of classical music ever. For tonight it's fitting, and as I listen the Mockingbirds slip away. The trial, the crime, the enemies—they are gone. All that exists is all there should be—music, just music, filling me up.

Jones finishes. "I think music exists to express all the feelings we can't put into words. All the feelings there aren't words for," he says quietly.

"I was thinking the same thing," I say.

He bumps my shoulder with his own, and I feel the strangest sensation.

I feel a *zing*.

Jones turns his head to tune one of the strings and I sneak a peek at him, not his face, but his hands. His long fingers. His musician's hands. Hands that can do everything, hands like mine. An image flits through my mind. His hands on mine. Two musicians' hands, fingers against fingers.

Then I look the other way, my cheeks burning. No wonder Martin was cold earlier. Because Jones is like a flame.

◆ ◆ ◆

I call Martin on the way back to my dorm. He doesn't answer. But before I reach the steps, a text comes through.

In science lab. What's up?

It's weird that he'd text me back rather than just answer, since he's usually alone in the science lab.

Want a visitor? I type, and then wait for an answer. For a minute, then another, then another.

Finally it comes: *OK.*

That's it. Just *OK.* Not even *Okay.*

I double back to the science lab. Martin's alone, hunched over a microscope.

"Anything interesting happening there? Cells dividing or something? What's that called? Metamorphosis?" I joke.

"Something like that," Martin says, and looks up from the microscope. His expression is chilly.

"Or maybe you're splitting the atom," I suggest.

"John Cockcroft and Ernest Walton beat me to that years ago," he says, then peers back into the microscope and scribbles something in the notebook next to him.

There's a silence in the lab, and it's clear I must go first.

"You're mad at me," I say as I walk over to him and put my backpack on the floor.

"Why would you say that?"

"You're not denying it."

"How's Jones?" he asks, looking up. He's icy again.

"Fine."

"So you did see him after all."

"I ran into him," I say.

"Convenient."

"*Convenient*? What's that supposed to mean?"

"You said you weren't going to see him. Then you ran into him. That's convenient."

"Yeah, it was convenient, since we were able to *practice* playing music then."

"I'm sure. Is he still going through *stuff*?"

"Yeah, as a matter of fact."

"And were you able to help him?" Martin shoots back.

"What the hell? What are you trying to say?"

"Nothing. I'm not trying to say anything," he says through gritted teeth. He looks away from me and grips the edge of the black counter with hands pressed so hard against it I swear for a second the counter buckles under them.

"What is this about?" I ask, pushing the memory of the *zing* far out of my mind. "I've been friends with him the whole time I've been here. The whole time you and I have been together."

"I know," he says, clenching his jaw, then breathing out hard.

"So...?" I ask.

"It's just, you're always slipping off to see him. Running into him. Practicing with him. Talking to him. He texts you when we're together. You write back right away. You leave me to see him," he says, rattling off a litany of my sins. The day in the caf, the afternoon after the Faculty Club, the night in the library. That's why I don't say anything, because he's right. I don't defend myself because it's all true.

"I'm sorry," I say softly. "But I see you too."

He turns his gaze to me now, locking his eyes on me. His hands are still gripping the counter but not quite as tight, not quite as firm. Still, I can sense the strength of his whole body resting on those hands.

"*I see you too*? That's it? Most of the time I see you it's with the Mockingbirds. I want to see you without them. Do *you* want to see me without them?" he asks, and now his anger has turned to hurt. I step closer to him and take his hand.

"Yes," I say quickly. "Of course I do. How can you even doubt that?"

He laughs for a second and lets me hold his hand. Then he says, "Because I am not the superhuman person you think I am."

Now it's my turn to laugh. "I always suspected you had superpowers."

"But I don't," he says, and he runs a hand through his shaggy brown hair. "And I am insanely jealous of how much time you spend with him. *Alone.* And I don't want to be jealous. I don't want to be that guy. But I am. And I hate it."

"I kind of like it," I say softly. Martin's always been the pillar of integrity, honor, and character, and sometimes I can forget he is just a guy, a normal guy who gets jealous when his girlfriend hangs out with another guy. "I just kind of like seeing how normal you are."

"Oh, you do?"

"Yeah. I kind of do," I say as I reach for his other hand. He lets me lace my fingers through his. I look down at our hands together and though they're not musician hands, they're *his* hands. They're the ones I want to be holding. He's the one I want to be touching. He's the one I hurt. But even more than that, he's the one I want. And I want him. I want him now. "It's kind of sexy."

"Is it? Sexy?" he asks playfully.

"Yes," I say slowly in a whisper, and pull him near me. "I want to kiss you. And then I want to do more than kiss you. Because you're the guy I'm in love with."

Then he groans, a low sound that tells me he wants exactly the same. But before he gives in to me, he turns around and opens a drawer in the lab. He pulls out one of those long lighters, like the kind for a fireplace, with a blue plastic handle.

"You going to burn the joint down?" I ask.

He shakes his head and reaches into another drawer. There's a bag of cotton balls in the drawer. He takes one out and pulls it apart, breaking off a feathery bit of cotton. He dips his hand back in the first drawer and now he's got a long metal stick that looks like a barbecue skewer with a bulbous wick of white fabric at the tip. He flicks on the lighter, leans into the wick, and lights it. The next thing I know, he's moving his other hand into the flame, peeling off a fireball into his palm, then dropping it into his mouth. He keeps his mouth open for a second, showing me his tongue on fire, then closes his mouth and smiles. He turns the lighter off, then takes the cotton ball out of his mouth.

To say I am amazed would be an understatement.

"How did you do that?"

"Simple physics," he says. "The moisture in your mouth starts to douse the flames. Then you take the air away like this," he says, closing his mouth in demonstration, then opening it again, "and the flame is killed."

"You can eat fire."

He nods proudly.

"My boyfriend can eat fire."

"There's more where that came from," he says, and proceeds to show me how he can rub the flame against his jeans without setting the denim on fire, how he can shift a flame back and forth between his hands, then how he can lean his head back and eat the flame that's burning at the end of the makeshift torch.

"How did you learn to eat fire?" I ask.

"Alex, I've been playing with fire for a long time."

"C'mon. Seriously. How do you do all this?"

He shrugs happily, that familiar Martin shrug. "What can I say? I'm a science geek. You watch a few Web videos, try a few things, you teach yourself how to eat fire. I've been doing it since I was twelve."

"Amazing," I say.

"Want to try?"

"Not for a second."

"You can do it. I'll walk you through it."

"You're crazy."

"C'mon. You're not afraid of anything," he says, and I feel myself bending.

"Fine. But just that little cotton ball."

"I wouldn't let you use the torch. The torch is only for seasoned pros," Martin says. Then he walks me through the cotton-ball trick. I hesitate the first time, blowing it out. The second time I hand it off to him and he douses the flame with his tongue. The third time I just do it. I pop the lit cotton ball in my mouth and clamp my lips down on it instantly.

My eyes light up as I take the cotton ball out. "I ate fire!"

"You ate fire," he says.

I put my hands on his face and kiss his lips.

"Your mouth is warm," he whispers.

"So is yours," I say. But, really, *hot* would be a much more accurate adjective right now.

Chapter Twenty-Two

BACKFIRE

I am a fire-eater.

I am a stealthy spy.

I am the defender of the powerless.

I am the protector of the student body.

I am Robin Hood.

That is what I tell myself the next day. All day long. In every class. To steel myself for my mission tonight.

I say the words under my breath in English class as Mr. Baumann scoots up on the edge of his desk and pushes up the sleeves on his blue button-down shirt.

"Power," he begins. "Tell me about the kind of power *The Chocolate War* addresses."

Maia—shocker—is the first one to raise a hand.

"The power of fear. The Vigils exist solely for the purpose of pushing others around," she says, referring to the secret society in *The Chocolate War* that makes other students do their bidding. "Their only mission is to keep other students on edge, and they do it through psychological intimidation. The most masterful and chilling psychological intimidation. I wouldn't want to cross their leader."

"Is that enough to maintain a hierarchy? Fear?" Mr. Baumann asks.

"Yes," Maia answers. "The Vigils set the rules. And everyone else follows them. And if you don't follow the rules, then, like Jerry, you lose."

"Mr. Cormier was not one for happy endings, was he?" Mr. Baumann asks.

Anjali raises a hand, and he calls on her. "That's where I disagree with Cormier. You said you want us to find truth in fiction, and I think the ending is needlessly depressing. I think you can stand up, you can disturb the universe, without just winding up back where you started. Isn't that where all good revolutions come from? From someone standing up to the way it's been and saying, *No, let's change things. Let's make them better!*"

Maia swivels around to look at Anjali, the sleek, black-haired Brit taking on the wispy, blond French girl. "Are you honestly saying you think Cormier should have written a happy ending where Jerry just trots off without selling the chocolate and everyone follows him, doe-eyed, into the happily-ever-after?"

"I don't know that everyone would follow him. But I think some would. I don't think everyone wants to sell chocolates.

And I think people are strong enough to say no to chocolate-selling."

Whoa.

Could there be more of a double entendre to their conversation? I glance around at the other fourteen students in the room, wondering if they too are picking up on all the undertones between Maia and Anjali, who might as well be talking about the Anderin case.

"What would happen if you said no to chocolate-selling? Would anyone listen? Would the teachers listen?" Mr. Baumann asks.

Theo answers immediately.

"Not in Robert Cormier's construction of this universe, where everything is bleak and everyone is violent and everyone gives in to all their baser instincts. Because the teachers succumbed to cruelty too. They were fully complicit; they allowed the Vigils to operate. They didn't even turn a blind eye. They let Vigils do their bidding, making them their own personal army of sorts."

No wonder the debate team is winning. That stuff works.

Then I flash on something. Theo *only* talks like this in class. He doesn't talk like this, all sharply cut and smooth as glass, when I see him in the dance studio. He's muddier then with words, but softer too. He must be taking the Annie right before classes and right before Debate Club practice. But in the studio, he's not on anything. In the studio, he's still trying to be himself.

"But step aside from this book. We're talking about *you*.

That's the theme this semester. Truth in fiction. Your truth. What would happen if you said no to chocolate-selling? Would the teachers listen?" Mr. Baumann asks again.

I cock my head to the side and consider Mr. Baumann, the gray streaking through his hair, the casual way he sits on the desk like he wants to be part of a circle with us, like he wants to connect with us. Could I talk to him? Could I tell him what's going on right under his nose? Could I tell him what I know about the student who just answered his questions? Would he listen? Could he act? He is the Debate Club advisor, after all, and this case should be his jurisdiction, not mine, not ours.

I start imagining how good it would feel to slough off this role, to push it onto him, to let the teachers carry the yoke. I find myself wiggling my shoulders ever so slightly, once to the left, once to the right, as if I just let go of something very heavy.

But there is no letting go. There are no teachers to talk to. There is no dean who cares. We are the only ones.

When class ends, I head to the music hall for a private lesson with Miss Damata. And even though she's the only teacher I trust, I can't talk to her about this. I might have told her what happened to me last year, but I've never told her about the Mockingbirds. Besides, what could she do? I've practically told Ms. Merritt and she was more concerned about my college apps.

Miss Damata listens to me play Ravel's one-handed song.

"Technically it's pristine. But I can't help but think

something's off. It's as if something is missing, not in the music, but behind the music," she says. "It's as if there's a layer of emotion left unexplored."

I try the piece again, but as I play, the music sounds empty.

"We'll return to Ravel. Let's hear your Bach," she says.

When we're done, I think back to what Mr. Baumann said earlier about teachers, when he asked if they'd listen.

"Miss Damata, what would you do if you found out that, say, one of the other teachers was doing something wrong?"

She smiles. "That's kind of a broad hypothetical, Alex. Can you be more specific?"

"Well, what if a teacher were supplying drugs?"

Miss Damata places a hand on my forearm. "Alex, if there's a teacher here who's supplying drugs of any kind to students, I need to know. We need to do something about it."

Then I laugh. "No! That's not what I meant. What I meant was what if a teacher were supplying to other teachers? Like selling and stuff?"

She relaxes a bit. "There is a code of conduct for the faculty. It outlines ethical guidelines we must adhere to in teaching and in our conduct with one another. How we behave, how we treat one another, how we treat students. And it governs anything that's a criminal act, like *selling and stuff*, as you say."

"But does anyone enforce it? Because a code only matters if it's enforced."

"Absolutely. There are clearly spelled-out sanctions and

disciplinary actions. Obviously we all strive to the highest standards, but there have certainly been punishments doled out. Ms. Merritt is very involved. She spends a lot of time with the teachers, and she listens to us. She listens to concerns we share with her and she can act upon them. The code is very important to her."

I go cold all over because the faculty has a code.

A code that matters. The dean enforces it, she disciplines, she does more than slap hands. But only with her peers. What does she do with us? She leaves us to the wolves—we are the wolves. She won't fight for us; she won't protect us; she won't help us.

"Why do you ask, Alex?"

I can't speak right now. If I open my mouth, I will breathe fire. I will burn the music hall down in a towering blaze. I place my left hand on the keys while my right hand lies limp, lifeless on my leg. Useless, like the faculty with us. The left does everything. The left hand bears all the burden.

I look down at my hands, one working, one not, and then I explode through the music. I storm across Ravel, a general on the battlefield, tearing over it, marching forward, plowing down enemies, leaving nothing behind but charred earth. That's how Ravel meant the music to be played. With rage, with unbridled, all-consuming, red-hot, fiery, flaming fury. After all, who wouldn't be pissed to have only one hand?

When I stop, Miss Damata says, "I believe you've found what's missing."

My anger carries me into the night like a wave hurtling

toward the shore. It carries me from my dorm and across the quad and into the administration building to the mission I have been plotting all day. I turn a key in the lock and let myself in. Anjali gave me hers to use. She has one, being a runner.

The building is dark, except for a few hallway lights. I walk down the hall, glancing back and forth at the portraits of past headmasters and headmistresses dating back to the founding of Themis in 1912. I want to rip every one from their gilded frames. I want to slash the canvases with a razor blade. I want to leave them all in a pile of mangled portraits outside Ms. Merritt's door for her to discover. What's the big deal anyway? So what if I slice a bunch of dumb portraits? It's not like I'd get in trouble. It's not like I'd be disciplined. I'm not a teacher. I don't matter.

At the end of the hall, I make a left and reach a dark wood door with a pewter half-circle knocker. I don't knock. No one's in the Faculty Club right now. It's only fitting that my meeting is here in the seat of their self-congratulatory power. The place where they make us perform for them.

I sit down on a high-backed leather chair, then survey the room—the shelves stacked with bound books, the rich mahogany walls, the blue Turkish rug. I envision taking it over, camping out here and protesting their illusions. Holding up picket signs and shouting through bullhorns. But they'd never notice; they wouldn't care; they'd just hand me a self-help book on growing out of teenage rebellion. As if that was all that ailed us. Knowing this gives me strength to do the thing I'm about to do.

My eyes adjust to the dark, since I didn't turn on a light. Beat doesn't turn one on either when he joins me a minute later.

"You got my note," I say, and gesture to the chair across from me. After I borrowed Anjali's key, I slipped a note under Beat's door instructing him to meet here.

"I did and I'm here," he says, and sits down in the darkened room.

I cross my legs and place my hands together, painting my own false front of steady calm. But inside I am a jangled box of exposed nerves, and when I look into Beat's dark brown eyes and see the tiniest bit of fear, my resolve weakens. But then I think of the brochure, of the code, of Ms. Merritt's concern for the school's record, rather than us. What choice do I have? What choices have we ever had? If she had done her job, I wouldn't have had to snoop in Maia's things, lie to the board, look through Vanessa's phone, or do this. So I plow onward, venturing into territory I should be straying far away from, but doing it anyway, violating all our rules.

Even unwritten ones. We've never expressly forbidden *entrapment*, but that's probably because no Mockingbird would ever do that to a witness.

But I'm about to be the first. I'm wiretapping, I'm profiling, I'm demolishing every shred of our guidelines.

"I know you're involved, Beat," I begin, unspooling a lie. "I know Theo's forcing you to share your supply with him for the Debate Club. He's trying to mix it up, to get some from you, some from Jamie. I'm not going to let Jamie be the only one to take the fall for him. And I've got other students who'll say all this on the record."

I'm completely bluffing. But I have got to get the right guy on trial. The end justifies the means, I tell myself. This is the lesser of two evils. This is my only choice.

Beat's face turns ashen. "You do? They will? They're going to point fingers at me?"

It's like weeds are twisting inside me, hooking into me, trying to stop me, but I push through them, stepping closer to the cliff, to the edge of the lie that could make this all worthwhile. "They are. And I know you're not trying to hurt anyone. I know you're just being victimized. So I think we'd all be better off if you just coughed up the information now. And then I really can protect you. I'm going to need you to testify. Because we know it's Theo. We know he wants to win the Elite. So you can either corroborate that and testify or it might be hard to keep the immunity promise."

I am sickened by what I'm doing. But what else can I do? Really, what else can I *possibly* do? This is what happens when no one will help.

He runs a hand through his tousled curls, closes his eyes, exhales. When he opens his eyes, he says, "Fine. I'll tell you everything."

Then the words spill out.

"You're right. Well, almost right. It's not Theo. But it is about the Elite. It's Maia. Maia Tan is behind it all. And I will testify to that. I will tell you how she operates, how she supplies, when she distributes. And I will bring other witnesses too. I will call them right now before we all leave for Miami in the morning for our next debate competition," he says.

I put my head in my hands, and the weeds shoot up, snaking around my whole body now, pinning me down in their grasp. I deserve this. I set him up. I lied to him. I am no different from the students we try.

An hour later Beat delivers two other Debate Club members to testify. He brings them to a board meeting that I hastily convene. They tell their stories. Not a single, solitary piece of data about my roommate's supposed sick quest to win the Elite is left out.

I guess when you play with fire you get burned.

Chapter Twenty-Three

REASONABLE DOUBT

Nothing at this school stays secret very long. I'm reminded of this when I bump into Natalie on the quad the next day. This time, she pokes me in the chest, her right index finger banging into my sternum.

"Can you keep your hands off me?" I say, and I push her fingers away.

"But of course. I wouldn't want to get in trouble with your little clubhouse there for inappropriate poking," she says. "Because that's what you're running. A clubhouse."

"What are you talking about?"

"Let's see," she begins, raising her index finger. "You run the group with your Goody Two-Shoes boyfriend." She adds the middle finger. "He rooms with Senator Dickhead's son, who also just so happens to be on your dumb board."

Ring finger now. "And to top it off, their *other* roommate is now the prosecutor." The pinkie finger for the finale. "Who, natch, is practically engaged to that soccer bitch."

"Watch it, Natalie," I say.

"What are you going to do?" she asks, and leans in closer to me, her chest about to bump mine. I take a step back. "You going to sue me? You going to put me on the stand again? Because I would *love* to take you down again."

"If memory serves, you didn't take me down last time, because you defended the wrong guy," I say, and my latent anger over her testimony rises up. "You defended a rapist."

"Whatever," she says, and then waves her hand in front of me. "And now I hear your *other* roommate is about to get what she deserves." Then she starts cackling. "You know, I'm going to have to campaign to have your trials opened to the public. Just like on TV. Because that I would love to see. That I would love to be in the audience for."

She snaps a finger, swivels around, and walks off.

As I head to the caf, I notice a flyer on a tree. Something about it catches my eye, so I walk over to it, wrapping my arms around my chest because the October air is growing chilly. When I reach the tree, I place a hand on the flyer to smooth it out. It's a drawing of a dog, a cartoonish-looking canine, but something about it bothers me. Maybe it's the strange smile on the face that's almost a sneer. Or the words I spot underneath it—*coming soon*—like a cold wind that just whipped by out of nowhere. It unnerves me, the message that's like a warning, a stranger flitting through a dark alley at night. I glance around and see students streaming by but no one paying close attention, so I take it down, fold it up, and put it in my back pocket.

I head to the cafeteria and join Martin, Sandeep, and T.S. at a table.

"Do dogs in Brazil think in Portuguese?" T.S. is saying as I sit down.

"Dogs don't think, T.S.," Sandeep says in a deadpan voice.

"I know that," she says, and rolls her eyes. "But if they could, would they think in Portuguese? Or maybe French? Or how about Russian? Does it depend where they live?"

"Actually," Martin interjects, "there have been studies showing that apes and dolphins are able to process information and even consider several options before making a simple choice. So it's possible we could learn that dogs can think."

"Dude, you're embarrassing me," Sandeep jokes. "You're like a walking encyclopedia of scientific studies."

"Why are you guys talking about dogs?" I ask suspiciously.

"Because dogs rule," T.S. says.

"Did you see that sign or something?" I ask.

"What sign?" she says.

I reach into my back pocket and smooth out the paper to show them.

T.S. wrinkles her nose. "Eww! That's kind of a creepy Snoopy."

"So is that why you're talking about dogs?" I ask again as I put the paper back in my pocket. Maybe they saw the sign too. Maybe they know what it means.

"No. My mom just sent me pictures of our dogs from this morning. They're catching Frisbees in tandem on the beach!" She takes out her cell phone and shows me a photo of her border collie/Lab mutts. "It's like synchronized Frisbee-ing!"

"But what does that have to do with Brazil or Portuguese?" I press.

"Jesus, Alex. We're just having fun. One thing led to the other, you know?"

"Yeah, okay," I say, and try to shake it off. Obviously T.S.'s dogs have nothing to do with that freaky dog sign. Still, the words *coming soon* worry me.

I head to the food line. As I'm waiting for the pasta primavera, I overhear some students behind me.

"That's how you qualify. You have to be in the *circle* of friends."

"And if you're not, they hunt you down. So don't piss them off."

"Yeah, but did you hear one of their own is selling her stash?"

I cringe at the words but keep moving through the line.

"I bet they won't even try her. There are benefits to rooming with the leader, you know. Membership has its privileges, as they say," the student says, scoffing.

I contemplate turning around to see who's talking about

me and maybe confront them too. But what can I say? Fact is, they're right. Fact is, Natalie's right.

I leave the line and return to the table. When I sit down, T.S. says, "For the record, I think dogs think in Sumerian."

"No, they don't. They think in Etruscan," Martin says with a wry smile, and pushes a hand through his shaggy brown hair. He leans back in the chair, pleased with his contribution to the ancient-languages trivia match.

Sandeep shakes his head, then says with a straight face, "You're both wrong. Dogs think in the Illyrian languages."

T.S. lights up and smacks the table with both palms. "You *so* win!" Then she leans over and gives him a big kiss, pausing to linger on his lips for a moment before she pulls back. Then she looks at me. "That is, unless you can beat him."

"No," I say.

After lunch, I walk with Martin to Morgan-Young Hall, where I have advanced calculus and he has superstar biology, or something like that. We pass the bulletin board in front of McGregor Hall and there's a new drawing hanging up. This one's of a tree house, and it's in the same style as the picture I took down. The tree house has a sign on the door drawn to look as if it was written by a child—SECRET CLUBHOUSE. A bird perches on top of the tree house.

I point to it. "Look. That's us. Students are talking about us again," I say. "Not *us* us. Us as in the Mockingbirds."

"I know," he says. His voice is oddly serious. "You can't let it get to you."

"Who said I was letting it get to me?"

"Maybe the fact that you were incredibly testy at lunch was the giveaway."

"I wasn't testy."

"You were," he says.

"Because I didn't play *what obscure language do dogs think in?* I don't feel like talking about *dogs* right now."

"Case in point," Martin says.

"Anyway, people were talking about us in line."

"Saying we're all clubby, right?" Martin says, and it's like he's reading my mind.

"Exactly."

"People always talk about the Mockingbirds, Alex. There's always something they don't like."

"Yeah, but I don't think it was ever like this."

"You're noticing the talk now because you're in it."

"No, that's not it. There's more chatter now than there's been before," I say, and tell him what I overheard in the line, then what Natalie said.

"You can't let Natalie get to you."

"But what about the others? Those students I don't even know?"

"Same thing. Same advice."

I stop before we reach the steps to Morgan-Young Hall. "Actually I'm not looking for advice."

"Okay."

"I was telling you, and then you started offering advice, and I didn't ask for advice."

"Okay. Gotcha," he says. "Why don't we go to class now and I'll catch you later?"

"What does that mean? Are you blowing me off?"

He laughs, and I feel small. "Alex, I'm just following your lead."

"Fine. Go, then."

"Okay, I will," he says, and gives me some sort of tip-of-the-hat gesture. It irks me, the way he's so casual, so been there, done that.

I grab his arm before he can leave and pull him to the side of the building.

"If you want to skip class with me, all you have to do is ask," he says, and runs his hand down my arm and to my waist. He tries to pull me close to him as he says, "I'm always up for skipping for the right reasons."

But I resist. "Martin, listen to me. I'm not going to try Maia. I don't care about the evidence. I don't care what people are saying. I don't care what Beat and his friends said last night. I'm not going to do it."

"Alex, there's a lot of evidence."

"You think she did it?"

"I think there are a lot of students who say she did."

"They're setting us up. I know they're setting us up, Martin. They're liars," I say, even though I started the lies.

He sighs heavily. "Be that as it may, there are three of them."

"But you know she didn't do it, right? Please tell me you know she didn't do it."

"What I think doesn't matter, Alex. Don't you get it? The Mockingbirds aren't about you or me. They're about something much bigger. They're about all of us. And they're about us—you and me and Parker—not inserting our own opinions or feelings onto a case."

"So now you're accusing me of favoritism too, just like those students in line."

"Right. Yeah, that's exactly what I'm doing. I'm just like everyone else. Just like the guys down the hall who say it to me. Or the people in bio who whisper behind my back. Or the people who come up to me face-to-face and say it too. You're not the only one people say crap to. They say it to Parker. They say it to me."

"And now you're letting them get to you, aren't you?"

"No," he says emphatically. "I'm not. I'm used to it. Every year it's been something. This is what they're saying now. I saw the sign on the bulletin board. I know what it means. I hear people say stuff too. That's why I said you can't let it get to you."

"You keep saying that, Martin! Like you're the expert and I'm just the new kid on the block," I say, even though I am the new kid and Martin would never have backed a student into a lie.

"You know that's not how I feel or how I think, so don't try to put that on me."

"So stop saying it, then. Stop telling me not to let them get to me."

"Fine. I won't say it," he says. "May I go to class now?"

I'm not ready to let this end. "I'm not going to try Maia," I say again. "And it's not because of what people are saying."

"And this is where I disagree with you, Alex. And it's not because of what people are saying either. But I think we need to try her. The evidence against her is no less compelling than against Jamie."

"There's physical evidence against Jamie!" I point out.

"And there are *three* students who are saying Maia's involved."

"And one of those students is someone you don't trust— Beat. You said not to trust him from the start."

"You're missing the point. The point is, this is when you have to be objective. This is when you have to move beyond you and your world and your friends and your feelings. It's about the group having integrity and doing the right thing. It's about the whole student body, not our favorites. It's not a personal decision. We don't get to pick and choose who's potentially guilty or innocent based on who we're friends with. If we do that, we might as well be the little clubhouse they all think we are," he says, and pauses to look straight at me, his gaze sharp and fierce, his eyes full of steady quiet. "And now I am going to class."

He turns around and walks away. Before he can go, though, I blurt out, "I'm leaving for Juilliard tomorrow."

He looks back, slightly puzzled. "I know. You've told me before. I remember it's this weekend."

"I'm taking a tour," I say.

He nods. "Right."

"And then there's that jam fest thing."

Then he gives me a curious look. "And I hope it goes great."

I haven't mentioned I will have company. Every time I've tried, something came up, made me stop. My stomach curls, and I feel like I might throw up.

"Are you okay?"

"Jones is going. Miss Damata invited him too."

Martin doesn't say anything for a second, then a minute, then what feels like an hour, a day, a week. I watch his eyes as they cycle through a myriad of reactions. Why I didn't mention it before, why I'm mentioning it now, but most of all he wants to know if something is going on with us.

"Why are you telling me now?" he asks slowly.

I shrug. "I just remembered."

"Really? You just remembered?"

I gulp, then nod.

"You just remembered? Like just now? Like just this second? You remembered you're going away for the weekend with the guy I told you two nights ago that I am insanely jealous of and you said there was no reason to be insanely jealous?"

"There's not a reason," I say, and the bell rings for class. But neither one of us makes a move to go.

"There's not?" he asks, giving me a sharp look.

"There's not."

"So why didn't you tell me?"

I toss my hands up. "I don't know. I forgot. I've been

busy. This case is all freaking consuming. My roommate's mad at me. The dean cares more about my college apps than a cheating ring. And I'm busy chasing down suspects because Parker's not doing his job. Maybe that's why," I say, feeling like everything is falling onto me, everything that shouldn't be my responsibility, so then I really start going. "Oh, and I forgot. I also have classes too. I have an English paper due. And a history paper. And I still have to finish my Juilliard audition CD. That enough for you?"

He holds up a hand. "You can just spare me the details, okay? Because the same applies here. I go to the same school. I'm in the same group. I have the same crap to deal with, and I would have remembered to tell you if I was going away with some girl for the weekend to visit MIT."

I close my eyes at the words *some girl*, picturing Martin with *some girl*. Walking around MIT, touring the campus, working on science experiments together. *Hey, come watch this cell mutate.* He nudges the microscope closer to her and leans in as she peers through the lens. I walk into the scene and yank her hair back. *Get away from my boyfriend.*

"I'm sorry, Martin. I should have told you," I say softly.

"How long have you known?" he asks, his voice bursting with an uneven mix of hurt, anger, confusion.

"A few weeks," I admit.

"Alex," he says in a low voice as he shakes his head. He turns away for a minute, and I watch how his broad shoulders curve into his back. My hands have touched that back, touched his naked skin. I know that back. I know the freckle under his left shoulder blade. I've traced it with my index finger. I've run my hands along the length of his smooth skin and pulled him closer to me.

He looks at me and pushes a hand through his hair. "Don't make me say this."

"Say what?"

"Don't make me be this guy."

"What do you mean?" I ask, and for a second I'm scared. I'm scared of what he's going to say.

"I don't want you to go," he says, and I can tell the words taste bitter, like vinegar to him.

I have done this to him. I have made him do something he hates doing. I have made him be that guy.

"I don't want you to go away with him," he says again, and holds up his hands in a terribly defeated gesture. "There. I said it. And now I am the guy who tells his girlfriend what to do."

"Martin, I can't tell him not to go. That's not fair," I say.

He says nothing.

"And I can't not go. I mean, I've been dying to go."

He still doesn't speak.

"Please don't make me choose," I say.

"I'm not making you choose."

"Yes, you are," I protest, and I clench my own hands into fists, and suddenly I build up my defenses, I assemble bricks around me, stacking them higher, walling myself in as I say, "I just feel like you want to come between my friends and me. You want to try Maia because it's the supposedly noble, unbiased thing to do. And then when I am going away to New York for the weekend and not even staying with Jones, just going to a performance with him, you're like a different person and you say no."

"I didn't say no, Alex. I said I don't want you to. There's a difference."

"But is there?"

"You tell me. Is there a difference? Do you like Jones?"

"Of course. He's my friend."

Martin points a finger at me. "That's not what I mean at all, and you know it. Do you like him, Alex?"

I fumble for a second before I answer, asking myself if maybe I do, if somehow all along this is why I haven't said anything to Martin, because of the *zing* I felt that night, because of the way Jones's hand felt on my shoulder that afternoon before music class. "Not like that," I answer, and I'm not lying, I'm telling the truth, I know I'm telling the truth, but I feel like I'm lying.

"It took you long enough to say it."

"Well, I'm sorry. I'm sorry I'm not all levelheaded and reasonable like you and sure of all my convictions and beliefs every single second of the day."

He closes his eyes, exhaling heavily. "But I'm not like that, okay? I wish you could see that. I wish you could see that this—you—is the one area that I am not Mr. Calm-and-Cool and whatever it is you think I am."

"What does that mean?"

He softens for a second and takes a step toward me, reaching his hand out to my shoulder, holding me there tight. "You," he whispers. "You are the thing in my life that I am not levelheaded and reasonable about. And I'm sorry, but I'm not sorry. Because I am fucking in love with you, okay? And that makes me not want to see you get on a train with another guy and go to New York. The thought of you on that train with him, with Mr. Guitar Hero, Rock Star, whatever, makes me absolutely crazy."

I am torn between wanting to fold myself into his arms and let his intensity, his desire, his strangely sexy jealousy envelop me, and needing to take a stand for myself, for my friends, for my own convictions.

"I can't just ditch Jones, Martin. You have to understand," I say quietly.

"I'm sure I would understand if you would tell me. But you won't tell me. You won't tell me why you're always racing off to see him. And you didn't tell me you were going away with him when you've known for a while. And you tell me now. You tell me now like it's a confession. Like you know you should have told me. Like you know you should have said something. And you should have, Alex."

"Well, I didn't. And I can't go back and change it. So I'm sorry, okay?"

"Okay," he says, but what he really means is *whatever*.

"So, what now?" I ask.

"What now?" he repeats.

"Where does this leave us?" I ask, and I am terrified of the answer.

"I don't know," he says. "But I am late for class and I need to go."

I watch him the whole way, till the door swings shut behind him. Then I go to my room and I get into bed and I pull the covers up over my head and I cry. This year is turning out to be nearly as crappy as last year, and that's saying something.

Chapter Twenty-Four

STOLEN KISS

"More than two hundred and fifty pianos. The school has more than two hundred and fifty Steinway grand pianos. It's like I've died and gone to heaven, only better, because I'm alive and playing music," I tell Jones.

I've just finished an official tour of the Juilliard campus, which didn't take long because the school is actually quite small, just a few buildings and only one residence hall. But size doesn't matter in this case. *Location* does. The school is next to the Metropolitan Opera House, the New York City Ballet, the Lincoln Center Theater, and the New York Philharmonic.

Jones strokes his chin. "Hmm...where have I heard this before? Let me think. Could it be from you? The seventy-five or so times you've told me this before."

"I know, but here it all is in person! And I just walked

through it," I say as I sit down next to him at the fountain in Lincoln Center. It's not the first time I've toured the campus. But being here doesn't grow old. Being here is also the only thing that can distract me from thinking about Martin, from thinking about whether we're even together still. He didn't call me after class yesterday. He didn't text me. He didn't come to see me. But I didn't do those things either.

So I focus on what's in front of me, what I can see and touch and hear. It's Saturday afternoon and the October sky is painted a perfect powder blue. The air's crisp but not chilly. Lincoln Center is filled with people heading to their Saturday matinees. Here in the epicenter of the arts, where I want to be next year, surrounded by all those glorious Steinways. I watch a stream of theatergoers pour into the Vivian Beaumont Theater for the two o'clock curtain. The crowd is filled with pretty women in autumn coats and crisp heels, handsome men in pressed suits and sharp ties, tourists in sneakers and JCPenney jackets, and everything in between. New York is truly for everyone. It's also the furthest thing from Themis Academy that I can imagine. I might as well be moons away, galaxies even. There are no Mockingbirds here, no underground student-justice league at Juilliard. Why would this school need one? Juilliard does not labor under the same delusions that Themis does.

Coming here, going anywhere, will be a relief.

Jones places a hand on my thigh. "We'd better get going. Our jam fest starts in an hour."

"Which means we can soak in this ambiance for another

few minutes and still be early," I say as I twist around to watch the fountains spurting water behind me. "This is really perfect, isn't it?"

"If you like this sort of thing. Culture, that is," he teases. As I turn back, I notice his hand is still on my thigh. I don't move his hand. I look at it, drawn again to his fingers.

"Jones, do you think we should try Maia?" I ask quietly, and it feels so good to unburden myself. It feels so good to share all these things I've kept from him. "These three debaters came to us and said it was her. And they went into all this detail, and the other board members say we can't just ignore it. They say we can't ignore three people."

"You can't try her, Alex," he says, his hand gripping my leg more firmly as he speaks. "Friendship is more important than your code. Besides, there are other codes that matter, and that includes the one that says you don't do dickhead stuff like try a friend in your mock court. It all comes down to the kind of person you want to be, right?"

I nod. "I'm glad you agree with me."

"Why are you glad I agree?"

"Because you have your own moral compass or something that has nothing to do with what other people think."

"Funny. I'll often imagine a hot girl telling me I rocked the guitar, or she likes my blue eyes, or she dreams about what I can do with my hands. But liking my *moral compass*? First time for everything."

I blush for many reasons. For *hot girl*. For *blue eyes*. For *hands*. For all the times I've noticed parts of Jones. When

I shouldn't notice parts of him. Especially not here in New York City, far away from Themis, so far away it isn't just in another galaxy, it's in another universe, maybe even an alternate one. Not here on the steel edge of the fountain, the water shooting up behind us, making its own sort of aquatic music. Not here where I want to escape to and escape from everything I left behind for the weekend.

But I want to know if Martin was right to ask if I liked Jones. I want to know if maybe there is something more. If I do have feelings for my friend, feelings I haven't acknowledged.

So I look up, but not at him. I don't ask if he's calling me a hot girl. Because I don't care about that. I don't tell him his eyes are beautiful, because that doesn't matter now either. What I do is this: I lean my head back. I let the sun warm my face. I imagine. Turning to face him. Looking into his indigo eyes. Closing mine as I let him kiss me. It's like a rock song, a guitar riff, fingers spreading across strings, stretching to reach faraway notes, strumming them in ways they've never been strummed. He kisses like he should kiss—hot and electric and alive and solo.

How utterly easy it would be for me to kiss him. No one would know. No one would have to know. It could be our secret stolen kiss by the fountain in Lincoln Center.

Fountains don't talk.

But if I'm going to be the kind of person I want to be, that person doesn't cheat. That person doesn't give in to a fleeting thought, however momentarily tempting. I'm sure it would be a delicious kiss. I'm sure there are many boys all around the world who kiss deliciously. But that doesn't mean I am going to test the theory, especially when I already know a boy who kisses deliciously and I am *so* in love with him.

"Hey, Moral Compass. Let's get the hell out of here," I say.

We catch the nearest subway down to the Village, where the Juilliard alums welcome us into their inner circle as if we're just like them, as if we're equals. As we play I have this fleeting image of how it could be, how it should be. Adults and teens in concert, as equals, striving for the same goal— for now it's musical harmony. And it could be so much more.

Chapter Twenty-Five

PEACE OFFERING

When I return Sunday afternoon, my mission is singular and it's Maia.

On the way upstairs I overhear other students talking about how the debate team not only placed first but crushed the competition in the tournament in Miami this weekend. I open the door and she's there, lying on her bed reading *A Separate Peace*, the next book on our English class syllabus.

"Maia, I can't fight with you anymore," I say.

"I'm not fighting," she says coldly. She doesn't look up from the book.

"You know what I mean," I say as I shut the door behind me.

"No, Alex. I hardly know what you mean about anything anymore." She turns the page and keeps reading.

"Maia, you're more important to me than the Mockingbirds," I say, keeping my voice calm and steady, so she knows I mean everything I'm saying.

She raises an eyebrow. "Oh, really?"

I sit down on my chair. "Yes. Our friendship is more important than the stupid case."

"And when did you decide this?" She closes her book and turns to look at me.

"Now. This weekend. Always. I'm just saying it now because I've said it badly before. And I've acted badly before. And I should never have looked in your bag. I never should have pried. I never should have thought for a second that you'd be connected to the case. I know you'd never sell drugs. I know that, Maia. I know that like I know the Ninth Symphony cold."

"I wish you'd acted like it," Maia says, and she shifts. She's not cold anymore. She's wounded. This is the side of Maia I have never seen.

"I know, and I should have. I should have done a better job at so many things, but especially this. And I am sorry. I am so sorry."

"Why'd you snoop, then? Why did you look through my things?"

I run a hand through my hair. "Because I feel completely alone. I mean, it doesn't matter that there's a board. It doesn't matter that Martin's on it. At the end of the day, we're all alone. Ms. Merritt won't do a thing," I say, and then tell her about the brochure, about Ms. Merritt's comments outside the Faculty Club about how Anderin abuse might be distracting me from more important tasks, even about the *shared culpability* dig.

"No. Bloody. Way," Maia says, shaking her head. "She's hell-bent on her record, isn't she?"

"Yes. And that's why I felt all this pressure to do *something*. Because she does nothing but smile and cheer and look the other way. And then all these students were coming up to me and telling me stuff. Here I was, fresh off my own case and thinking how I had to give back. I mean, I never expected to be leading the Mockingbirds. I had no idea that's how they worked. And I wanted to do right by them, like what they did for me. So when students came to me and pointed fingers at the debate team or Theo or whoever, I wanted to do what I could to figure it out. I wanted to solve the case. And you were saying students were playing me; then I saw you putting the pills in your bag and it looked like you were hiding them. So then I thought you were playing me, and that's why I looked in your bag. And I'm sorry, and I feel terrible because I know you would never do that."

"I wasn't playing you, Alex. I was just trying to keep it private. And I meant it when I said something about the case seems dodgy."

I snort. "Oh, trust me. It's *all* dodgy," I say, and I decide to take a chance. I decide to sit down on her bed next to her. I brace myself for the possibility of her kicking me off. But she doesn't, so I continue. "Maia, the thing is, it's all gotten worse. Because right before you left for Miami—" I hesitate for a second, because I'm too embarrassed to say how or why

I tricked Beat, so I censor that part and continue. "Beat said you've been supplying to the whole team, and of course I know that he's lying."

Her brown eyes widen. "Beat Bosworth? What a twat."

I laugh lightly. "I'm glad to see your sense of humor is intact."

"He is the biggest poseur I have ever met. He only joined debate because the Mockingbirds busted him for that idiotic Benadryl act last year. I've never considered him one of the true members of the team."

I tell Maia he brought two other teammates to us, figuring this will only incense her and turn our tacit truce back to ice. But she laughs again, a deep, hearty chuckle.

"Those losers. No wonder he picked them. They're the worst performers on the team."

"Really?"

"He is totally trying to set me up, Alex. I will smother him," she says, and raises an eyebrow playfully. I'm not quite sure how to react, so I say nothing. But inside I'm thinking maybe Beat *is* the one who's setting us up. Maybe he's been toying with me all along to get to Maia. "You are going to let me have my day in court with him, right?"

"Um, no! That's what I'm trying to tell you. I don't believe him. I'm not going to press charges against you. I'm not going through with this. I don't care how many people he brings. I won't do it. That's why I said you're more important to me than the Mockingbirds. I love you, my crazy British roommate."

She waves a hand in the air. "You Americans. You're always so emotional with your professions of love. You need to adopt more of my British coolness."

Then she reaches out to hug me. "Shhh. Don't tell anyone I bestowed a hug," she says.

"Your secret is safe with me," I say, because she is who I will protect. She is who I will defend. I have crossed so many lines, but this line—my friend or the Mockingbirds—this is the line I will not cross. I side with her. I stand by her.

Except she doesn't want to have it my way.

"Now, listen to me. You *are* going to let them file charges against me. You are going to serve me. You are going to write my name in that book. And then I am going back into the laundry room—where, I might add, I had some of my finest oratory moments last year—and I am going to smash those thespian bastards to a new level of rhetorical oblivion. Got it?"

"Maia, I don't want to try you."

"Oh, but I want to be tried."

"I can't let that happen."

Maia reaches over and squeezes my hand. "Let's go to the cafeteria. It's dinnertime," she says with a look of mischief in her eyes.

Midway through the meal, Maia stands up and clears her throat to get everyone's attention. It doesn't take much for the noise and the chatter to die down, because Maia is imposing, her voice carries, and she has that indefinable thing called presence.

"I want you all to know that for the next *mock* debate,"

she says, pausing on the word *mock* to make it clear she is talking in code, "I am going to be defending myself in the *Pharming* case, and I am going to win."

Then she walks out. It takes me a second to process what she just said and how she did it, pure 100 percent Mockingbirds-style. Then I race out of there and follow her.

"Are you crazy?" I call out.

Maia shakes her head and slings an arm around me. "I am *ebullient*," she says, and flashes me a big, brilliant smile. "I enjoyed every single second of it."

After she writes her own name down in the book in the library, we return together to our room. T.S. is there and declares she has news.

"Parker and Anjali were totally flirting last night," T.S. says.

"Shut up!"

"Yep. Anjali had one of her chess parties. I stopped by with Sandeep. Parker was already there, and I swear, Alex, he was freaking glowing."

"He has a massive crush on her."

"Evidently it's mutual. He kept leaning in to whisper to her, and she was laughing at everything he said and she kept touching his leg."

"She could do better than him. Much better," I say.

"I, for one, think he could do better than her. She's a snot," Maia chimes in.

"You're just saying that because she's the only one who'll ever disagree with you in English class," I point out.

"And really. How dare she? Doesn't she know better?" Maia says with a wink, and I am glad everything is back to normal with Maia.

If only I could figure out what I want to say to Martin. But when it comes to him, I have no idea.

Nor does he. Because when I text him the next day, saying *Sorry about our fight*, he writes back *Me too*.

But that's it. Neither one of us says anything more, and I don't see him much as the next week passes by in a blur.

I call Theo to ask him point-blank if he's going to let someone else be tried for his crime or if he's going to own up to it. But when he answers, I don't even have a chance to ask because he tells me he's not at Themis right now. He's home in New York. Before I can ask why, he says he has to go.

I track down Delaney, but she doesn't know much more than I do. She tells me he left campus a few days ago with barely a word, saying only that he'd be back in a few weeks.

I try him a few more times that week to no avail, so I do the one thing I still do well. Piano. I finish my Juilliard audition CD, and when I record the Ravel, it's my residual anger at everything—Ms. Merritt, the Mockingbirds, Parker, Theo, even Martin—that propels me through the piece. I pop the CD in the mail and as I watch the envelope slide into the mailbox, I am keenly aware of a phantom beside me—my own wish that Martin were here with me, that we could send it off together.

We don't have many Mockingbirds meetings, though we do hear a few minor complaints, like when a freshman comes to us when her shampoo has been replaced with green dye. Martin explains that pranks are pranks, and those are still allowed. Then I tell her she should embrace the new look, that some people look great with rainbow-hued hair. She stares at me like I can't possibly understand the horror of her new hair color. I shrug my shoulders. What can you do? Some people can rock a cool do, some can't.

When the official meeting ends, Martin and I make small talk, but there's a distance between us now—and maybe I was wrong when I thought the Mockingbirds were coming between us, when I thought our different codes were dividing us. It seems Jones, or rather what I would or wouldn't share about Jones and when, has become the wedge after all. Maybe we are just normal teenagers, not merely idealists, not simply caped crusaders who have adulthood thrust upon us prematurely thanks to an administration that either trusts too much or cares too little. But, really, we are just your average seventeen- and eighteen-year-old boys and girls who fight and love and feel.

◆ ◆ ◆

The night before the trial, I slide into bed with *A Separate Peace*. As I read about the prep schoolers holding a midnight trial of one boy for causing the accident that broke his friend's leg, I realize maybe there is truth in fiction. Because here is a student tribunal just like ours.

I close the book and peer out the window. White flakes

drift down. Then I glance over at Maia, who's sound asleep. I wonder if she's nervous about tomorrow. I wonder if she's worried about the trial. Sure, she'll be in her element— talking, arguing, examining. But this time she's playing for keeps. Because it's not just another argument on foreign policy or politics. This time it's for real. She's fighting for what she loves. If she loses there's no more debate team, no more Elite, no more love of her life.

If she loses, she could be like Theo.

But that won't happen. This isn't risky; there isn't a bad landing.

Maia was made for the courtroom; she was bred to be a champion. She'll be fine. Everything will be just fine, I tell myself as I fall asleep, the rest of the student body sleeping soundly too as the snow turns everything white.

Chapter Twenty-Six

MISSING

It's the calm before the storm. An illusion.

Because when I wake up at seven on Saturday morning, a full two hours before the trial starts, I find five text messages on my cell phone. All from Martin. All telling me to meet him right away. His notes are sloppy, full of spelling errors and abbreviations.

I slam on clothes, pulling and yanking in record time, and race out of the room. I run across the quad, making a clompy path through the newly fallen snow to his dorm. I grab the heavy door, and Martin's on the other side, his hand pulling open the door, ready to find me too. His eyes are solid brown, like a wall, a sheet of monocolor.

"The evidence is gone," he says.

"What do you mean?"

"The bag. In our room. Gone."

"Who took it?"

"No idea," he says, and runs a hand through his hair. He screws his lips together, breathes heavily, shuts his eyes. I feel like I'm watching a pot about to boil over and scald everything in its path.

"Okay," I say, taking a deep breath. "Walk me through this. The bag was there in the closet yesterday, right?"

"Checked it like I do every morning. But this morning— gone," he says, each word like a brick in his mouth.

"So it could have happened anytime in the last twenty-four hours."

He nods.

"Well, what were you doing yesterday?"

"Class. Lab. The usual. Sandeep and I went to Williamson last night and watched football with some friends there."

"Did Parker go with you guys?"

"No. He stayed behind in the room."

"Does he know what happened?"

"Yes. He's freaking out and crying," he says.

"He's crying?"

Martin nods. "Makes me sick. Dudes shouldn't cry unless it involves dead pets or dead people."

"But why is he crying?" I ask.

Martin twists up the corners of his lips, a scornful look meant for Parker's tears.

"Seriously. Why is he crying?"

"I don't know, Alex. Maybe because the case is blown? Think that might be it?"

"You don't have to yell at me. I'm trying to understand everything."

"He's freaking out because the evidence is gone and—"

"He took it."

Martin says nothing.

"Parker took it," I say again. "That's why he's freaking out. That's why he's crying. I'm telling you someone has been trying to set us up all along. And I bet it was Parker."

Martin shakes his head. He doesn't want to believe it.

"He took it and hid it. He took it and destroyed it. He took it and did something with it while you guys were at Williamson. I never trusted him."

Martin breathes hard. "I don't think he did it, Alex."

"Why not? He was there. He had access. He's crying now, probably to cover it up."

"It wasn't him. I know it wasn't him."

"How did it happen, then?"

"I don't know how it happened. Maybe someone broke into our room and took it."

"Broke into the room?" I scoff. "I don't believe it. It had to have been Parker."

"It wasn't Parker."

There's a sound above us, someone walking across the hallway. We're silent until the footsteps fade. The pause in the action is enough to soothe tempers.

"Either way, let's just figure out what to do next," Martin says. "Because we have no evidence."

"We'll have Calvin and his testimony. That's powerful, right?"

"Yeah. And what else are we supposed to do? I mean we're not going to just call it off two hours before."

"I guess the show must go on," I say, but I have a deep, twisty feeling in my gut that it will be a show. That Jamie will likely get off, and that it'll just be Maia on trial.

I look at Martin, and there's this hard silence between us, a weight in the air like the sky itself is filling up, and I am sure this is the moment when I am supposed to apologize, or he is, or we are. This is the moment when we both forget why we've been barely talking for the last week and when he pulls me against him right here in the stairwell, presses his hands on my back, holding me tighter, tighter, tighter, finding ways to bring me even closer, compressing all the millimeters that divide us.

But we're still here, still standing feet apart, still not saying the things we really want to say. I look into his eyes, those brown eyes I desperately miss, his hair I want to breathe in.

And if this were any other day, any other hour, any other moment, I'd tell him I miss him terribly and we'd tumble through the requisite *I didn't mean to*s and *it wasn't like that*s and *I shouldn't have*s, and they'd rush by so quickly, like soap bubbles floating away and popping until they're gone, and I'd put my hands on his face and bury him in my kisses.

But there's a trial starting in two hours. My roommate is about to face a student tribunal that'll determine if she is allowed to do the thing she loves most or not. If she is allowed to be Maia or if she could become Theo.

I tell Martin I'll see him in the courtroom, and I leave.

Chapter Twenty-Seven
THE SPOTLIGHT

The room is ready. The dryers are running. A witness chair waits for students who'll testify. And while I didn't take Natalie's advice to open the courtroom to public viewing, it feels like everything is open. It's as if the basement laundry room is the heartbeat of the school, a gigantic, pulsing organ beating, ticking, making that *buh-bump, buh-bump* sound.

Three council members sit at the head table at the back of the room. Courtney Jaynes, Eric Bonner, and Lon Reid. Two long tables face the council. Sandeep sits at one alone. He's not even thrown by the missing evidence. He is the picture of calm, a doctor in an operating room repairing a patient's broken hand while discussing his kid's soccer match with a nurse. When Martin told him what happened, Sandeep simply nodded, in the same way he'd nod if the nurse told him she'd just lost his only scalpel right before surgery. He'd find another way to put everything back in place.

Martin and Parker tell me the defendants and their attorneys are coming. "The defendants are entering now," I announce in a voice that surely doesn't belong to me.

Maia walks in first, past the washers and dryers, to the other table. She nods to each of the council members, then sits down. Jamie follows. Her straight black hair is cinched back in a clip at the base of her neck. She wears flats, a dark blue denim knee-length skirt, and a beige cardigan. I have this fleeting image of her on a prairie, some sort of innocent pioneer girl. She looks so unbelievably young, so unbearably innocent, so fourteen years old. McKenna is next to her, her wild black hair tamed back with a red headband. But the headband can only do so much. The curls have a mind of their own. She wears pressed black slacks and a white button-down shirt.

The two sisters take their seats at Maia's table, but it's not as if the three of them now form a united front. They're not really on the same side; we're just trying Jamie and Maia together because they've been accused of the same crime.

I shut the door and walk to the middle of the room. I open my notebook and read from it.

"The function of the council is to listen to the evidence presented in this case—the students of Themis Academy versus Jamie Foster and Maia Tan. The charges are selling and trafficking in prescription drugs with the intent to cheat. The council will listen to the *evidence* and determine the verdict for each of the defendants based on the *evidence* against each of them. The punishment for Jamie Foster will be voluntary withdrawal from VoiceOvers as well as regular and random checks to ensure the activity in question has ceased. The punishment for Maia Tan will be voluntary withdrawal from the Debate Club as well as regular and random checks to ensure the activity in question has ceased. Both Jamie Foster and Maia Tan have been offered settlement options. Both have declined. They have signed the papers and agreed to these terms. If Jamie is found not guilty, we will remove her name from the book and enact appropriate restoration measures. If Maia is found not guilty, we will remove her name from the book and enact appropriate restoration measures."

I look to Courtney and say, "Courtney Jaynes, I turn the proceedings over to you."

Courtney gives instructions to each side as I retreat to the doors, where I will wait and watch and listen for the rest of the morning.

Sandeep goes first, calling Calvin to the stand. Calvin is not as self-assured as he was the night we met him. He stumbles more, turns red at times, and trips on his words. His high-pitched voice doesn't help. He looks even younger than Jamie. As I listen I realize that Calvin doesn't have much to contribute without the evidence. Sure, Jamie approached him, Jamie made him an offer. But that's it. That's all he can say, because that's all he knows. Without the evidence that documents her crime, his words fall flat.

It's only when the evidence is off the table that I see how

much of the case against Jamie relied on that Ziploc bag he found on her desk, waiting, calling out, begging for discovery.

The hair on my arms stands on end. I begin to realize what is happening and how we were set up, like a spotlight pulling up onstage and revealing just a sliver of the scene. The light grows stronger when Sandeep calls Beat's buddies to the stand. They present a long and detailed account of Maia's alleged activities, coupled with descriptions of inspirational speeches she gave to the team on "winning at all costs."

Beat is next, and now the stage is practically bathed in light, all of it glowing on its star, with his high cheekbones, his wavy brown hair, and those deep brown eyes. His palms rest on his legs, and his chin is lifted up, a pose that seems to say, *I'm open, I'm here, I'm ready whenever you are, so take your time.*

He waits patiently for the first question from Sandeep.

"Tell us how it started."

"It began late last year," Beat says, like a storyteller of old. "It was the last week of school, and Maia was giving us a pep talk for the summer, to keep us energized and ready, she said." A pause. "*Ready*," he repeats. "That was the word she used. She wanted us *ready* for the Elite. I wasn't sure what we were *supposed* to do. I didn't really know what she meant. So I asked. And she answered. She said we needed to do"— he stops, winces on the next words—"*whatever it takes.* That was her saying. We had to do whatever it takes to win the Elite."

A question—what did that mean specifically?

"We weren't sure. We discussed it," Beat answers, gesturing to the other witnesses who went before him. "We talked about it. We wanted to do well. And I'll be honest," he says softly, calling on his best shamed look, "it's no secret that I don't have a perfect record. You know what I did and what I'm trying to make up for."

He takes a deep breath. The whole process of coming clean is so difficult, apparently.

Then he continues. "But when the new year started and we had our very first meeting, there were no longer any questions about what she meant. She took out her pill bottle and said, 'These help me, and they'll help you too.'"

Maia objects, but the council overrules. They want more; they lean in closer to the campfire, eager for the next chapter in the tale.

And Beat provides it, ably. "It all happened so quickly, and pretty soon she was producing forged prescriptions for some of us."

Maia objects.

The council doesn't even look at Maia. Courtney just waves her off, like she's a minor annoyance, and keeps watching Beat, entranced by him, as if he's some sort of magician in a turban, luring her into his tent.

"For others, she taught them how to doctor shop. That's when you visit different doctors and get prescriptions from a bunch of them. So you stock up, essentially," he says. "Some of us already had ADHD, like myself, and to be honest, I even thought about sharing some of my own pills with my friends." He takes a deep breath, places his hand over his mouth for just a second, as if the memory itself still hurts. "The directive was just too strong to ignore," he adds, shrinking back in the chair a bit. Then he straightens himself. "But I couldn't do it. I crossed a line last year and I did something wrong, and I knew it. And I just didn't want to be that kind of person again. I learned my lesson, the lesson the Mockingbirds taught me."

It's like a stake in my heart.

It's like a twisted, rusty stake the way he is using *us* to play *us*. The way he is taking his past with the Mockingbirds to paint a new present for himself. Beat, the bad boy turned good. Beat, the reformed.

And I fell for it all. I fell for it when he called me to the theater. I believed him. I wanted to believe him. But it was all an act, just like this is all an act now.

"And soon, half the team was hooked. Half the team was either sharing someone's pills, or using her fake scrips, or getting their own. And then they were snorting too. If you walked into our practice room, you could smell it on us. We were coated in the stuff, it seemed. And it worked. We were confident. We were on fire. We were winning. We were taking down other teams left and right. We were untouchables."

"So why did you come to the Mockingbirds then?" Sandeep asks.

"It wasn't easy. I mean, it's not like I'm on the list of their favorite people," Beat says.

The council members nod sympathetically. They under-stand how terribly hard it must have been for Beat to come forward.

"But it's just wrong," he says, and looks to the council. "You have to play fair. You have to do the right thing. Right?"

He waits for them to respond. And they do respond, they do nod, they do understand every single thing he is saying.

"That's why I came here."

Here, cloaked in the immunity I granted him, safe from another black mark on his record because I backed him into a corner the one night when I tried to act.

But Beat is a far better actor than I am.

He is also a better liar than Maia is an orator.

Because he has an answer to everything she asks.

"Beat, you said I showed my pills to the team, but yet they never left my bag. How can you explain that?" Maia begins.

"Maia." He says her name like a gentle chide. "You know that's not true. We all saw them. You get them from the pharmacy in London."

"That's a lucky guess, Beat. Of course I get them from a pharmacy in London. I'm from London, and so is my doc-tor."

He just shrugs and gives a smile, waiting for her to ask a question, because it's still her turn to ask a question.

"Let's go back then to this *whatever it takes* directive that I issued," she begins as she walks across the linoleum floor, her soles clicking against the tiles. "Are you aware that *what-*

ever it takes is a common phrase that doesn't specifically refer to cheating, drug dealing, or other insidious measures to get ahead?"

"Of course. But that wasn't really how *you* used it," he says, managing another dig.

"I used it to refer broadly to the idea, no, the *ideal*, of doing your best. Of working very hard to achieve something we all want," she says sharply.

"Yes, something you wanted badly," he says, and lowers his eyes momentarily like he's ashamed to point out this supposedly sordid truth.

"I was saying it in the way that a coach would encourage a team to go out and do their very best."

He pauses, shrugs his shoulders, and twists up his mouth for a moment. "But when you couple that with showing us the pills and teaching us how to doctor shop, it's pretty clear that you wanted us all to cheat right along with you."

Maia's eyes flare at the audacity of the accusation. I watch from my post, my heart caving in more as she struggles to contain her anger, to put out the fire that he's fanning with his lies. She takes several seconds to collect herself, then continues. "And this doctor shopping. When did this supposedly occur?"

"It was the third week of school, I believe," Beat says, looking up at the ceiling like he's trying to recall the details. He scrunches his forehead for a second. There, yes, he's got it. "It was shortly after our first tournament, where we barely squeaked past Andover, and you said you were very concerned and we needed a much larger margin of victory."

Maia gives him an incredulous look. "I never said that!"

"Maia," Beat says again in that concerned voice.

"I never said a thing like that. I told you all I was extraordinarily proud of you for the Andover victory," she says, but it's not her normal cool, calm, and collected voice. It's a defensive voice. I want to look away, to turn away from this scene, but I can't stop watching her having to defend herself rather than question him. Because that's what he's done. He's turned the tables. He's turned her into a witness rather than an attorney.

"Not exactly. You said you were proud of us, but you knew we could do even better—*loads better* was what you said," he adds, and he even says those words with a British accent, imitating her perfectly, scarily, so spot-on that the council is convinced he is telling the whole truth. "And you added that we were all, in effect, performers, so there was no reason why if we could talk circles around opponents that we couldn't surely do the same with doctors."

I cringe because even though it's a lie, he uses the exact words that Maia would use. He has mastered her speech patterns, her vocabulary, the way she strings words together, and he is using this to take her down.

"I never said that!" she shouts at him.

I want to run past the dryers and the washers, run past the tables, and grab her, wrap my arms around her, put a blanket on her shoulders and take her away. Because she shouldn't even be here. She's only here because I pushed Beat into a lie. Because I went too far.

But Beat's not done. Vengeance, or drama, runs deep in him.

"And you even asked me to share my supply too. You said if you were sharing, it would be the *magnanimous* thing for me to share as well," he adds.

I watch as the word *magnanimous* slices into her like an arrow. Because that's just the kind of word she would use too, the kind of thing she would say.

She hasn't met her match.

She has met her vanquisher, and he has learned from the master; he is defeating her by playing her part. He is Maia right now. He is better than Maia.

For a second, just the tiniest hair of a second, I understand why he drugged the seniors last year. Because he has unparalleled talent. Because he deserved the lead. He deserves all the leads, all the roles, all the parts ever. He has charisma, he has presence, he has the council in his hands as he unfurls this beautiful, seductive, magnetic lie.

Maia calls her character witnesses, two other debaters who testify that she didn't do what Beat said she did. But their words fall flat. The damage has been done.

When the council adjourns, there is no reasonable doubt.

When they return the next morning, the verdict is everything I expect to hear.

They find Maia guilty. They find Jamie innocent.

What they don't say is the part I know to be true beyond a reasonable doubt—it is all my fault.

Chapter Twenty-Eight
SCHOOL RIVALS

Maia is a zombie.

She barely speaks, barely talks, barely looks at anyone. It's not because she's mad anymore. It's because she's broken.

This is what happens when we take away. This is what happens when we punish. This is what happens when the innocent are found guilty.

Fine, it's *only* debate. But it's *not* only debate. It's Maia's love. I would be a zombie too if someone took the piano away from me. I would be Theo, homeless, helpless, the inside of me cratered.

Because we are what we love. We are the things, the people, the ideas we spend our days with. They center us, they drive us, they define us to our very core.

Without them, we are empty.

Maia lies in bed, still wearing her courtroom attire hours later, as the sun sinks low in the sky and the evening chill sets in. She returned to the room after the trial and she hasn't moved from her bed all day.

"Maia, I'm so sorry," I say again.

"S'okay," she mutters, the only words she's said all day.

Her black hair spills out beneath her, a fan around her face.

"Maia, I'll get to the bottom of this. I promise, I will."

"S'okay."

"I will figure out who set us up."

"S'okay."

But nothing is s'okay or okay or anything. Because she didn't just lose. She was humiliated, called out publicly, branded a cheater. But so much worse—a cheater who forced her whole team to cheat, a dealer who made her whole team take drugs to win. Word travels fast at Themis Academy.

And like me last year, her private life has become public. Only, I chose to step forward then. Maia didn't choose; she just had to defend herself, her secret, the thing she didn't want anyone to know.

If I ever questioned whether I would be good at leading the Mockingbirds, if I ever wondered if I was cut out for the administration of justice, I don't have to ask anymore. The answer is clear.

I have failed spectacularly.

One innocent person has been found guilty. One alleged

perpetrator was wrongly accused. Score: two screwups for the price of one. Three, if you count the fact that we were played, faked out, clearly set up by someone. Or by several someones. I already have a growing list of suspects and I am adding more by the hour.

Was it Beat? Or Theo? Or Beat *and* Theo? Or Calvin? As remote as that possibility sounds, I can't discount it. Or perhaps Delaney protecting Theo somehow? Or Natalie, that loose cannon Natalie who's had it in for me, and for the Mockingbirds, since last year? Natalie, who mocks me when she sees me, who jams her elbows into my body? Or Parker? I can't help but think Parker is responsible. Parker cried over the evidence. Plus, Parker was tasked with tracking Theo and he came up short. It took me only a few nights to find him dealing. Parker has always been the weak link on the board. To top it off, he's always questioned me, tried to undermine me. Maybe Parker has been playing me all along. But why? As he asked during our first board meeting before classes even started, what would the *motivation* be?

What would anyone's motivation be?

What scares me is not that I don't know who's behind the setup but how many valid options there are, how many students might want to take us down.

And how I played into their hands.

But I have to find a way to fix the mess I made. And that mess isn't just Maia. It's Jamie too. So I pay her a necessary visit.

McKenna is with her. If I had a younger sister who'd

been accused of masterminding a drug-using cheating ring, I probably would be all mama bear with her too. I probably wouldn't let the big, bad Mockingbirds talk to her without being there either. I'd spit it back in my face and be all, *I told you so. I told you she was innocent.*

McKenna doesn't say that. Neither does Jamie. When I visit them, Jamie invites me into her room, and McKenna offers a chair. I sit down and begin. "I want to offer my sincerest apologies for the accusation that prove to be false," I say, though it's more a recitation. I practiced before I came over, reviewing the section in our notebook on how to handle accusations that prove to be unfounded. I suppose it's no different from a real court. Some are found guilty; some are found innocent. And I suppose too that having a mechanism in place in case the accused is found innocent keeps things fair, so we don't simply favor the victims all the time.

Still, none of this makes it any easier to say the words that come next.

"We are truly sorry for all that you went through. I will remove your name from the book, restore all your points, and announce that you will indeed stay on in the VoiceOvers as a member in good standing, which will signal to the student body that you were found innocent," I continue. I have this strange sense of déjà vu, but it's not that I've been here before; it's that I somehow *knew* I would be here.

"I would also like to offer you an advisory post on the Mockingbirds," I add. "You would essentially become a de facto board member, and in this capacity you can help us better consider the rights of the accused. Would you like to join us in this post?"

Jamie nods enthusiastically, and I find myself thinking, yet again, how young she is. There's this softness around her, a sweetness almost, that doesn't fit the evidence I saw, the stories I was told.

Then again, nothing fits.

"I'm excited to join the Mockingbirds," she adds, and she's smiling brightly, back to the Jamie I had dinner with, the Jamie I asked to mentor.

McKenna gives her a cutting look, then speaks for the first time. "Thanks, Alex. For handling this with such grace. I know it can't have been easy," she says.

I wish she'd just be a bitch to me.

◆ ◆ ◆

The next day at lunch I feel like I am eating sand as I stand up and say, "Maia Tan has an announcement to make."

She isn't stoic or tough or cool. She's dead. She's a shell as she delivers words I know have to be eating her alive.

"I'm withdrawing as Debate Club captain effective immediately and for the rest of my time here. If you want to know why, the answer is in the book."

Then she walks out. I don't follow, though I desperately want to. I want to do all the hard work for her, to bear the burden. I want to turn around and shout at the top of my lungs, "I did it! I was the supplier! I'll take the punishment."

But she would never let me. See, that's the difference between us. She would never have put me in a position where I might have to take the fall. Last year she stood by me, shoulder to shoulder. She went to bat for me, and she knocked it out of the park.

When it was my turn to protect her, I struck out.

As she leaves, heavy, empty, gone, I begin the next part of what I have to say, the part about Jamie staying in the VoiceOvers—crystal clear code for her being innocent—then the part about her becoming one of us. I finish and I've just had a brief taste of what it's like to be on the other side. To be the one standing up in front of the crowd, admitting she was wrong.

It feels awful.

As I walk away I catch a brief glimpse of Carter seated next to that red-haired girl, his arm draped around her, a smug smile on his face.

◆ ◆ ◆

That evening, I sit alone on the steps outside my dorm, trying to figure out how I can prove Maia's innocence, how I can prove she's *not* responsible. It's late and it's cold, but I'm not alone. Because Martin texts me to tell me he has some info, then joins me a few minutes later.

"You were onto something with those signs," he says.

"The creepy cartoon dogs?"

Martin nods. "I did a little recon on my own, and I found out what they're about."

"You did?"

"This dude a floor below tipped me off. Said there are some students trying to start their own group. That's what the dog signs are all about. Been recruiting quietly for the last couple weeks."

"Like a rival justice system?"

"Evidently."

I pause for a second, considering this. A rival justice system. Another underground secret court. Isn't one enough? Isn't one more than enough? But then I think of D-Day, of the Faculty Club, of Ms. Merritt, and how one or two or all the underground justice systems in the world will never be enough. They will always be pale facsimiles of how right and wrong, good and bad, should be handled. And neither of them can do what really matters: rebuild, repair.

I think of Theo, the broken boy who got off scot-free. I want to confront him, shake him down, get him to fess up. But he's not even here. And I've done the shakedown. I've done the spy thing. They didn't work. Nothing I do works.

Besides, Theo's already lost the thing he loves most. Our justice doesn't work for him.

"Some days I wish I was just in public high school," I say.

Martin leans back on the steps, stretching his legs out in front of him. "I don't think it's a picnic there either."

I suppose we could kiss and make up right now. I suppose

now would be as good a time as any. We're not fighting. We're not even distant anymore. We're just us, sitting here alone on the steps in the dark. We might as well be boyfriend-girlfriend again. But I don't think I can do that. I don't think I can let myself feel good, feel something, feel hands, kiss lips, run fingers through hair, escape, escape, escape into him. Not when Maia feels nothing right now.

And not when there are other things I need to do first. Like tell the truth.

"It's all my fault," I say, and the admission at once embarrasses me and frees me. I have been carrying this around for the last few weeks, and now I am letting it go.

"What do you mean?"

"I lied to Beat. I set him up. I told him I knew it was Theo and I needed him to back me up, otherwise I'd take the immunity offer away."

"You did?"

I nod. "I'm the reason he lied about Maia. I'm the reason he brought those others in to say it was Maia. I totally and completely subverted everything we stood for."

"Wow," he says under his breath.

"Do you hate me?" I ask, and I don't feel so lightweight and unburdened anymore. Because I can't stand the thought of Martin hating me. Not being with him is hard enough.

"God no," he says.

"What do you think?"

"What do I think?"

"Yeah."

"I think we all messed up."

"*We?* You don't have to take the fall for me. I'm a big girl. I can handle it. I know what I did. I did it because I wanted to nail the right guy. I did it because I'm not so sure this whole honor code means more to me than anything else."

"I'm pretty sure none of us are perfect. We all made mistakes. Parker sucked at following Theo. I spent more time talking about the case than doing legwork. You, at least, were trying. Besides, who ever said an underground, unofficial justice system was easy?" he says, and his lips curl up in a small smile. I smile back as he adds, "But whatever went wrong, let's try to fix it."

Let's.

It's not quite a *let's get back together*. It's not even close. But for now I will take it.

Chapter Twenty-Nine

TORCH SINGER

I bake Jamie cookies.

Trust me when I say the kitchen is not my forte. But Amy gave me an awesome recipe—one cup brown sugar to a half-cup white sugar makes all the difference—and I managed to pull off an excellent batch, along with help from T.S.

"Aren't you just a little Holly Homemaker?" T.S. teases when I drape Saran Wrap over the cookies.

"Just don't tell anyone I baked, okay? I don't want word getting out that I have a shred of domesticity in me," I say.

"The internationally renowned world-traveling concert pianist would never deign to use a stove when she performs around the world."

I point a thumb back at myself. "This girl is ordering up room service all the way," I say, then head across the quad to Jamie's room.

She opens the door when I knock, since she's been expecting me.

"Cookies!" she says, and then claps her hands together. She takes the plate and reaches for one. She bites into it and then says, "Dee-lish."

"I'm glad you like," I say.

"Do you want to sit down?" she asks, and points to a chair.

I tip my forehead to the laptop on her desk. "You like Diana Krall?" I ask, since the torch singer's voice is oozing out of the computer's speakers.

Jamie's brown eyes light up like stars. "I love love love her. And I love Ella and Rosemary and Billie and all the first ladies of song."

"Favorite song?"

"Oh, definitely it would be 'These Foolish Things' by Billie Holiday," she says, and then hums the first line or so. "God, I *love* that song so much. I love Billie and I just love those lyrics. They're so like one of those 1940s movies where there's an overhead fan just slowly turning and this woman in a slip walks across the hardwood floor and she's just missing this guy, some guy she was never supposed to be with in the first place. But she can't help herself. She loves him," Jamie says, and she's lit up like a sparkler. I wouldn't be surprised if she twirled right now, like a preschooler.

"That's what I picture too when I hear the song. That kind of rose-colored old-time wistfulness for the one who got away," I say. Then I add, "It's a good piano song too. You know, Jamie, it's not the same as a cappella, but would you want to sing while I play?"

She presses her palms together, a plaintive yes. "Like a duet! This is exactly why I wanted you to be my senior mentor!"

"Let's go," I say, and we hit the music hall. I settle in at the bench, and Jamie stands next to me. As I play the first few notes, something changes in her. She stands taller, her face settles into an almost brooding expression, and she sways her hips ever so slightly as I play.

The torch singer. She is the torch singer.

Who'd have thought this wide-eyed freshman could be a torch singer? Because when the lyrics start, it's clear she's got a serious set of pipes. I expected a standard musical-theater soprano to come out of her, but her voice is all edge, smoky and sexy. I see her in a slinky wine-colored dress, pouty red lips, her black hair high and teased, the lone microphone in her hands the conduit between her and a gauzy, hazy, jazz-club audience.

"You sure can sing," I say when the song ends.

She smiles bashfully. Now she's Jamie again, perfect white teeth, big brown eyes, shining, simply shining. Then the smile fades to black.

"Why are you being so nice to me?" Jamie asks.

"Because you went through a lot, Jamie. We put you through a lot. And we owe you a lot." Her face sinks again when I say that. I quickly add, "But I'm not doing this because I owe you. I actually really like hanging out with you."

She grins now. She tries to contain it, but she can't. "You do?"

I nod. "Yeah, I do. And I think you deserve a nice time right now too. An easier time than we gave you."

◆ ◆ ◆

The next day is Saturday. The debate team returns from Dallas. They lost the Elite, and word in the cafeteria is that Beat Bosworth performed poorly. I have a feeling it was intentional. I overhear someone mention that Theo's back on campus too. I want to know the details of both of their performances, but I'll have to find out later because we have our first meeting with Jamie right after lunch.

"The big question we want to get at, Jamie, is what could we have done differently?" I ask as we settle into the Knothole in the back of the basement laundry room, Jamie next to me, Parker and Martin across from us.

"Um," she begins, and shifts uncomfortably on the pizza-stained couch. She looks down, eyes fixed on her fingernails. "Well, I guess I didn't really like having my name in the book," she says. Then she picks at the skin on her left index finger. She is determined to remove an errant cuticle.

"Do you think there is a better option than writing names in a book?" Martin asks carefully.

She shrugs. "Um..."

"Well, obviously the better option would be if we didn't

have to have an underground justice system at all," Martin adds with a laugh, to lighten the mood.

"Yeah," Jamie says, pulling at her fingernail, trying to turn her other nails into makeshift scissors.

"Do you think we should wait until verdicts are decided to write the names in the book?" Parker asks, now taking his turn. The thought crosses my mind that I haven't seen Parker and Anjali flirting or hanging out since T.S. told me about that night. I wonder what the story is there.

"I guess," Jamie says as she finally snags that hangnail. But then her finger starts bleeding at the cuticle. She makes a fist with her left hand to hide it and pushes against the skin to stop the blood. I reach into my backpack and riffle around for a tissue. I find one and hand it to her. She nods her thanks and then wraps the tissue tightly around her index finger.

Maybe it's the room. Maybe it's being in the courtroom again that's throwing her off. Because she's not the same Jamie she was last night when she was singing with me.

"Maybe we just shouldn't have trials altogether," she says.

"Maybe," I say.

"That, I think, is what we all aspire to," Martin adds.

When the meeting ends, I walk out with Jamie, leaving Martin and Parker behind. I put a hand gently on her back. "Are you okay, Jamie?" I ask.

She shakes her head.

"What's wrong? Was it just hard being there and kind of having to talk about what it was like?" I ask, because now

I'm thinking how crummy she must have felt the whole last month. Having her name smeared into the book, having her fragile, barely formed reputation on campus merge with the one we created for her—that of a drug dealer, a shady, nefarious, opportunistic mastermind at the center of what might have been the next big school scandal. When she's simply a young girl who got framed.

"C'mon. I'll walk you back," I say as we cross the quad.

"Alex," she says in a tiny little voice.

"Yes?"

She doesn't respond right away. We keep walking and now we're nearing her dorm. I notice a sheet of paper taped to the door. In fact, all the dorms have sheets of paper taped to their doors.

"I have to tell you something," Jamie says.

I look at the paper closely as I wait for her to talk. It's that dog again. But now it's holding a gavel. A smiling cartoonish gavel. Like the one McKenna drew for her student council.

Images fly by: a movie montage, flashes, photos, scenes. Every click, every frame, they lock into place, and the audience knows who did it.

I turn to Jamie, but before I can speak, she does.

"It was my sister. She's behind it all. She was the one who set up the Mockingbirds."

Chapter Thirty

SISTER'S KEEPER

It takes a minute to fully register that McKenna Foster is the one who set us up. But when it does, it makes perfect sense, dating all the way back to the start of the school year, when McKenna *swooped* in to save me from Natalie—a known enemy. She wanted to make me think she was on my side.

It worked. I believed her.

Other details that seemed off fall into place—how McKenna asked me to be Jamie's mentor. McKenna must have planned that, must have wanted her sister close to me. And why would she want that? I snap my fingers, realizing McKenna must have wanted someone she trusted on the inside. And who could she trust more than her own family?

Pieces are coming together, but there are details I need to know for sure, so I point to the music hall. When we're inside, I begin. "You were always the one who was supposed to be tried, right? She set it all up to look like you. She put all that evidence together to look like you. But it was never you, right?" I say, the words coming out like lashes of hard rain.

"It was never me. It was Theo, but she made it look like me," she says, wincing, like she's biting into a bar of soap, like the admission tastes that bad.

I want to pound my fist against the wall. I always knew it was Theo because of Delaney, then because I saw his pills, then because I saw him deal. Now I know where he was getting them from—from McKenna, who had access, who was forging the scrips from her parents.

"She set it up with him over the summer after his knee injury. McK said she'd keep him in anything he wanted as long as he'd sell to the team," Jamie says, and I jerk my head at the sisterly nickname, pronounced like "McKay." "As long as he'd get himself on the debate team. He was her *point person*. That's what she called him."

Another puzzle piece shifts into place—those e-mails Delaney saw must have been between McKenna and Theo as they plotted this over the summer, as they planned to hit the ground running the *second* the school year started. That was the blueprint, the road map, and Theo's job was to get himself on the debate team, then convince the others to start using Annie too. The team didn't need much convincing to get hooked, not when Ms. Merritt was harping about the Elite. It never takes much convincing here at Themis. We are all preprogrammed to win, win, win.

I bet McKenna protected Theo too. I bet she was his

shield, making sure he was never implicated, always getting people to point fingers at others at just the right time. But never at him.

"What about all the evidence it was you? I bet you planted the evidence for Calvin to find. He said he saw it in plain sight in your room. You did that on purpose so he'd come to us, right?"

"Yes," she admits in a broken voice, and I feel like a total sucker. Because every move I made played into McKenna's hands. I sought out evidence, I solicited it even, and she served it right up. All to make her sister look guilty. And there's only one reason you want someone to look guilty who's not—so she can be found innocent and get inside. Which is where her sister is right now.

"She wanted you to be in the Mockingbirds as her spy?"

"I never wanted to do it. I swear I didn't. But she asked me and she begged me to and then just said I had to. And then you and I hung out and you were so nice to me, and I can't do this. I can't be her person on the inside."

But why would she want someone *on the inside* so badly that she'd engineer a whole case? I hold those words in front of me—*on the inside*—lasering in on them, and then it hits me hard in the gut. The creepy cartoon dogs. The rival justice group. The fake case was a means to an end. The drug ring was supposed to be the means to *our* end—a ruse designed to take the Mockingbirds down and lift her group up, with its creepy cartoon gavel and dog.

No wonder McKenna loves government; no wonder she

loves studying how power is assembled. She figured out how to systematically undermine our power by turning everything that was good about us against us. By using everything we tried to uphold to take us down—our checks and balances, since we give board posts to people we wrongly accuse. But she's not the only one who wanted to take us down, I'm betting. Because Beat clearly played us. As I remember his pitch-perfect performance in the laundry room, I can picture McKenna recruiting him early, knowing he'd want revenge against us.

"She lined up Beat, didn't she?" I ask, assembling the rest of the pieces.

Jamie's voice is strained as she coughs up more details. "He was at our house a few times this summer. He even got himself a real prescription from a real doctor in his hometown so he'd look like he really had ADHD."

"I bet he loved every second of that performance," I say. I bet he relished walking into that doctor's office and playing the role of a teenage boy suffering from ADHD. I flex my fingers, digging them into my palms, as if I have to restrain myself from slamming my fist into his nose even though he's not here.

"Is Natalie Moretti involved?" I say, thinking of all the bumps and bruises she unleashed on me.

"She's the heavy. McK brings her along when she needs to get people to agree."

"She's building her own mafia, your sister," I say.

McKenna is the godfather, the don, the head of the family.

Fat and happy, smoking a cigar, counting her money, directing her underlings to carry out her wishes. She never dirties her own hands.

"Who else? Who else is working for her? And if you say Delaney, so help me, God, they will hear my screams in the next solar system," I say, praying that my decision to trust her was not in vain.

"Not Delaney. McK can't stand her because she was always telling Theo to stop. Plus, McK hates Delaney's hair."

I give Jamie a curious look. "She hates her hair? Her purple hair?"

"Yeah. She thinks it looks stupid. She said one night she wanted to shave it all off. And her eyebrows too."

"Her eyebrows too?"

Jamie just shrugs.

"Tell me who else is involved," I say insistently, but before she can say a word I hold my hand up. I know who it is. It's the girl who talked to Theo after English class, the girl who said Jamie would be at the chess party, the girl I wanted for the third board slot. "Anjali."

A final nod.

McK has a lieutenant on the inside.

Chapter Thirty-One

ONE BAD LANDING

So much for instinct. So much for anything.

I don't even have to ask why. I don't even have to wonder what Anjali's motivation is. The fact that I am instantly sure of her motivation says nothing about Anjali but everything about us. She was dying to be a board member and she wasn't chosen—another flaw in our system. Mockingbirds start as runners, then some move to council, then even fewer to the board. Most council members never graduate beyond their roles on the juries, though. Most council members never get to lead, choose cases, or investigate. Those are all the things that, frankly, are *cool* about the Mockingbirds. But only a select few members can do them. The rest fall off like damaged parts on a conveyor belt, dropping down to the factory floor to be swept away.

One of our soft spots.

McKenna poked and prodded until she found *all* our soft spots. She turned every weakness into her advantage. She will make a great campaign strategist someday, a magnificent advisor to a world leader.

"Do you want me to resign?" Jamie asks quietly. "You probably don't even want me to resign. You probably want to fire me or kick me out."

"No, I don't," I say, the answer coming more quickly than I expected. "We accused you, and you didn't do it. I'm not going to rescind the offer just because it was a setup. The rule's there for a reason. To keep us in check. To balance out our power. If I break that rule, I'm just as bad as"—I stop myself before I say *your sister*—"they are."

"I want to stay, Alex," Jamie says, and she clasps her hands together and looks up at me with those puppy-dog eyes. "I know you probably hate me, though."

I don't hate her. How do you hate a pawn? Besides, she may have done the hardest thing of all. She turned against her family. She returned to herself.

"I don't hate you, Jamie. Oddly enough, and I'm not entirely sure why, I still kind of like you."

"I'm going to prove myself to you," she tells me, a new determination filling her, like a paint can being poured over a canvas, a new color covering the old.

A flash of doubt streaks by. This could be another setup, another layer to another intricate lie. But now is not the time to ask. Now is the time to confront.

"I have to go see Theo," I tell her, and I leave for Richardson Hall.

I bang hard on his door, waiting, ready, eager to pounce on him.

But he's not the one who answers.

When the door opens, I'm greeted by my informant.

I give Delaney a quick nod and turn to Theo. He's sitting on his bed. I glance around his room and notice there are two suitcases pulled out. One is a hard-backed navy suitcase, the other an army-green duffel bag, the kind that comes to your chest if you stand it on end. "So you skipped out on the trial but managed to travel to Dallas for the Elite."

"I didn't go to the Elite," he says.

"Why not? Wouldn't that be your moment of triumph? Isn't that what you wanted all along?" I say, because now I don't feel any sympathy for him. I don't feel any sadness. I am nothing like him. "How could you miss it? You were training, prepping all along."

"I withdrew," he says.

"Oh, how noble of you. To withdraw from the competition you practically rigged."

"Alex," Delaney says in that raspy voice of hers, butting in. "He's not talking about the Elite."

But I barely hear her words. Just the sound of her voice, that husky voice hunting me down in the student-activities office, brings me back to the night this all started, and she was the one who set it all in motion.

She was the first domino.

292

"You always told me to keep you out of this. You always said you couldn't be associated with this," I say to her, holding up my index finger. "And now you're in this. So which one is it, Delaney Zirinski? Were you in on this?"

"You asked me that before, and I told you. No."

I wait for her to say more, to explain herself.

"He told me everything just now when he got back from New York. All the details I didn't know and didn't want to know before. And I told him I went to you. I told him I was the one who tipped you off."

"That is so sweet. The two of you comforting each other in your mutual confessions," I say to Delaney, then I swivel around to Theo. "Does that include how you let someone else take the fall for you? Does that include how you let Maia take the fall?"

"I was already gone. I had no idea she was being tried until I got back."

"Yeah, but would you even have confessed if you knew it was going on? Would you have confessed it was you?"

He looks straight at me, his eyes worn out but painfully honest when he says, "It's not like I have a track record of making good decisions. But I'm hoping that changes."

"Why is that going to change?" I ask, because all I can think is he should be standing up in the cafeteria and taking his punishment.

"You know our English teacher? Mr. Baumann?"

"Of course."

"I started talking to him about it a few weeks ago."

I take a moment to process what he just said. That he confided in an adult, a teacher, no less. Just like when I told Miss Damata last year what happened to me. "He's been helping me," Theo adds. "With everything. Not just the Anderin, which I stopped taking, but everything. How to deal with what happened to me. How to move on. I started seeing a counselor. Someone he put me in touch with. That's why I was gone for the last few weeks. I was back home with my parents."

"I'm glad to hear that," I manage to say, and for the first time all year, I feel like maybe we—the Mockingbirds, the students—don't have to do all the heavy lifting. There are teachers and parents who care.

I watch Theo's eyes travel to the suitcases. Delaney's gaze follows, but I speak next. "You're withdrawing from Themis, aren't you?"

Theo nods. "Yes. Mr. Baumann is great, but he made it pretty clear he won't sanction cheating."

I think back on the honor pledge for a second. Maybe it does work.

"Did he turn you in to Ms. Merritt or something?"

Theo shakes his head. "No. Because it doesn't matter. I'm leaving Monday. I just came back to pack. It was my choice. But I told my parents what happened, and I'm going to finish high school at home in New York and keep seeing the counselor there."

"There's something you have to do before you leave," I tell him.

"I know."

"Are you going to?"

"Yes," he says. "Tonight at dinner."

I want to reach out and grab his shirt by the collar, twist it, push him into the corner, and make him swear on it. But I know those tactics don't work. They won't do any good. I can't control him. I can't control anyone here.

I learned my lesson when I lied to Beat—the lie that ricocheted back with so much collateral damage, hurting my friends, the Mockingbirds, and me. So all I can do is wait, because dinner, and a certain someone's regular chess party, won't start for a few hours.

I look over at Theo, remembering the way he danced for me, the way he favored his right knee. It strikes me as almost funny that one bad landing was all McKenna needed to set in motion a drug ring that turned dozens of Themis kids into buyers, dealers, addicts.

Then again, we are all addicts here. We are all hooked on something, whether it's the piano, or the microscope, or the soccer field, or one another. This school lures us in like magnets, the overachievers, the ambitious of our world, and we spend our days and nights here aspiring, wanting, desiring like we've never done before.

Chapter Thirty-Two

GIRL POWER

Delaney catches me on the way out. She grabs my arm, and I turn around to look at her, her blue-gray eyes tough and steely through her silver glasses.

"I wasn't jerking you around. Ever," she says. "I wasn't in on it. I always wanted it to end. I always wanted it to stop. For me and for him."

I look at her, at the way she wears her convictions on her sleeve. I know she's been telling the truth all along. "I know. Sorry I said that. So what happens to the two of you?" I ask, nodding back at the room.

"I don't know," she says. "It's not like I'm going to see him much now."

"Will you miss him?"

She nods. "More than you know."

"Are you in love with him?"

"Ridiculously."

"Are you glad he stopped?"

"Immensely."

"Are you addicted to adverbs all of a sudden?"

She laughs. "Evidently."

Then it's my turn to laugh. "Can I touch your hair?" I ask.

She laughs lightly and nods. I reach a hand out, thinking it'll feel like straw from all the bleach and coloring, but it's silky.

"You really can rock the purple hair," I tell her as I pull my hand back.

"Not everyone can pull it off," she adds playfully. "But you would kick unholy ass with a blue streak."

"I would, wouldn't I?"

"Do you want to do it?" she asks conspiratorially, like she's offering me drugs, a pill, something that tastes good. But this is her drug; this is what she plays with—color, style, boldness. And maybe it's not a drug. Maybe it's just who she is.

"I've got three hours," I say, and it's that easy. I don't worry about drawing attention to myself anymore, because I'm already public and that's just the way it is.

Delaney takes me back to her room, where she gathers her supplies, bleaches and dyes and shampoos and other assorted bottles and potions, then to the girls' bathroom in her dorm. She drags a chair in and positions it against the sink. She won't let me take a peek until she's totally through, which includes blow-drying my hair. When she's finally done, she spins me around to the mirror.

I touch the blue streak on the side of my head. It's like a badge, a medal of honor, a declaration even. It makes me look tough; it makes me look cool.

"Now, if you'll excuse me, I have to go kick unholy ass," I say, and return to my dorm. I don't go up the stairs. I go down the hall and toward the common room on the first floor, and my instincts were right. They're here, getting ready for a chess party.

Anjali has a bright orange scarf with tiny white flowers patterned on it wrapped around her neck and silver flats on her feet. She even has a clip in her hair, a shimmery blue one with a metallic butterfly. She looks so celebratory. She sets up tables and boards and wineglasses for her famous lavender, rhubarb, and vanilla organic sodas. I briefly entertain the idea of smashing a few bottles together or just knocking them over and letting them break, the bubbly liquid spreading into the Themis Academy common-room carpet. Who wants lavender soda, anyway?

McKenna is there, lounging on the couch. Where she was tightly wound a month ago, calm and gracious a few days ago, now she is loose and languid. She wears formfitting jeans and a long, slinky gray shirt, her feet perched on one end of the couch, her head on a pillow, and an arm dangling to the side. She might as well be holding a cigarette, carelessly letting the ashes fall to the ground. Instead, it's a remote in her hand. An iPod remote. She uses it to change songs. She has on a beige cap with a dusty rose pattern, and its job is to hold back that wild hair.

I am muted in comparison—jeans, sweater, Vans; standard gear—except for the blue streak in my hair.

"I guess it's a good night to have a party," I say as I step inside. "Lots to celebrate, right? I mean, chess is really working out for you, isn't it, Anjali?"

They both turn to look at me.

"At last! You're finally taking me up on my invite for a chess party!" Anjali says. She doesn't realize I was being sarcastic. She is still playing me.

"I think I took you up on that earlier this semester without even realizing it. And I think you won the first match," I say.

She widens her eyes. Then they register that I know. I detect the slightest bit of embarrassment in her when she looks away. Good. She should be embarrassed. She should feel bad.

"Hello? Were you going to say hello? I'm here, people," McKenna says, clearly not bothered at all to have been found out, perhaps even wanting it to have happened. I wonder if she knows her sister was the one who ratted her out. But it's not my place to let on how I know.

"Hello, McKenna," I say. "I think you guys are missing someone, though. Aren't you a threesome after all? Where's your heavy?"

"Right behind you." It's Natalie and she's carrying more of that vile soda as she walks in. I look down at the six-pack in her hand. Lemongrass flavor. In her other hand she carries seaweed chips. Thank God I never said yes to an Anjali chess party. Natalie plunks the six-pack down on the counter and taps one, then looks to me. "If they were beer, I'd give you one. Oh, wait, your drink of choice is vodka, isn't it?"

I don't respond. I don't bother telling her I don't drink and I won't drink ever again. Instead I say, "That's why you did this, Natalie? Because the horse you bet on last year didn't win?"

Natalie snorts in response. "So typical, isn't it?" She directs this to her cohorts. "She thinks it's all about her."

"Speaking of, your hair looks stupid," McKenna says to me, then stretches like a cat. I half-expect her to start cleaning herself like a feline would. She starts by licking one hand, then uses that hand—no, paw—to reach behind her ear. Then the other. Her tail swishes side to side.

I've never been one for cats.

"So does yours," I say back.

McKenna doesn't respond, just flicks the iPod controller and picks a new song. "I get so bored sometimes with the same songs over and over."

I stare at her, at McKenna the Cat changing the music. "Is this all just a game to you? Is this because of student council? Because it has no power?"

"If only I were that petty. But I'm not that small, Alex. This is much bigger than student council," she says, then crosses her feet at the ankles and stretches her arms above her head. "It's about responsibility. And not that collective responsibility crap you espouse. But *personal responsibility.* That's what we believe in."

"Oh. That makes perfect sense. You believe in personal responsibility, so you set up a drug ring. Naturally."

"Maybe you should never have looked into it in the first place. Maybe not everything should be in the Mockingbirds' jurisdiction. But you have to stick your nose in everything. I mean, a cheating ring, Alex? This is the kind of thing no government or group should be getting involved in. But that's why it was so *easy* to trick you. Because we knew you Mockingbirds weren't going to be able to resist waving your holier-than-thou flag."

"But yet the students thought we should get involved. We took a vote," I point out.

She waves a hand dismissively. "A vote. Ooh. That proves so much. You know what it proves? It proves the student body is afraid of *one* group ruling it. That's what we call an oligarchy, Alex. And that's what you guys have been. Besides, it was all too easy to take down the Mockingbirds, because your group had a lot of holes in it."

"It was like a sieve!" Natalie says, and laughs at her own lame joke, then takes a swig of her lemongrass swill.

"You should have picked me as the board member, Alex," Anjali says, and her voice is cutting now; her eyes are cruel. She stands against the sink and the cupboards, her arms crossed in front of her. Gone is the bubbly, enthusiastic, happy-to-help girl. "But you passed me over for Parker

Hume, the senator's son. I never liked Senator Hume, and I never liked his son either."

I laugh then. "Why'd you flirt with him at your party?"

"They didn't just flirt!" Natalie says with a snort. "They made out in your boyfriend's room the other night too."

Then all the girls laugh, enjoying their power, the way they play people. "Sometimes you have to take one for the team, as they say," Anjali says. "So when your boyfriend and Sandeep were watching football the night before the trial, I spent a little one-on-one time with the boy whose job I should have gotten. God, he was so easy! First he practically announces Maia's under investigation that day after English class. Then he tells me at my chess party that he's keeping the evidence in his room! He made it so easy to go back and get the evidence."

I grit my teeth, wishing there'd never been a third board member at all. Because it was Parker's faux pas that tipped off Anjali to Maia being under investigation in the first place. That's probably why they coached Beat to claim Maia was the mastermind.

"So you made out with him just to take the evidence from his room?"

Anjali nods proudly. I imagine her with hidden fangs, standing outside a doorway, waiting patiently to be invited in, like a vampire. Once inside, she sinks her teeth into Parker, the weak link as always. He turns away, a look of rapture on his skinny face as she grabs the evidence she planted in the first place. "Though the evidence was ours to start with."

"Since you planted it in Jamie's room."

"And lo and behold, Calvin walked right into our little trap, the one you helped me set up with those posters," Anjali says, smacking her palms together to emphasize her point. "Of course, I'm not surprised, since I knew he'd fall for it."

"That's what you were doing when you were investigating for us," I say. "You were just scoping out who actually had enough morals and decency to turn in a dealer."

Anjali rolls her eyes. "You guys are so self-righteous."

McKenna sits up on the couch, like those words from Anjali are her call to action. "My point exactly. You're always trying to force your choices on the whole school. Because that's what this is all about. Choices. Personal choices. Because you know what? I never cheated. I never forced pills down anyone's throat. I don't drink, I don't use, I don't smoke, and I don't cheat. Anjali doesn't. Natalie doesn't. It's not that hard to do the right thing. You just make smart decisions. You resist temptation."

"Do the right thing? You engineered a cheating ring! And you're getting all over us for being too involved?"

McKenna arches a well-groomed eyebrow. "But sometimes the end justifies the means, doesn't it, Alex? You can't really come in here preaching your *do-the-right-thing* ways when you lied to Beat. He told us everything about your meeting in the Faculty Club."

I slice my hand through the air. "Let's not start acting like Beat Bosworth is some poor, meek soul I manipulated."

She tilts her head to the side and gives me a fake smile.

"Whether he's defenseless or not is beside the point. You manipulated him. You entrapped him. And so we may have gotten our hands a little dirty too—"

I interrupt to scoff, "Euphemism."

"—the point being that you had your goal when you lied to Beat, to prove Theo was the supplier. So you can't really come around and accuse us of being manipulative too. You don't have the moral high ground."

"And you do?"

She nods. "We are doing this for the greater good too. Because if you've studied government as closely as I have, you would have recognized a common thread. And that is when there is too much power vested in too few hands, you have the makings for change, the seeds of a revolution perhaps. Some might even call it a coup."

"A coup? Really? This is a coup? Your little group is a coup?"

Natalie marches forward and grabs my left wrist. "Little group? *Little* is a diminutive word, Alexandra Nicole Patrick." She yanks my arm behind my back, twisting my wrist so my shoulder lurches forward and my hand torques up. Her cold brown eyes bore into mine, and I stare right back, my steely blankness matching hers each time she twists harder. All those muscles in her body are spectacularly powerful, and she's hurting me like she's a paid professional. But I will not show an ounce of pain in front of Natalie, in front of this girl who ripped me apart last year and who's hitting where it hurts most right now.

My hands.

"It'd be really hard to play the piano with one hand broken, wouldn't it?"

I grin wickedly then, unable to resist smirking at her error. How could she know after all that I can play one-handed? But I say nothing. Because what happens between the piano and me is still mine. It's still separate from the Mockingbirds· and therefore separate from these three. It is the part of me they cannot know, the part that drives me, that gives me strength—I have years of training too; mine is on the bench.

Natalie doesn't like my smile. She cocks her head to the side, narrows her eyes. "Something funny, Alex?"

She twists harder, her arm a corkscrew, cranking deeper, further than it needs to go, so far the cork starts to splinter. Each hand has nineteen bones, twenty-seven if you count the wrist too, and Natalie Moretti is using every single one of the hundreds of muscles in her sculpted, sinewy, track-star body to crush them all, maybe more. Maybe she'll even shatter bones that don't exist.

"Enough," McKenna calls out lazily, and Natalie lets go just before she breaks anything.

I want to cradle my left hand, to touch it, stroke it, hide it. But I grit my teeth and hold tight, the pain shooting to my fingertips and back up to my shoulder.

"I mean, really. We want this to be a fair fight, don't we?" McKenna says. Then to me, "But it doesn't have to be a fight. We know, in a lot of ways, you didn't really have a choice about becoming a Mockingbird. You were a victim, and you won your rape case, and all of a sudden you became a Mockingbird. So we'll give you a choice. You can leave them. You can leave your past behind and we'll just let you go. I'm sure you've had your doubts about the Mockingbirds just as we have."

It's kind of like when someone else insults your mom. You can say crap about your mom all you want, but it's never okay for someone else to. Because while I have had more than my share of doubts about the Mockingbirds, a bolt of loyalty shoots through me, rooting me to the ground.

"I'm not leaving the Mockingbirds, McKenna. And if I were going to, I wouldn't need your permission. And I don't care if the whole school knows, because I'm not a victim. I'm a survivor. It's part of me and so are the Mockingbirds."

McKenna takes out an imaginary bow and plays a fake violin for a moment while Anjali and Natalie bestow exaggerated claps.

"Then if you're going to exist, we're going to exist," McKenna says. "It's sort of like that law of physics—for every force, there is an equal and opposite force. You were the only force for a while." She holds up her palms like scales, the left one high, the right one low. Then the right one rises and they're equal. "But science won't allow that." The right hand is above the left one now. "So we're here."

"Physics. Government. You're mixing metaphors," I say.

McKenna nods to Natalie, who understands the directive immediately. She grabs my other arm now, administering the same torture to the right one. She even adds a little spice to her routine, jerking my middle finger back. It's perpendicular, then a little more.

"Apply consistent pressure," McKenna says with glee, then claps her hand to her mouth. "Oh look! Now I'm mixing medical terms!"

Natalie's eyes burn with delight. "Harder, Alex? Want it harder?"

I won't respond. I can't respond. I refuse to respond. I squeeze my eyes shut, taking the pain, sucking it in, not showing them I am breaking. Then I scream silently when she jacks the finger so far back, I hear it snap for real this time. "Please stop," I whisper, but with the quickness that's earned her victories on the field, she does the same to my ring finger, then my pinkie.

Snap. Snap. Snap.

She lets go, and I am hating them, hating the pain, hating their power.

"How does it feel to have the thing you love taken away?" McKenna asks, her words a final kick in the gut. They're her encore, her last reminder of how she has undermined us once again.

"Did it hurt?" Natalie asks as I open my eyes.

"Yes." It's throbbing, to be precise. It's burning up my freaking body.

"Good."

"So now you understand us better, Alex," McKenna says, and stands up for the first time, sweeping her hair back off her shoulders and padding over to me on those cat feet of hers. "We're here to keep you in check. To keep the Mockingbirds in check. That's why we're the Watchdogs."

If I had any energy left in me, I'd laugh at the name.

"Though you can really think of us like the Vigils," Anjali adds.

I guess there is truth in fiction, after all.

I'd say something about life imitating art if my breathing wasn't growing shallow and my vision wasn't feeling blurry and the pain wasn't radiating from my right hand in sharp stabs. I turn to leave, my left hand holding the right one as if it might fall off, because it feels like it might fall off, when McKenna speaks again. But she's not talking to me.

"I told you Theo would blab in under a week now that he's *seen the light*. He was such a pansy," McKenna says. "So pay up, bitches, 'cause this bet is mine."

I hear Natalie and Anjali reaching for their money when it hits me—McKenna has no idea it was her sister who sang.

Chapter Thirty-Three

MIDNIGHT TRAIN

I desperately want to see Jamie, call Jamie, text Jamie. I want to ask her if she'll tell McKenna, and I want to ask her *not* to tell McKenna. But my hands feel like limp rags, my fingers like poison, so I find my way across the quad to Martin's room. I want to see him—I want to fall into him, knowing he would let me, knowing he would take me back if I just ask—but I *need* to see his roommate.

I knock with some clumsy combination of elbow and forearm. Martin answers. Sandeep is there too, but Parker is gone.

"Are you okay?" Martin asks immediately.

I shake my head. "No. It's my hand," I say, my voice breaking for the first time. I still hold back the tears, but I no longer fake it, I no longer pretend this doesn't kill me.

Sandeep springs to attention. "Let me see," he says. He takes my right hand gently in his, then asks, "May I touch?" I suck in my breath, gasping as he touches the middle finger. "Does this hurt?"

"Yes," I choke out.

He does the same to the ring finger, then the pinkie.

"Can you move them? Can you gently try moving them?"

I lift my fingers slightly, screwing up my eyes, grunting a bit as I try to move them. I look at Martin, his face wracked with worry. "What happened, Alex?"

"I'll tell you later" is all I can manage to say.

"Who did this to you?" Martin says, and the worry vacates. The seeds of anger take its place.

I can't answer yet. There is too much to say, too much to tell.

Sandeep looks at Martin. "She needs to see a doctor. Her fingers are fractured."

"Can she go to the Health Center?" Martin asks, referring to the on-campus medical clinic.

"It's after hours. Only a nurse is on duty. The nurse will have to call a doc to set her fingers."

"Let's go, then," Martin says quickly, grabbing his keys, not bothering with a coat.

"Where are we going?" I ask.

"You need to go to a hospital," Sandeep states.

"No," I say weakly as I lie back on Martin's bed. Its familiarity is comforting. I know this bed. I've been in this bed. I can curl up here.

"You need to see a doctor," Sandeep says clinically.

"Please don't take me to the hospital," I moan. "I'll be fine."

"You're not fine," Martin says insistently. "I will carry you there if I have to."

I would wave them off if I could move my hands. I try to shift over to my side, away from them, away from everyone, calling out to sleep, to sweet slumber, to anything that'll take the pain away right now. I close my eyes and feel Martin's strong hand on my shoulder.

"Alex," he says gently. "We need to get you seen."

"How are we even going to get to the hospital?" I mumble as I consider counting sheep so I can float away and forget all this. But Sandeep is already calling a cab.

◆ ◆ ◆

I tell Martin everything on the way to the ER. I even manage to come up with a cover-up too, so the doctor who evaluates me thinks I tripped on a patch of ice and broke the fall with my hands. He nods, saying that, after sports injuries, falls are the most common cause of broken fingers. I suppose that is a bit of serendipity. That, along with having a fall birthday. I'm eighteen now, so the hospital doesn't have to tell my parents. I'll tell them soon enough but not tonight.

"You have three fractured fingers," the doctor informs me. But that's really just a nicer way of saying broken fingers, because when it comes to hands, *broken* and *fractured* are the same.

Then he tells me I can't play for four weeks. Four long weeks. Four long, miserable weeks. He says my fingers will be back to normal then. But will they? And what is normal in this doctor's world may not be *normal* for me. I need my fingers to be more than normal. I need them to be extraordinary.

So I ask him, "Can I play the same?"

His answer: "You'll be fine."

But "fine" isn't good enough. Theo can dance fine, and that's not good enough.

Then I'm sipping orange juice and walking out of the emergency room, three fingers on my right hand in a splint.

"Now I really can play that Ravel piece the way it was meant to be played," I joke to Martin. His arm is wrapped around me, and he manages a smile. I don't know if his arm is wrapped around me because my hand is broken or because we are done being mad. But whatever the reason, I'll take it. Because it's the only thing that has felt good in hours. The immediate pain is gone, replaced now by an ache that is not dull but is, in fact, rather insistent. It occurs to me that the phrase *dull ache* may not be so apt after all. "Good thing I already sent in my CD, huh? The audition won't be till January, if I get one."

"*When* you get one."

Martin is gentle with me as we slide into the backseat of another cab, but I know he is seething inside. He wants to crack heads or snap wrists or do something. He wants retribution. So do I, but not tonight, not yet. For now I am exhausted.

"You're staying with me tonight," he says as we near campus. "I already told Sandeep and Parker to find another place to sleep."

"I'm staying with you?" I ask, but stop at that, not daring to ask what else it might mean.

We pull up to campus and walk to his dorm. I sink down on his bed. Martin sits gingerly on the edge of his bed, afraid he might break me.

But he can't break me.

No one can break me but me. If I wasn't broken by what Carter did to me, I won't break myself by what I have done, and I won't let those girls break me either. I will put all of this back together, everything, starting with Martin. Because I can't remember, nor do I want to, why we weren't together for the last few weeks. He is here and I am here, and this is where I came when they broke my hand, to him, the pull irresistible.

"I miss you," I say.

"You have no idea how much I missed you," he says, and like that, with words—words that stand alone and stand together—everything is behind us, and we move forward, only forward.

"Come closer," I say as I manage to kick off my shoes. I slide my feet, then my legs, under his covers.

"Are you sure?"

"Lie down next to me," I say.

He takes off his shoes and follows my lead, sliding under the covers. He pulls the blankets up to our chests, careful not to jostle my right hand that's resting on my stomach. His shoulder touches mine and it feels so good and so different from how my shoulder felt in the common room when Natalie jammed it.

"Mmm," I say. "Tell me something nice. Tell me a story. What would we be doing tonight if we weren't at the ER?"

"Ah," Martin says. "I had planned to take you to a movie."

"Oh, you did?"

"There's some new movie out with talking animals. You'd like that, right?"

I laugh. "Talking animals. Perfect escape."

"And I wouldn't just take you to some crappy Providence theater. I'd take you all the way to Boston."

"Ooh, fancy."

"That's me. Fancy," he says. "We'd take the train to Boston."

"I like trains."

"No one would ask where we were going. No one would care."

"Of course not. There are no rules here."

"We could do whatever we wanted. Slip away and no one would notice. Wouldn't even have to use our points. And when we got to Boston, I'd take you out for dinner."

"A proper date."

"Well, if you call a greasy pizza joint a proper date," he teases.

"I love greasy pizza, the kind you can fold."

"Folding pizza is the only kind I permit. And maybe we'd get cannoli after."

"I don't like cannoli," I say.

He places the back of his hand on my forehead. "I think maybe you did hit your head when you took that *fall*."

"How about ice cream?"

"Mint chocolate chip for you."

"Of course."

"Then we'd see the talking animals and you'd laugh the whole time."

"Would you laugh too?" I ask.

"Oh sure. What's not to like about talking animals? Especially raccoons."

"Raccoons are the best kind of talking animals," I say softly. "Martin?"

"Yes?"

"Nothing happened. Nothing ever happened with Jones. It's his—" I get the first letter out of *dad* before Martin places a finger on my lips.

"It's okay. You don't have to say anything."

"But..."

"But your blue streak is totally hot. And I'd be touching your hair the whole way on the midnight train back," he says, returning to our fantasy as he traces my cheek with his finger.

I wriggle closer to him. "Would it be empty?"

"Of course," he whispers.

"What would we do?"

"Whatever you wanted to do," he says.

"What would you want to do?" I ask.

He brushes a strand of blue hair from my face and leans in to my ear, then says something that's so ridiculously sexy, so incredibly hot, that I feel like I'm melting from the inside out.

"Please kiss me," I say.

He props himself up on an elbow, bending his face to mine, his lips brushing me softly, starting with my eyelids, then down to my cheeks, then finally my lips. He kisses me tenderly, and it's the sweetest kiss in the world, the softest kiss any girl has ever gotten. I close my eyes, drifting into the kiss, into his touch. He runs his hand gently down my left arm, then moves his lips to my bruises, to the black-and-blue marks Natalie left on my hand. I imagine him taking the pain away with his kisses, the opposite of what the Watchdogs did to my hands.

This is how I fall asleep, damaged, bruised, broken, but completely peaceful and wholly content in my own way.

Chapter Thirty-Four

TAKING SIDES

I don't wake up for a long time. I sleep through breakfast, then brunch, then lunch. When I wake up, Martin is there with Jamie.

"We've been busy," he says. He's holding an ivory enve lope in his hand, the kind society women send thank-you letters in.

I sit up in bed, self-consciously patting my messy hair.

Jamie shows me her right arm. There's a black twisty ponytail holder on it. "Want it?"

"Yes, please," I say, and hold out my left hand. She drops the black rubber band into my palm and I try to pull my brown and blue hair back, but it's awfully hard to do one-handed.

"Let me help," Jamie says. She scooches next to me and twists my hair neatly into a ponytail.

"What's going on?" I ask.

"Theo stood up in the cafeteria at dinner last night," Jamie says. Her smooth black hair is long and sleek against her shoulders, and her brown eyes are as innocent as they have always been, but somehow savvier too. She's aged a few years overnight.

"He did?" I ask cautiously, eagerly, waiting to hear.

Jamie nods. "He said it was him after all, not Maia."

"Holy crap," I say. "He really did it?"

"He said that the wrong person was accused, the wrong person took the fall, and that it should have been him."

I try to say something, but I am speechless. If I could form words, if I could give voice to the swirl of thoughts racing in my head, I'd say something about bravery, something about hope. Because Theo may have been point zero in all of this, but maybe he can change. Maybe, in some way, justice has been served after all. A new kind of justice. The kind that matters, the kind that helps you become the person you can truly be, the kind that helps you overcome the person you're leaving behind.

"Was Maia there?" I ask.

Jamie shakes her head. "No. But I suspect she's heard the news by now. News travels fast at Themis."

"But that's not all. We have a double agent," Martin adds proudly, nodding to Jamie.

"Really?" I ask.

Jamie nods. "I was going to tell McK today that I was

done with her side, but Martin found me first and told me what she did to you."

"Your sister didn't do this," I correct her. "Natalie did."

"And we need to get back at her," Jamie says firmly.

I snort. "What are we going to do? Try Natalie? For us to be the good side, *others* have to believe in what we do," I say.

"There are other ways," Martin points out. His eyes are sparkling, though, and he's clearly been working on those other ways.

"And what are those other ways?" I ask.

"We paid a visit to your dorm this morning. Well, to the first floor, to be precise," he says.

"To the scene of the crime," Jamie adds.

"And we asked around. Knocked on doors. Went up and down the whole hallway. Turns out there were a couple of sophomore girls on the first floor who saw what happened," Martin explains. "Maxanne Braff walked by when Natalie broke your fingers. She texted Rory Bell and told her what she saw. Rory showed us the text, and Maxanne told us what she saw."

"So now what? Like I said, Natalie would never consent to be tried by us."

"I know, Alex," Martin says heavily. "We're not talking about going to *us* on this matter."

I shake my head in disbelief. He can't possibly be suggesting I go to Ms. Merritt. Besides, I didn't go to her last year.

Last year.

I feel like I've been plunged back in time, the victim again.

But then just as quickly, I return to the here and now, because this *is* different. Not the crime but the environment. Last year, there were no Watchdogs to give Carter other options. Last year, the Mockingbirds were the *only* option for any of us.

Now there is a new threat.

And because of them we are not the same. We have to change. But I don't know how exactly we should change, so I shift gears.

"Can we go back to this whole double agent thing first?" I say, and turn to Jamie.

"I don't want to be like them anymore. I want to be on the good side," she says, and I want to say I'm not even sure we're the good side anymore. I'm not sure if we did any good this semester. It seems that all we did was weaken. The termites got into the foundation and ate it away little by little.

But then again, here's Jamie. Here's the girl who *chose* another path. Here's Jamie actively *choosing* the Mockingbirds. "I don't want to be on the same side as someone who'd break your hand," Jamie continues.

I glance down at my splint, at my fingers that may be *normal* soon, but may not ever be good enough. A fresh surge of anger courses through me, and I am ready to jump up and find Maxanne and Rory and then tell everyone—every single last student and teacher here—what happened in the common room.

But I need a plan. I need to be methodical. I need to be smart and strategic every step of the way, because that trio of girls is dangerous.

"They had their spy. Let me be yours," Jamie pleads. "I can help you even more this way."

I want to ask how I will know she's not playing me. But there's no test to show loyalty. I can't prick her finger with a needle and then run her blood through a machine that'll tell me it's okay to trust her.

I have to rely on instinct, and instinct can be wrong.

"Alex, you know how I said I was going to prove myself to you?"

"Yes."

"You know that redheaded girl who's been seeing Carter?"

"Yes," I say tentatively.

"I know who she is. She's a freshman. She didn't know what he did to you last year. Now she does," Jamie says.

"You told her," I say, and I can't resist—the corners of my lips curl up.

Jamie nods proudly. "I didn't rub her face in it. I just took her to the library and showed her his name in the book."

"What did she do?"

Jamie shrugs. "Let's just say they're not together anymore."

"Jamie Foster. You little vigilante. You Mockingbird."

"So, you're not going to kick me out?"

"Jamie, I already told you I wasn't going to kick me out. I meant it. You're in. You're a Mockingbird."

"And?"

"Fine. Take advantage of me while I'm down," I tease. "If you want to be a double agent, Jamie, it's your choice. It's going to be risky, very risky. You're going to have to be amazingly careful. And you're going to have to watch your back every step you make."

"Sounds like just your average day at Themis Academy," she says wryly.

"Yeah, it does," I say.

"There's something else," Martin says.

"Oh, joy," I say.

"You'll like this one," he adds, and hands me the ivory envelope.

My name is written on the front in sharp black letters. I slide a finger under the flap and open it. It's a letter from Parker Hume.

Dear Alex,

Please accept this as my official letter of resignation from the board of the Mockingbirds effective immediately. It was a pleasure serving with you, and I wish you all the best in your future endeavors.

Sincerely,
Parker

I laugh out loud. "This is brilliant. Did you see it?" I ask. Martin shakes his head, so I hand it to him. He grins as he reads it, then narrows his eyes in a faux serious gesture. "Very professional."

"I'm sure he learned it from Daddy."

"Speaking of, that's why he quit. He told me this morning. He said what happened to your hand freaked him out too much. He's too worried about Daddy finding out about the Mockingbirds."

Because of my hands, he quit. I look over at Jamie. Because of my hands, she stayed.

Sometimes instinct can be wrong. But sometimes it can be right too. And sometimes you just have to take it on faith.

I reach up and run an unbroken finger through my blue streak. Then it hits me. "Jamie, I have your first official assignment."

Chapter Thirty-Five
HER GOOD NAME

I have another assignment too, and this one's for T.S. and me to handle, because I need to pay my debts to others first.

"I bet you learned a lot from having three brothers," I whisper to T.S. when I find her in the library studying.

She gives me a look and raises an eyebrow. "What *sort* of things do you think I learned from having three brothers?"

"Like how to cause trouble," I say.

"What sort of trouble?"

"Fun trouble."

"Like giving someone a wedgie?" she asks eagerly.

"I'm thinking wedgie times one hundred," I say.

"Dude, I'm in," T.S. says.

And it's that simple with T.S.

Even with my broken hand, we manage the assignment

in under an hour because T.S., as she always does, comes through. She knows how to take what we need, flit by unseen, and do the dirty work without making a sound.

"My brothers would be so proud," T.S. says when we're done. "I'm so going to have to take pictures. This is exactly the kind of stuff they trained me to do."

"Let's show Maia," I say, and we return to our room to fetch our other roommate. She is resistant at first and this—this spark in her, this tiny little fire—is how I know she is coming back.

"Now? You want me to go outside now? It's practically freezing," she protests.

"Here's a coat," I say, handing her my fleece as we walk down the steps and into the November night.

We reach the theater, and the doors have a new look. Like a string of lights at Christmastime, a line of black boxer briefs has been draped over the curved archway. Maia steps closer to get a better look. There are maybe twenty or so pairs of boys' underwear hung up. She leans in, not wanting to touch the undergarments, but close enough to see that each one has a label sewn on the inside: *Property of Beat Bosworth*.

I wait for Maia to say something.

"His mom sews his name into his underwear? Like who'd take them? Who'd want them?" she says.

"I know, right? But thank God for Mrs. Bosworth."

"And who wears black boxer briefs *only*?" she adds. "And where did you two loons come up with this idea?"

"Look," I begin, "it's not the Elite. I know it's not even remotely close to a replacement for the Elite, but it was all we could do at this point. It was all I could think of to do."

"No, it's not the Elite. And, don't get me wrong, I wanted to feel that bloody trophy in my hands like I've never wanted anything before in my life. But you know what? There was something I wanted more. Or less, really. Because when I heard what Theo did last night in the cafeteria—and incidentally I still think he's a total wanker—I realized it was actually more important to me that the rest of this school know I'm not a cheater. And he let them know that. That was the worst part of all this, even worse than not debating, even worse than losing the Elite. That's why I was so miserable, because I didn't want people thinking that about me. I didn't want the whole school thinking I'm someone I'm not."

"We're not done clearing your name, Maia. There's more we will do," I add, though I know it'll take a lot of work to undo the damage I've done. I'm up for the task, though.

"But there's something I have to do too," Maia says to me. "And that's to say I'm terribly sorry for not seeing what you were going through as head of the Mockingbirds and the risks." She looks down at my hands.

T.S. jumps in quickly. "I'm sorry I gave you a hard time too. I know you were just trying to do the right thing."

I wave my good hand in the air as if all of this is just no big deal, but mostly so I don't choke up. Because it is a big deal, all of it. But whether I'm a public person or a private person or some cocktail of the two, the goal is the same: to do the right thing. I don't always hit the mark, but I plan to keep it in the crosshairs.

"Let's just enjoy the view for now," I say, and we take a few steps back to get a better look at our handiwork. The three of us stand on the quad gazing upon a doorway decorated with black boxer briefs.

"I've always thought we've never had quite enough pranks at Themis Academy," Maia says.

"And let us never forget that pranks should always be allowed. In fact, they should be encouraged," I say.

We head to the cafeteria for dinner, where I take my usual spot. Jamie's across the cafeteria with a group of girls I presume are her freshmen friends. She laughs at something funny someone must have said. Then she makes a goofy face at the person.

I turn back to my friends and take a bite of my salad. The lettuce falls off the fork, which is surprisingly tough to use with three immobile fingers.

Maia laughs at me. "Maybe next time you'll get a sandwich."

"Maybe next time you'll get it for me."

When Martin finishes eating, he stands up and taps his fork against his glass, quieting the room. "Just a brief update to the recent announcements. Wanted to let you know that Maia Tan has, if she wishes, been fully reinstated to the debate team."

We didn't plan this, but this is part of the restoration. This is part of how we can make good again. He turns to Maia. "I'm assuming you'd like to return."

She nods, the epitome of class and grace.

"Good. Then let's move forward and look ahead to Nationals next semester, where I'm sure you'll lead the team as only you can."

Then there's clapping. Not everyone. Not even most students. But enough. And even though my fingers are too broken to hold a fork properly, I'm pretty sure I'm the loudest of all.

As the clapping subsides and Martin sits back down, I spot a mane of flaming red hair a few tables away. Carter's former girlfriend. She's looking at me, watching me, and when she knows I see her, she nods and mouths, *Thank you.*

◆ ◆ ◆

On my way back to my dorm after dinner I see Delaney and Theo across the quad. They're walking and holding hands on their last night together before he leaves for good. As I watch them I remember holding hands with Martin the night after I played *Boléro* for him. I feel a pang, knowing I won't be able to play again for a while. But then the emptiness subsides, because that night wasn't just about music. It was about something more. I still have that something more, and that's another thing they can't take away from me.

As they walk past the music hall and the dance studio, I

flash on my conversation with Theo earlier this year when he mentioned Ms. Merritt e-mailing him.

She was saddened—*that was her word—to learn that my dreams might not materialize. And she had some* suggestions *for what I might be able to do with my* creative energy.

Suggestions. I bet she had suggestions. I bet she *suggested* the debate team. She was needling him, poking him, pushing him. She was stirring up all our competitive spirits, stoking the flames so we could do her bidding—perform, perform, perform and help bring the J. Sullivan James trophy home.

So she could win. So she could beat her biggest rival. So she could bolster her record in every way.

Then I laugh. Because I doubt there's any trophy coming for her this year. I bet Matthew Winters will claim it after all. God, I hope they beat us. I hope they take the trophy home and gloat over it, lord it over Ms. Merritt's head.

I rush over to Delaney and Theo, needing to confirm my suspicions.

"Hey," I say, knowing I am interrupting but knowing this is vital. "Ms. Merritt suggested you go out for debate, didn't she? That's what was in the e-mail she sent you over the summer, wasn't it?"

Theo nods. "Yeah. She said she knew I was good with politics and thought debate would be a good outlet for me."

I look at my hand again, and my resolve to do something about it deepens.

"Hey, guys," Delaney says, and points to the time on her

phone. "I have to go. It's time for me to meet Jamie for our *assignment*."

Then she winks at me. "I guess I'm an honorary Mockingbird," she adds.

"You absolutely are, Delaney," I say.

"I guess that's all out in the open now too," Theo says to her, then leans in to plant a kiss on her cheek.

"It is," Delaney says. Then to him, "I'll meet you in your room when I'm done."

She dashes off, and I'm standing under the night sky with Theo McBride.

"I'm sorry about your hand," he says softly.

I look at my hand again; my eyes keep drawing me back there, like it's a new tattoo.

"Can you play again?" he asks.

"That's what they say. But who knows if it'll be the same, right?"

"Yeah. Who knows," he says, and he doesn't need to say anything more, because we will always be speaking the same language; we will always understand each other. "I'll listen to you play anytime."

"I'll watch you dance anytime," I say, and this is a promise I will keep for my whole life, because it's not about this school; it's not about the here and now. When I am twenty, thirty, forty, when Themis is in my distant past, when I look back on high school through the gauzy haze of memory, I know that *this* promise will matter, that this promise will not be forgotten.

Then I walk to the nearest drugstore, buy some facial-hair remover, and return to my dorm. When all the lights are dimmed, when quiet descends on the building, I head down to Anjali's room and quietly, carefully, and ever so quickly apply the cream to her eyebrows while she sleeps.

I do the same to McKenna.

Their naked eyebrows will go great with their new hair color.

Chapter Thirty-Six

BIRDS CAN FLY

When Monday morning rolls around, the Watchdogs have made their mark on campus. Every tree on the quad has been tacked with a flyer that says *Join the Watchdogs* next to that nefariously grinning dog holding its gavel. Its mouth is kind of smiling and snarling at the same time. A *smarl*. Then there's a time and a place for a meeting—three nights from now. A recruitment meeting. The bulletin board has an extra-special sign on it. A picture of the dog gobbling up one of our birds. The bird's head is in the dog's jaw; the wings and body and feet dangle from its teeth. Then the headline— as if it needed one—*Dogs Eat Birds.*

If I had a Sharpie, I'd scrawl some graffiti on their drawing. I'd march right up to the tree and even with my bad hand I'd uncap the marker and scratch in the words *But Birds Can Fly*.

Instead I go to the cafeteria and I search for the Watch-dogs. They're not going to miss their moment in the spotlight even *without* eyebrows, even *with* their new hairstyles. My eyes scan the cafeteria and land on the most brightly colored crowns there. Sure, McKenna has that stupid hat on again and Anjali's wearing a scarf on her head. But the scarf can't hide Anjali's new red hair. Bright strands the color of a fire engine poke out. As for McKenna, her wild mane is a bitter orange, like a burned Popsicle.

They look like clowns.

I walk straight over to them and grab a seat.

"Nice scarf," I say to Anjali. Then I turn to McKenna and give her a shrug. "Don't feel bad. Not everyone can rock a rainbow-colored shade," I say as I twirl my own blue streak.

Look, I'm not saying pranking their hair and their eye-brows is the same as breaking fingers. But you can't stoop to that level. You have to fight fair, and just because your op-ponent uses deadly weapons doesn't mean you have to. You use the weapons you can live with yourself for using.

Like hair dye and bleach from an honorary Mockingbird. Like a double agent who added those extra ingredients to two girls' shampoo bottles—red dye for the blond Anjali, bleach for the black-haired McKenna. Like facial-hair re-mover for the pièce de résistance.

Before either of them can speak, before either of the clown twins can sneer or spit, I continue. "It could be worse. Your bones could be broken. Hair grows back."

Then I turn to Natalie, the third musketeer and the only

one whose hair is still its natural shade, whose eyebrows are still intact.

"You, Natalie, are a bully," I say. "And you won't get away with it."

She laughs at me. "I already got away with it."

"That's what you think," I say. "But I know something you don't know."

Natalie tenses and narrows her eyes for a second. Now I am the one going rogue. Now I am the one she has to beware of. But I don't play by her rules. I play by mine, by the Mockingbirds'. Our rules may be changing, but they are still good.

♦ ♦ ♦

In English class that morning, Mr. Baumann chuckles when he sees Anjali. Then he covers his mouth with his hand and turns around. But his shoulders are shaking and he's still laughing. That makes me happy. I glance at Maia, and she's grinning too.

When English class ends, Mr. Baumann calls me aside. "How's your hand?" he says.

"Fine," I say.

"Do you need any extra accommodations for assignments?" he asks.

"No, thank you," I say, because I don't, and if I did I wouldn't take them anyway. I'd grin and bear it, even if both hands were broken, even if my hands were covered in casts. I shudder at the image of me clunking around, my prized possessions encased in plaster, knocking glasses off tables, frames off mantels. But even as they crashed and shattered, I'd still be stubborn enough to insist I could do it all myself.

Then again, maybe I wouldn't. Maybe I would accept help. Maybe I would accept Mr. Baumann's help, like Theo did.

"I'm glad to hear you're well, then," he says. He takes a beat and in his pause I decide to ask *him* a question.

"Are you upset that the Debate Club didn't win?"

He shakes his head. "No. Not in the least."

"Why not?"

"I'm not teaching them to win. I'm teaching them how to compete with grace."

I let those words sink in. *Compete with grace.* If only everyone here was teaching that. But maybe it's enough that some are. Maybe it's a start.

Then it's his turn to ask me more questions. "What did you think of the books this semester?"

He knows what I thought. I've written papers. I've analyzed scenes. I've contributed to classroom discussions, maybe not as much as Anjali, definitely not as much as Maia, but enough. But I have this feeling he's not asking the question in a teacherly way.

"I think some boarding schools are scary places to send your kids," I say. "Midnight trials, groups like the Vigils."

"Indeed," Mr. Baumann says. "Indeed. But maybe that can change."

Maybe. Maybe it can.

I think about one of the last lines in *A Separate Peace*, when Gene says, "I was on active duty all my time at school." Indeed, we all are on active duty here at Themis. We are all fighting. Sometimes we know the enemy. Sometimes we don't. Sometimes the enemy is us. And sometimes the enemy hides in her office.

But I know where her office is, so I drop by to see Ms. Merritt, showing her secretary my splint, like it's a first-class ticket to let me in the dean's office. It does the trick, and I sit down across from Ms. Merritt.

"I'm so sorry to hear about your hand," she says. Her hair is tight against her scalp, pulled into her trademark braid, and her hands are clasped in front of her, resting on her massive oak desk. "How are you managing? Is there anything at all I can do for you?"

"Are you sorry?" I ask pointedly. "Or are you just sorry I can't play the piano?"

She's momentarily taken aback. She's not used to students quizzing her. She recovers quickly, though. "Alex, I feel awful that you're hurt. I feel awful *for you* that you can't play right now. It's a terrible accident you had. Snow can be such a vicious thing."

The lies we tell ourselves.

"It wasn't snow, or ice. It wasn't a fall. It wasn't an accident."

She raises an eyebrow, almost daring me to go on.

"What would you say if I told you another girl did this to me? Another senior? The star of your lacrosse team that's in line to three-peat for Nationals?"

She reaches for a lipstick on her desk and applies a fresh coat of peach to her lips, then rubs them together. When she's done, she speaks. "I would say that's quite the allegation you're talking about. And with such an allegation, you'd need to think seriously whether pursuing it is in anyone's best interest. It could be very complicated and difficult to go through. Perhaps it might be best to find a way to put the bad blood behind you and move on."

I'm not surprised, not in the least. But her words don't eat away at me like they did earlier this year. They strengthen me. "I had a feeling you'd say something like that. So let me rephrase." I hold my right hand up. "The only *shared culpability* here is yours. Because if you had done your job, this would never have happened. Oh, and there's one more thing: a brochure on broken fingers isn't going to fix this. It isn't going to make this or anything better." Then I tip my forehead to the empty space on her shelves. "Looks like that spot will be empty for some time. Maybe you should just get a nice vase of flowers instead. *Fake* flowers."

"You may leave now," she says.

"I will."

I continue on to my classes, then to my private lesson with Miss Damata later that day. There's not much to do. So we talk. We discuss music theory and music history, and I find with Miss Damata I truly can learn as much by listening as I can by playing.

Then she says something random.

"You don't have to do it alone," she says.

I give her an *I don't get it* look. "Do what?"

"Be the good for the school."

I turn back to the keys, hitting a few notes with my left hand. She lets me run through some chords, then a few more, before she lays a soft hand on mine, silencing my music.

"Alex," she says in that gentle voice of hers. A few blond strands from her pinned-up hair shine as the sunlight streams through the window. "I know about the Mockingbirds. I've known for a few weeks now. I know you're leading them. And I know you're trying your best, because the school is an absolute failure in protecting and helping students."

I consider denying it. I consider walking out. I consider playing dumb.

But there is no point. She knows, and I can't make her *unknow*.

She tells me how she put the pieces together. First there was the remark I made last year about a group of us "together accusing another student," then the Faculty Club stunt, and then my questions about codes sealed the deal.

Part of me waits to be reprimanded. But another part, a stronger part, knows that's not what Miss Damata is here to do.

"I'm not the only one who knows, Alex. Mr. Baumann does too, and we've talked about it. We want to help you. We want to work with the students and with the Mockingbirds. To make things better."

"Why?" I ask, and it's the first time I've verbally acknowledged our existence to a teacher, to an adult.

"Because I would never send my own children here," she says, an intensity bordering on anger in her voice.

"You wouldn't?"

"Not a chance. I don't like how the school looks the other way. I don't like how the record and the accomplishments matter more than anything. I don't like how the administration infantilizes the student body, how it puts you all up on a pedestal, and in so doing how it fails to recognize you are all teenagers and you are all real people and you are all going to make mistakes. I want to teach at a place where I can send my own children when they are older. I want to teach at a place that isn't operated by blind idealization, but someplace that looks problems square in the face and tries to solve them."

"It's worse than that, Miss Damata. Ms. Merritt doesn't just think we're above reproach. She willfully chooses to look the other way."

"Yes, that too."

"So what does this all mean?" I ask tentatively.

"Mr. Baumann and I would like to meet with you and the other leaders if you're willing. We don't want to expose you; we don't want to turn you in," she says with a laugh. "We want to help and work with you. We want there to be a better system. We want to help you get there. We don't want you to have to do this alone anymore."

The plan is clear. This is what I need to do. This is how we need to change. And if these two teachers want to help, then there is a matter that needs to be tended to. It's one that has evidence, one that is clear-cut, and one that needs much more than our brand of justice. Because our brand doesn't work like it used to.

"You can help me with this, then," I say. "Natalie Moretti broke my fingers. Ms. Merritt isn't going to do anything about it. But there are two sophomores who saw it and are willing to say so on the record. I think Natalie should be kicked out. Can you help us?"

"I promise we will do everything we can."

"Let me ask the other board members about the meeting, then."

When I ask my fellow board members, the decision is unanimous. Martin and Jamie want to hear them out. So the next day I tell Miss Damata we'll take the meeting. "But it has to be on our turf," I say.

"Of course," she replies, no questions asked.

"We meet in the basement laundry room of Taft-Hay. Can you and Mr. Baumann be there at eight tonight?"

"We can be there at eight."

I leave the music hall, and Jones is waiting outside for me on the step. "You know, Alex, I've been thinking it's time to revise my position on something."

"What would that be?"

"It's a long-standing position, so you might want to sit down," he says playfully.

"I like standing. Actually I like walking," I say as we head to lunch.

"Well, I warned you," he says, and then claps his hands

together. Before he can speak, I stop and say, "Wait. Don't tell me you're actually secretly in love with the violin and this whole electric-guitar phase is over?"

"Never. That will never change."

"Then what is it?"

"Well, I kind of decided that I think you could really use my talents."

"I could?"

"Well, I think the Mockingbirds could."

"Jones, are you saying what I think you're saying?"

He shrugs and holds out his hands. "I'm saying if you need a runner, or whatever, I'm your man."

"You want to be a Mockingbird? Are you for real? You don't believe in the Mockingbirds."

"Last time I checked, it wasn't a religion, was it?"

I laugh. "Definitely not."

"Look, Alex," he says seriously. "Things changed. They broke your hand. I figured you guys could use all the help you could get."

I grin and hold out my left hand to shake his.

"Welcome to the Mockingbirds, Jones," I say, and as we continue on to the cafeteria, I think how some decisions are hard, some are easy, but either way it's our choices that matter. Who we choose to align with. What we choose to give in to. What we choose to resist.

And most of all, who we choose to be. Because it is always our choice.

At seven forty-five I leave my dorm to round up Martin and Jamie, then we walk together along the stone pathway on the quad as an early November wind blows by.

"Man, it's cold out," I say as I wrap my scarf—a warm, wooly one, not a flimsy Frenchie one—up and around my chin.

"I think it's quite balmy," Martin says. He's wearing jeans and a sweatshirt.

"Figures. Typical guy," I say to Jamie.

"Totally," she says, enjoying the camaraderie, the teasing, the small talk with us, her new friends because her old associates no longer fit.

Besides, Martin's the furthest thing from a typical guy. I wouldn't have it any other way.

He reaches for my left hand. "Your hands are cold," he says, and Jamie walks a bit faster, giving Martin and me some space.

"I know. I need gloves. I didn't realize how cold it was," I tell him.

"Actually, mittens might be better right now," he says. Then he reaches into the pocket of his sweatshirt and pulls out a pair of striped mittens—blue and green. "I got them for you. I figured you'd need them for the next few weeks. You have to take extra care of your hands now, so you're ready *when* you get your Juilliard audition in January."

I put them on and then hold up my hands. "I love them,"

I say. Then I stop walking and so does he. I wrap my arms around his neck and his warm lips meet mine and instantly the heat has been turned way up. My hands even feel warm. I wriggle my fingers a millimeter or two under the splint as far as they can go, picturing them in a month or so, maybe more, free and flying across the keys with abandon.

I will hold on to that image for as long as I have to—until it becomes real again.

We cut the kiss short and catch up to Jamie at the door to my dorm. She walks in first. Martin holds the door for me. Before I go in, I look back across the quad, quiet for now on this frigid night. I imagine it at the start of school, stirring with students, with all the people I have vied with, spied on, sided with, fought with, lied to, lied for, played with, ate fire with, escaped with, laughed with, and loved. I think about the kind of people they are.

Those who run when the going gets tough.

Those who make bad choices but then with grace start anew.

Those who break your bones.

And those who do the hardest thing of all, who mess up but have the guts to say, *I will not abide by it anymore*. Like Jamie. That, I think, takes real courage. That is something you don't learn. That is something you just do one day, and then when you realize you have it in your core to do, you keep on doing, relentlessly, ceaselessly.

Then there is Martin, who lives and loves with a gentle yet ferocious intensity, who can make integrity sexy, and who, at the end of the day, is just a boy who loves a girl. And that girl loves him.

I am somewhere in the middle of all of them, or maybe I am circling, or maybe I am even at the center, as I try to understand the kind of person I am and want to be. I wasn't always sure. But then I failed; I screwed up spectacularly.

Only, I won't stop there.

Because I won't let one bad landing define me.

And in trying again, I know who I am and I know who I'm not.

Because even though they took away the thing I love, I will not give in. I am more than just the thing I love. I am a friend. I am a girlfriend. I am a keeper of secrets. I am the girl with the blue streak. I am the one who confronted Ms. Merritt. I am someone who asks for help. I am the person who didn't cheat on her boyfriend. I am a one-handed pianist. I am the audience. I am a fire-eater.

I am a survivor.

I am a Mockingbird, and I will not look the other way, and I will definitely not go quietly.

I will fight.

Acknowledgments

I hereby toast the following people:

To Kate Sullivan, a rock star editor who is tough on manuscripts, gentle with writers, easy to talk to, fantastic to work with, and totally fashionable. (Ha, you can't edit that sentence, nor can Dale Snitterman.)

To Andy McNicol, thank you for being my shark and for your great taste in footwear, the two of which often go hand in hand.

To Caroline D'Onofrio, a fantastic teammate and one of the most astute readers I know. To Laura Bonner for bringing the Mockingbirds to the world.

To Nancy Conescu, who helped shape the world in this novel.

To Little, Brown and the whole team, including Lisa Sabater, Megan Tingley, Jennifer Hunt, and Dave Caplan.

To Gale Fraley for her insight on hair color. To Christa Fletcher for the aha moment. To Brian Brushwood for the how-to on fire-eating. To Jill Ciambriello for educating me about dance. To Doug Walker for his torch singer picks. To Scott Meldrum at Pollin8 for building an awesome Facebook page and being the best guy in the digital-media business.

To Courtney Summers and C.J. Omololu for their early reads, invaluable insight, and limitless putting-up-with-the-crazy capacity. To Suzanne Young, Victoria Schwab, and Mandy Morgan for always cheering me on. To fellow YA writers Kiersten White and Stephanie Perkins for friendship and access to their e-mail inboxes. To Zoe Strickland, my official teen reader and my friend.

Most of all, to Theresa Shaw for being the best of the best of everything and for always getting the *and* credit.

To my parents, Michael and Polly, for your faith in me and support. To Barbara, Kathy, Garry, and Jill for letting me be the rare person who has cool in-laws. To Cammi and Ilene for being my everyday go-to gals.

To the readers who embraced the first book—you make it all worthwhile. Keep those e-mails coming. To the librarians and booksellers who get books in the hands of readers—you make the world go round.

To Mighty Leaf green tea and Hello Panda cookies—I drive up the *P* in your P&L every day when I write. Please consider sending me a gift basket of goodies.

To my dog, Violet, who despite what the dedication says, is definitely one of the loves of my life.

To my children, who delight me with their love and their ability to distinguish between *lay* and *lie*.

And most of all, always and forever, to my husband, Jeff—the world's greatest humor producer.

Oh, and please go read or reread or re-reread *The Chocolate War* and *A Separate Peace*, because those are some seriously great books. Even if they don't have totally adorable Lab-collie mixes named Violet in them.

Last word goes to the dog!